CHASING A DREAM

CJ BOERGER

Marilyn,
Hope you enjoy the book!

Merry Christmas!

C.J. Boerger

For my Dad and Mom for their guidance.

For my kids for their inspiration.

For my wife for always believing in me.

Chapter 1

New Britain, CT

Two balls, no strikes on the right-handed hitting Rivera. Becker winds-up, and the pitch. Line drive single to center. This will score two. Johnson scores. Evers scores. And the Thunder increases their lead to 4-1. Becker is getting hit hard out here tonight. He just doesn't seem to have it working today.

"You're a bum, Gramps!"

"Time to retire, old man!"

"My kid throws harder than you do!"

Charlie Becker used to be able to tune out the crowd. He could put himself in a zone where he was in his own world. He'd only hear the thump of the mitt, the strike call of the umpire, his catcher giving encouragement. He'd breathe in and breathe out, and be completely at ease and calm. The only thing he'd see was the catcher's mitt and his entire focus would be zeroed in right there. It was almost like he was throwing the ball down a long, dark tunnel that ended in his catcher's mitt. It was his world of peace and serenity.

Now he hears and sees everything, and the crowd sure seems to be on him today for some reason. Oh, the words don't bother Charlie. He's been around too long and has heard too much for it to bother him. It is just noise. He almost finds it humorous. What bothers Charlie is the inability to just be in the game; to not have a world around him; to be lost in baseball with nothing else there. It's a great feeling to be lost in the game; to not have the pain and hurt of the past to deal with. But lately there is no relief, and no escape – at least not on the ball field.

Becker deals. Ground ball to short. Santiago with a nice, backhanded grab and they'll get the force at second. Wow! Another gold glove type of play by Santiago. And there are two outs in the fourth.

"You can do it, Charlie!"

There wasn't a doubt in Charlie's mind where the encouragement was coming from. At least Charlie knew he'd always have one fan up in the crowd. Two fans, really. His wife, Karen, never misses a start. She doesn't miss a start in the summer anyway. She's a second grade teacher in Charlie's hometown of Spring Valley, Minnesota, and from

June through August she follows the New Britain Rock Cats, a Double-A affiliate of the Minnesota Twins, all over the country with little more than their three year old son Timmy in tow. This year it's the New Britain Rock Cats, anyway. This being Charlie's 12th minor league team in his 10 year baseball career – if you can call this a career. Karen is now six months pregnant, and not exactly comfortable in the 90 degree late-July heat, but she's up there in seat 5A behind the home dugout trying to keep cool – not an easy thing to do with Timmy climbing all over her. This summer the Becker's are renting a small apartment in New Britain not far from the stadium. By now Karen has become accustomed to essentially living out of a suitcase for the summer months and then returning to relative normalcy during the school year at their home in Spring Valley.

Becker comes to the set. And the pitch – no it's a pickoff. They have Martinez picked off of first. Phillips throws to Santiago at second, and Santiago tags Martinez out. Martinez is not a happy man. He wants a balk called there, and he's letting the second base umpire know about it. I don't think he's going to win that argument. So, we go to the bottom of the fourth with the score Trenton 4, New Britain 1.

"You know that's a balk, don't you Gramps," Phillips barked as Becker walked in.

"It's not a balk if they don't call it. I've been making that same move for 10 years now and only been called on it twice. One of the advantages of being a southpaw."

"Yeah, I keep forgetting that you're 100 years old, and you was 'round when they created the balk rule. Next inning why don't you try and keep it under 30 pitches. I got a date tonight, and I know you got no kinda social life. If I were managing this team you'd of been out of the game two innings ago, but then it's probably too far for the crazy old man to have to walk out to the mound to pull you. Bunch a fuckin' losers on this shitty team. Can't wait 'til they finally move me up to the bigs where I belong."

"Thanks for the support, Benny."

Benny Phillips is a more typical version of what a minor league player is supposed to be. 19 years old, Benny stands about 6'3" and has almost unnaturally huge forearms. Benny is on the fast track to the majors, and not shy about sharing it with anyone that will listen to him. His cockiness is only matched by his abrasiveness. Benny is the youngest buck on a team full of young bucks. At 33 years of age, Charlie has 8 years on his next oldest teammate, which means a completely different lifestyle. That gap might as well be 100 years. The kids would be out late. Drinking. Socializing. Doing what kids do. Charlie would be home searching for a way to get some sleep before his personal demons appeared, knowing that Timmy would be waking him up at 6 AM to play.

Don Scott, the Rock Cats manager, can relate with Charlie's age difference plight. Don has been involved in baseball for over 60 years, and at age 75 shows no signs of retiring anytime soon. His hair is almost bleach white, and the baseball uniform doesn't look quite right on his aging and 25 pounds overweight body, but there's still nothing he'd rather be wearing. Forty years ago Don was a firecracker of a manager, yelling and screaming his way through the minor league coaching ranks. Before that he played three seasons as a back-up catcher for the Detroit Tigers before his knees wouldn't allow him to play the game he loved any longer. Now he has mellowed in his older age, and after a couple of knee replacement surgeries kind of walks like an overweight penguin. He is almost a grandfather figure for a lot of the boys, and is generally well liked and respected by his players.

"Give me the rundown Becker," Scott said as he waddled over to Charlie. This was Scott's way of asking for information.

"Well, you've seen the gun. The whole stadium's seen the gun. Wish someone would break that damn thing. I just don't have much today," Charlie replied.

The new radar gun at New Britain Stadium was always a hot topic with the Rock Cat players. The youngsters loved the thing. They'd throw a pitch, and immediately look up at the scoreboard to see the numbers flash. The boys in the bullpen even kept a running count of how fast the pitchers were throwing. Most of the coaches liked having the data available immediately to see how strong their pitcher's arms were on that specific day.

Charlie, on the other hand, loathed it. All it did, in his mind, was create a distraction for the pitchers, and give fans some ammunition for their attacks when things weren't going smoothly. The fact that Charlie could push the 100 mph mark 10 years ago, and now could barely top 86 didn't help.

"I've got the curve working, Skip. My slider is moving a little bit, and the changeup is fine. But without my fastball it's going to be a struggle." Charlie had so many coaches and managers over the past ten years that they'd all just been known as "Skip" to Charlie.

"Well, we need at least seven innings out of you. The bullpen is shot, and with a double header tomorrow we're running out of arms. Better find a way," Scott said.

This is another way that Charlie was different than any of the other pitchers on staff. The young arms were coddled. They were the future, and you couldn't risk overusing a strong, young arm. Charlie, on the other hand, was expendable. Charlie was only on the team to eat up some innings over the course of a long 140 game minor league season. Coach Scott would never send a youngster back out to the mound after throwing over 100 pitches or he'd end up fired. But Charlie was used that way all the time. In fact Charlie had already approached 125 pitches a couple of times this season when they needed him. Charlie understood, and Coach Scott knew that Charlie understood, and this made their relationship run quite smoothly. The fact that the two were both considered too old for their profession by many of their peers also helped them relate well with each other.

Charlie is by no means an elite physical specimen, but his strong conditioning program that he strictly adheres to keeps him able to perform at a high level. Standing about six feet tall with little body fat on his thin frame, he really looks more like a distance runner than a baseball player. The one facial feature that stands out about Charlie is his smile. He's able to disarm others by flashing the smile, and Charlie often uses that to keep people away from his eyes where the pain hides.

"Hey, Chuckster, when I put down one finger I'm calling for a fastball, not a changeup." If you met Dusty Timms on the street and someone told you he was a baseball player, you'd know immediately that he must be a catcher. Dusty is short, stocky, and talks nonstop. If Dusty's not talking, it means he's got some food stuffed in his mouth. Dusty grew up in New York City and has an edge to him that only living in the big city can bring. Charlie couldn't help but like the guy almost immediately.

"I've got one finger for you," Charlie laughed, giving him the one finger peace sign. "You should just be happy that I picked that guy off of first for you so you didn't have to see another 'stolen base allowed' number tacked on your stat line."

"How am I supposed to throw a guy out stealing when he's standing on second base before I even get the ball in my hand? I don't understand why they even lead off against you. Just wait 'til the balls in the air for 10 seconds and then take off. Even I could steal second off of you while carrying Benny's enormous ego along with me."

"Good stuff, Dusty. Anyway, Skip wants three more innings out of me, and I clearly don't have it today. Gonna have to use a steady diet of breaking balls, and hope they pound it into the ground in Santiago's direction."

"Sounds good, Chuckster. Nothing I enjoy more than blocking your slow-ass breaking shit in the dirt. Lucky for you I'm so young and spry."

"You forgot humble."

"Damn right, Chuckster, I'm that too."

So for three more innings that's how it went. Curveball, Curveball, Curveball, Changeup, Curveball, grounder to short. Over and over again. Fortunately for Charlie, Jose Santiago over at short has incredible range. He can't hit a lick, but anything on the ground in his general direction is going to find his glove. He's a great weapon for a team with a contact pitcher like Charlie to have.

Finally, after 7 innings and 121 pitches, Charlie's night is done. Not a bad night, actually, for a game pitched without his best stuff. 6 Hits, 4 Earned Runs, no walks and 1 strikeout. Even better yet, Dusty hit a 3-run homer (only his 2nd of the season) in the 7th inning to get Charlie the win, raising his record to 10-4 on the season, his best win-loss record in five years.

After 10 years trudging through the minors, a win doesn't quite carry the same joy that it previously did, but it still feels good to win. Actually, it's more a feeling of relief that he didn't take another loss rather than any real enjoyment of the win. Charlie used to live to play the game, and there was nothing he'd rather be doing. Now, it was a job and an obligation for him, and unfortunately not a great paying job, either. The sense of accomplishment, of relief, that he feels only lasts for a short time for Charlie. In fact, it typically only lasts until his head hits the pillow that night, and then the pain and hurt from the past comes flooding back again like a black cloud that hovers over him. It would take more than a win to make that cloud disappear. It's always out there lurking, waiting for its time to come back out again. After 17 years of its existence, it might not ever completely disappear.

Chapter 2

New Britain, CT

When you're a starting pitcher everything revolves around the five day cycle, and a monotonous routine begins to develop. There's not much mystery to what each day is going to bring, and for Charlie this is precisely what he loves. Charlie gets lost in the monotony and steady rhythm of a baseball season. He can program his mind to just focus on the individual day, and the work that needs to be completed to help him achieve his ultimate goal. Day 1 in the cycle is Charlie's recovery day which involves a 30 minute or four mile run, whichever comes first, as well as some light lifting.

Charlie likes to say 30 minutes or four miles, but it almost always ends up being four miles. He'll go into a run telling himself that it will just be a nice, slow jog. No need to hurry. But then, the clock starts moving and he just can't help himself. His competitiveness takes over and he starts mentally calculating what his pace would have to be to reach that 30 minute mark. Before he knows it there are five minutes left and Charlie has the speed up to 10 MPH trying to beat the clock while dripping sweat all over the treadmill. He could probably remove the clock by getting off the treadmill and running outside, but his obsessive compulsive personality loves seeing the exact numbers.

Charlie always waits until Timmy wakes him up at precisely 6:00 AM. He gets a cup of coffee and then sits with him for a while before the work of the day begins.

"Daaaad, I'm uuuup... Daaaaaad, I'm uuuuuuup!"

"Why don't you stay and get some more rest? I'll get some cartoons on for Timmy," Karen groggily whispers across the bed. "You weren't asleep until, what, 2:30 this morning?"

"No, I've got it," Charlie replied. "I'm not going to be able to get back asleep again anyway."

Charlie had a tough time winding down after a game, and since he stopped drinking this meant some short nights. But, at least without the alcohol in his system the nightmares were gone, for the most part.

For the first four years of Charlie's baseball career, the evenings went quite differently. Charlie would start drinking as soon as he got home, and wouldn't stop until he was passed out asleep. Waking up at noon was not an issue back then. Of course, Charlie might be pitching in the majors right now instead of packing for a three city, nine game bus trip if his routine was different at that time.

"Do you have your itinerary for the trip yet?" Karen asked.

"Yeah, I'll show it to you. Basically we're driving out to Altoona tonight after the game to play three, then to Richmond Thursday night after the game for three more, and then back to Altoona Sunday evening to finish the trip. We should be back home very late next Wednesday night. What are you and Timmy going to do?" Charlie asked while grabbing and throwing Timmy on his lap as the cartoons rolled on.

"We'll drive to Richmond Friday afternoon to watch you pitch that night, and then probably head back Saturday morning. I think we'll probably go to Altoona on Tuesday evening. I don't think we'll go to the game that night, just straight to the hotel. Then we'll be around to see you pitch Wednesday's afternoon game. It's going to be a lot of driving for us."

After five plus years of being married to Charlie, Karen understands how the five day cycle works as well, and unless there's a rain out she knows exactly when and where Charlie will be pitching. She also knows intuitively when something's bothering him just by watching and listening to him.

"What's wrong, Charlie?"

"Nothin'," Charlie said smiling up at her.

"You may be able to fool everyone else, but I know you too well. What's up?"

"I just hate being away from home so much. I've lost the ability to leave everything in my mind behind like I used to. So I don't get that feeling of release while I'm pitching anymore, especially when I'm on the road away from you two. The only time I feel that ease now is when I'm home with Timmy. And now, today, with us having that double header I'll be at the ballpark all day on my last day before our trip," Charlie said, getting up to grab another cup of coffee.

Karen followed him into the kitchen. "You don't have to continue playing, you know. You'd be a great teacher and coach, and I know you'd really enjoy it. We've been smart with our money, so you could stay home with our new baby for the school year and then look for a teaching job the next year. That sure sounds better than you being down in Mexico somewhere playing winter league ball again. You'll miss seeing the early years of our new baby and Timmy growing up."

"You know I can't do that Karen. I can't quit even if baseball is not always fun for me anymore. I haven't accomplished what I need to yet. That's not what Dad would want."

"Your Dad would want you to be happy. If he thought you'd be happier doing something else while being home with your family more, then he'd want you to do it, you know that."

"I can't just quit. I just need to buck up and do it. I don't want to talk about it anymore, honey. You know I don't like talking about it." And with that Charlie went back into the living room with Timmy and the topic was closed. Karen knew that there was no point in continuing the conversation as Charlie would just shut down at this point anyway. They'd been over this before, and Karen understood that she needed to be supportive, and so that's what she was. She never wanted him to feel like he had to quit playing because of her, but just wanted him to realize that there were other options if he wasn't enjoying himself. She really wasn't very excited about spending another winter apart from Charlie, however, especially now that there would be two kids to look after.

Karen met Charlie over six years ago after the baseball season had ended. She had started her teaching career the year before, and knew Charlie's mom, Ellen, from church. Charlie had just come back home from an especially disappointing and trying baseball season, and was attempting to get his life back in order. The drinking had to stop and he made a commitment to that, but Ellen thought his son needed something else, something to fill that void, so she brought him to church on Sunday.

Ellen was known around the church and community as the sweetest lady in town. She was widowed far too early, but instead of dwelling on her misfortune she spent her time assisting others in any manner that she could. Her once renowned brown hair was now graying and her eyes were starting to show the lines that come with age, but she still was a very attractive lady at 55 years of age and would have had no difficulty finding another man to spend the rest of her life with if she so chose.

Ellen says that it was just a coincidence, but on that gorgeous Sunday morning in early October she led Charlie to a seat in the pew right next to Karen. Karen's natural beauty and kindness took over from there. With long, blonde hair and clear blue eyes, she was not the picture of a typical lady at Our Savior's Lutheran Church. In fact, she may have been the only single lady in the entire church, besides a couple of widows and divorcees. Karen would come to church by herself nearly every Sunday, but the entire congregation knew it was only a matter of time before she'd be bringing a young man along with her. Like Charlie, Karen was also gifted athletically; having earned a volleyball scholarship at the University of Minnesota. So Charlie and Karen had that athletic component of their lives in common, and found that they could talk to each other easily for hours on end.

They dated for a year before deciding there was no point in delaying the inevitable, and got married there at that same church in a small ceremony. Small only because that's how they wanted it. Everyone in the town had some connection to either Charlie or Karen, and everyone was excited to see their local celebrity finally find someone to hopefully help ease his pain. They all knew of his pain, and all shared in the hope for him to find peace. The growing, young Becker family still attends church there in the winter months while Karen is teaching. Well, mainly Karen and Timmy attend church there with Ellen because Charlie is down south somewhere warm trying to jumpstart his baseball career. That time away makes the already tough Minnesota winters even darker and colder, but at least Ellen is around to help with Timmy.

"Has the Twins organization talked to you about what they want you to do this winter yet?" Karen asked trying to bring up a sensitive subject delicately.

"Not yet. You know they did put me on the 40 man roster this spring so I'm still hopeful that I'll get a call-up to the majors in September when the rosters expand. If I do, maybe I can make an impression and not have to hook up with a winter league team. It would be great to spend the winter with you, Timmy, and the new baby at home this year," Charlie responded trying to ease Karen's worries. Charlie knew, however, that the odds of getting called up were not great. He figured the only reason he made it on the 40 man roster was a lack of left-handed arms in the organization. He just had to keep on throwing, praying, and hoping for the best. Even if they did call him up he wouldn't likely pitch more than an inning or two. And, if he did impress someone, they'd just want to see more of him pitching in the winter leagues somewhere.

His closest call to the majors up to this point came in the disastrous season right before he met Karen. Charlie had been steadily climbing up the Phillies organization, and was the hot shot 26 year old pitching prospect for their Triple-A team. At that time Charlie was a dominant power pitcher. He'd rear back and toss it 98 or 99 mph and just try and blow people away. And, oftentimes, he would do just that. He really only threw two pitches at that point, and the curve only came out when a tough lefty was at the plate. He didn't even dream of trying to throw a changeup back then. Why do that when he could just overpower them all? All he had to do was rear back and let her fly. He was young, bold, and reckless with both his life and his pitching.

There was an open slot in the Phillies rotation that summer because of an injury. The Phillies organization moved Charlie's scheduled start back a day to line it up for him to move into that spot in the big league rotation. But, after he made what might have been his last minor league start ever, Charlie couldn't sleep, and so he did what he always did when he couldn't sleep – he hit the bottle. Normally, besides for the mental anguish and the deterioration of his body, this wasn't a big deal. Unfortunately, that night his roommate left his suitcase out where Charlie didn't see it in the dark, and when he fell over it he instinctively reached out with his left arm as he hit the floor, and he instantly heard a pop. The Phillies front office didn't keep him around very long after that. He was damaged goods. The doctors said that maybe it wouldn't have been such a serious injury if he hadn't been a pitcher who was hurling fastballs at an obscene rate. Maybe if he hadn't been drinking so much that night he might have been able to catch himself less clumsily. Maybe he would have made that major league start in five days, and been a big league pitcher with the Phillies for the rest of his career instead of a damaged minor leaguer. But, then again, maybe there would have been no Karen and Timmy, and that was a maybe that he didn't especially care to think about.

Chapter 3

Rochester, MN

"Shit! Shit! Shit!" Derek Morrison yelled as the van exploded onto highway 52 heading south towards highway 63. "How bad is it, Mike?"

"The bullet just nicked me in the arm. Hurts like hell and I'm bleeding like a stuck pig, but I'm not going to need a hospital or anything," Mike said through clenched teeth while his twin brother Matt held some cloth from his shirt over his arm.

"Damn right you're not going to need a hospital. You think you'd get through a hospital without having the cops all over us?" Tony yelled from the back of the van.

"We're fucked anyway. They saw our faces, and they've got Mike's blood. Our fingerprints ended up everywhere," Matt shot back, "and we've all got records. Anybody following us, Derek?"

"No, I think we're clear for now. Don't see any lights or sirens."

It was supposed to be a simple job for the Morrison brothers. In and out of the bank in five minutes. Masks and gloves donned protecting identities. A stolen van from an area farm to get them away quietly. It was the type of quick hit that they'd done three times already without any difficulty whatsoever. But now they'd killed three people, including an off-duty cop, and they were running for their lives.

"What do we do now?" Matt asked, looking pale and appearing as if he was the one that had been shot. Matt was the most anxious of the Morrison brothers and the most likely to be terrified and freeze up in the middle of a mission. Confidence was not his strong suit. It didn't help that he's always been the smallest Morrison and the most commonly picked on.

"We need to get off this fuckin' highway is what we need to do now," Tony said. "Why are we still on the highway, Derek?"

"Just shut-up Tony and let me drive. We'll take a left up here in Stewartville at the light, hijack a farm, and lay low for a bit. I've got a place that I know about already picked out. We're almost there."

Derek, at age 24, was the oldest and the brains of the operation. He had remote farms picked out all over

Southeastern Minnesota in case there were issues. On Saturdays he would read through the obituaries in the *Rochester Post-Bulletin*, and look for a widow left behind on a farm. It was incredibly easy to find an address, and then Derek, the clean cut Morrison sibling, would stop for a visit pretending to be giving a survey or something. Derek had the long, greasy black hair that the Morrison's were known for, but he was able to comb it back and look at least presentable, if not almost sophisticated. Most of the time he'd just be sent away immediately, but he was there long enough to check for any dogs or any other people that might happen to be living there. There was never a shortage of old farms and old farmers in this part of the country.

Tony, on the other hand, was just plain crazy and he looked it. Wild eyed with a gangly body that had been decimated by all of the drugs over the years, he hardly weighed over 100 pounds anymore. He was the one that decided they needed to start hitting banks instead of just relying on the drug trafficking that they had made their living on. They were making good money off of the drug trade, but that was not enough for Tony. He needed the rush of adrenaline that came from taking out a place with a loaded gun, and even the huge amount of various drugs that Tony consumed could not produce that kind of high. He already had been caught holding up a gas station, and Derek realized that the only way they were going to keep Tony out of jail was for him to start planning things. Tony was too reckless to be left to himself. He lived too much for the moment.

They continued straight through a stop sign out on an old dirt road for about two miles until they took a left down another old road and came up to a worn down looking farmhouse. The farm had once been a decent sized milking operation for that time period before the farms all got huge, but the years of decay with little work put into the upkeep had now just made the place seem small and decrepit. The paint on the buildings was peeling badly, and the house looked like it should just be razed to the ground. It was a sad reminder of growing old for the area neighbors that would occasionally drive by, but the Morrison boys didn't give that any thought.

"Alright, you three just wait in here a second. I'll be back after I take care of things," Derek said.

Tony jumped right in. "Don't mess around Derek. Just off the old lady. We can't keep a hostage right now. We're already in shit deep anyway."

"I know," Derek said calmly, "I'll be back quick."

After Derek left, Tony started working on the twins. "I'm not going back to fuckin' jail boys. If we're going down, we're going down in a blaze of glory. Guns firing. I won't go back there. We need to get high, have us some fun, and then just let it all loose."

"Settle down, Tony. We just need to let Derek figure things out, and lay low like Derek said," Matt said sounding terrified. "Besides right now we have to get Mikey all fixed up."

"Mike's going to be just fine. And, fuck Derek figuring things out. Derek obviously didn't figure things out so well this time, did he? We can't lay low forever. I'm telling ya boys, we're going to do something memorable. Somethin' they'll be talkin' about for years."

"We don't even know that they're on to us yet. We didn't see anyone chasing us and we're here safe right now. Maybe we'll get lucky. Let's just see what happens."

Matt and Mike, the two youngest at 19, had always just blindly followed whatever their older brothers were doing. They didn't have Derek's brains, and they didn't have Tony's passion. They were just consistently along for the ride, trailing their brothers wherever they would lead them. Neither one said much, but even if they did disagree with what their brothers asked of them they were loyal to no end. They just always seemed sad to everyone who knew them; like beaten dogs. It appeared as if they had no motivation to do anything other than breathe.

Five minutes later Derek came walking coolly back to the van like nothing happened. "Alright, let's take care of business. Tony, the twins and I will take care of patching up Mike, moving the old lady, and cleaning up the blood. You can park the van back behind the barn over there, and bring in our stuff."

"Yes sir, Mr. Boss, sir," Tony said sarcastically, taking orders about as well as he always did from his older brother.

Derek, ignoring it, said, "After we do that we need to have someone standing guard by the front door in case anyone shows up. Then we can give one of our neighbors a call from the old bag's home phone, and see if the cops are looking around outside our place in Rochester. Anything I'm missing?"

Tony never missed a chance to respond to a lead-in like that, especially when he had a chance to make Derek look stupid. "Yo, super smart genius, all we have to do is turn on the TV and we'll see all we need to see about whether they're on to us or not. We also better take the phone off the hook in case someone calls. Old people are always leaving their phones off the hook so it won't be too suspicious."

"Good idea, Tony," Derek said, passively placating Tony like he always did. "Let's get moving."

Tony, however, had other plans. As soon as the other three brothers started walking to the house Tony backed out of the driveway. The twins just stood there staring with their mouths open in disbelief. Derek, on the other hand, wasn't surprised by anything that Tony did anymore.

"Where do you suppose he's off to?" Derek asked with a strange calmness.

"I don't know," Matt said, "but he sure was all fired up in the car. Talkin' about guns blazing and getting high."

"Well, then my guess is he's off to Stacy's house. Nice of him to let us know his plans," said Derek wryly.

Stacy's house was where the Morrison's stored things that they didn't want found. The Morrison boys lived together in a beat up place not far from The Mayo Clinic in downtown Rochester despite the fact that they'd swindled enough cash to live in a much nicer place if they preferred. However, they never kept anything of value there. The risk was too great for a surprise visit from the local authorities.

They had at one point, three years earlier, tried living separately, but it wasn't able to catch. Derek got clean enough to take a sales position at a furniture place. He started renting his own apartment, and even had a girl that he was seeing. Not the usual drugged out girl looking for some free goods either, but a regular, smart girl. She was the kind of girl that he could have a normal life with. A girl that reminded him fondly of his own mom. But he couldn't keep himself together; his head was just too messed up from the events of his earlier days. The pain was too real and too heavy to hide without some sort of chemical assistance. Three months into his sales job he started casually doing drugs and drinking on the weekends. Then it crept into the week, and eventually, led to him being high at work. That was plenty reason enough to get him fired, and for his girl to see that she wasn't going to have much of a life with him, and so that was the end of that.

Derek thought of that as an experiment to see if he could make it in regular society. He wanted a regular job – a regular life, but he felt helpless to achieve it. Seeing that he couldn't, he found the place downtown to help centrally locate the drug trade for him and his brothers, and that's why they were still there today. It was the perfect location for shady looking people to come in and out of at all hours. Even though the twins were yet in high school when he bought the place they were essentially living up in Rochester already, and it was apparent even at that stage that they weren't going anywhere else with their lives. They might as well be part of the business operation. Of course, keeping everything there at the house just wasn't going to work, so luckily they had Stacy.

Stacy was a single mother with two elementary aged kids who happened to live only about five minutes from their current location on the farm. She was a receptionist at a dentist's office, and would be about the least likely person you'd expect to house thousands of dollars' worth of drugs, guns, and ammunition. Unfortunately for Stacy, she had a huge cocaine problem. She just couldn't help herself anymore, and eventually she stopped even trying.

The Morrison's had been selling to her for about two years when Stacy ran out of ways to pay them. Derek, however, had been to her remote house and seen the basement, and had the perfect answer. So, she got all the coke she needed, and they had a place away from probation officers to store the stuff that came in and out.

Tony took his time, and made it to Stacy's house without any issues. All he had to do was take that dirt road until it met up with County 1 and head south for a few miles. He knew he'd be fine and wasn't worried about it, but at the same time he knew Derek would never let him go, so there was no point in arguing with him. He'd just take care of things on his own. That's the way Tony did things when he knew Derek wouldn't like his ideas. Tony also needed some time to calm down and plan. He needed to get Derek to go along with him on his idea, and he had to come up with a way to make that happen. As much as he hated to admit it, this thing could never be successful without Derek's help.

He loaded up enough ammunition for a small army, and decided heroin would be the drug of choice tonight. He also raided Stacy's fridge and liquor cabinet for some booze and some food. He left a wad of cash on the table to hopefully keep Stacy from doing something stupid like notifying the police if and when their faces showed up on the news. Thirty minutes later he had everything he needed, and he was off again. Luckily, Stacy and the kids weren't around. Although, if they did happen to be at home it wouldn't have been a big deal. In fact, it might have actually been easier. He'd have just eliminated them as well. At this stage the body count was too big to control anyways, and he didn't feel like playing games. By the time that he pulled back into the old lady's driveway near Stewartville he had the hook figured out for Derek. He'd give Derek a little reminder of his past. By doing so, Tony could get the revenge from his own past that he desired. Oh, Derek would be in alright, and someday there'd be a movie made about the Morrison boys. Tony had a big smile on his face, the smile of an insane man, thinking about what was to come.

Chapter 4

Spring Valley, MN

Southeast Minnesota is filled with old farming communities just trying to hang on. The farmers are getting older, and the farms are getting bigger which means less of them. Spring Valley is one such town. Once a thriving community, it now has vacant buildings, empty streets, and a feeling of decay. Fortunately for the town it is close enough to Rochester that they get some commuters who enjoy the small town life enough to live in the community, and drive the 30 mile trip to Rochester and back every day. Those are the hardworking residents that the town loves – the Mayo Clinic doctors and nurses and the IBM engineers. But, unfortunately for Spring Valley, it also attracts individuals looking for extremely cheap housing. Combine that with the fact that the state has a very generous unemployment system, and a lot of Northern Iowans and Western Wisconsinites move into the area for their free lunch and low rent. Not exactly the clientele that the community would love to bring in, but right now they take whatever they can get.

Of course, if you're avoiding the Iowa state law enforcement, jumping across the border is a smart move as well. And so, eight years before the bank heist gone wrong, the Morrison's came north. Bill and his wife Jean packed all their belongings in their old beat up van; threw the four boys in, and away they went. The boys weren't exactly thrilled about being taken away from all they knew in Iowa, and they were quite vocal about that. Derek and Tony, a sophomore and freshman in high school respectively, were especially irate about the move.

"This is fucking stupid!" Tony said for the fifth time on the drive north.

"Stupid," Derek echoed on Tony's right.

"Just shut the fuck up!" Bill yelled from the driver's seat. "I'm tired of both your fuckin' mouths. Quit being such little bitches."

"What do you two want? Your Mom and Dad sitting in fuckin' jail?" Jean said back at the boys. "I'm sure that would be a great life for you."

Swearing was the norm in the Morrison household. It didn't matter who was doing the talking or who they were talking to, that was just the way that they did it, and not just with each other. They didn't even realize they were swearing. The words were just other adjectives. All four boys had been in trouble for cursing in school, and each time Jean would get the call she'd just be cursing right back at the principal for wasting her time. Jean was also intelligent enough to use the law to her advantage and throw around lawsuit threats whenever the school would discuss suspension or expulsion.

"Don't you think that perhaps you're being a little paranoid here, Mom," Derek said. "You haven't been formally charged with anything and you've been distributing for years."

"Look who thinks he fuckin' knows so much! It's Mr. Boy Genius using his big fuckin' words just like his mommy," Bill said angrily. "Here are some big words for you. We're under surveillance and it was only a matter of time before we were incarcerated. Plus, the business is dying down there. Here in Minnesota, I'm close enough to keep using the same supplier and I have a whole new group of buyers."

"And Tony," Bill continued now that he was getting fired up, "Grow a pair. I expect Momma's boy to be a whiny bitch about this, but you need to man up. When I was your ages I was working all day on the farm, and was nearly a dad. I wasn't no whiny little baby. Now, shut the fuck up!" With that Bill cranked up the radio and they listened in silence the rest of the way.

Bill and Jean started dating each other in high school. Well, dating is a loose term. They started having sex with each other in high school. They were 15 years old when Derek was born. 16 when Tony came along. They were married at 18, and then the twins followed a few years later. Except for the first pregnancy Jean drank right through pregnancies and never had any intentions of stopping. After all, it was her body. She did it by the book with Derek and got her baby. She wasn't interested in any more, and definitely was not trying to become pregnant. All three of the other kids had some of the tell-tale signs of Fetal Alcohol Syndrome – the small eyes, thin upper lip, and small head circumference. Jean really didn't care. They were just lucky that she didn't abort them as far as she was concerned. One baby was all that she wanted. Bill didn't want any of them, except maybe to do some manual labor for him. Even when they were infants they were just leeches to him, sucking all of his money away.

Neither Jean nor Bill graduated High School, or were even remotely close to graduating. Neither one cared. Jean could have gotten better grades in school if she chose to. Bill, maybe not. They had more important things to do anyway than care about that, like drink and party. That led to them needing money, and slowly the drug business grew from there. They each had worked part-time jobs at various stages in their lives as well, but neither could hold down a regular job. There was little chance of them ever arriving to work on time or in a coherent state on a consistent basis. Again, neither one cared.

They didn't love each other anymore, just tolerated each other. They weren't faithful either, and they didn't even sleep in the same bed anymore. It wasn't the kids that kept them together, however. In fact, at this stage in the kids' lives neither one really would have wanted the kids in a divorce, except maybe Jean wanting Derek. It was the business that kept the marriage together and the realization that if either one ever got caught they would sing like a canary to put the other behind bars if it would save their own ass. Also, Jean was convinced that if she ever tried to leave that Bill would track her down and kill her, and she was probably right. Jean was pretty sure that Bill had killed in the past. The fact that she suffered from battered wife's syndrome, was in no condition to go anywhere, and had no family support didn't help either. So she tried to lay low, keep her husband happy, and especially avoid him at all costs if he'd been drinking.

About four hours after the trip began the Morrison van made it across the Iowa border and into the town of Spring Valley. They decided to turn down Main Street and take a look at the downtown area. That jaunt lasted a whole 15 seconds as the downtown only encompasses two blocks of buildings. They only saw two people milling around, and those two had to be a combined 200 years of age. Bill and Jean shared a worried look, and without saying a word, they had the same thought. How were they going to find enough people in this community to sell drugs to? So, five minutes into Spring Valley a new business plan was formed.

"We're gonna need the boys to pull their weight, now," Bill said looking at his wife.

"The school," Jean replied, understanding what her husband was talking about without any other explanation. "We've talked about this before. You know I'm not that excited about that. The boys talk too much and are too hot-headed."

"I don't care what you're excited about. We'll just have to train them. I'll take care of that." For Bill, training them meant beating the shit out of them. He'd make sure that the boys feared him so much that they wouldn't do anything stupid. Bill was convinced he'd been too soft on them anyway up to this point in their lives. That wasn't going to continue. It didn't take a rocket scientist to sell drugs, so Tony would be just fine. Bill would just beat the hot-headedness out of him. It was Derek that he'd have to watch. Derek was still wasting his time trying to do school work and be one of the popular kids. He talked too much instead of just laying low and staying out of the way. Bill actually blamed Derek for them having to move. The sheriff's daughter was a classmate of Derek's and the surveillance started right after those two started spending time together. Might be a coincidence, but Bill didn't believe in coincidences. He'd rather just place blame and be angry.

For the first eight months in Spring Valley the Morrison drug ring thrived without a hitch. The boys had no trouble finding willing buyers in the school. Derek especially, with his good looks and charm, introduced kids to the world of drugs that would otherwise have never ventured there. He made the whole thing cool to a big group of kids. Word eventually leaked into the community so that people were actually coming up to the boys out of the blue looking for drugs. They would even use the high school locker room in the basement to conduct their business. They'd leave the back door to the locker room propped open in case the main door happened to be locked – which most of the time wasn't. With no windows, a musty dungeon-like feel, and practically no traffic it worked perfectly as a trusted exchange area. They'd sneak down there before school, after school, lunch time, between classes, even during classes – it was like their own little office. What did they care if they happened to be tardy or truant anyway?

The boys would mark up the prices and then only give their dad a portion of the sales. They finally had money to buy some of the necessities that they'd often gone without. Derek was now not just good looking and charming, but also had the nice clothes to match. And, best of all, they were still selling so much that Bill didn't know about the amount they were skimming off the top.

Even though Bill had money rolling in at a very profitable rate, he was not a contented man. Now that he was more of a hands-off member of the operation he was having difficulty with the lack of control, and the extra downtime. To deal with that he took to two of his favorite pastimes – drinking and fighting. Unfortunately for the rest of the Morrison's he was drinking at home, and was thus beating up his family. All four of the kids would get their share, but to the chagrin of Jean, Derek took the most abuse. Derek was too much like Jean for Bill. Too soft, not manly enough.

Derek would oftentimes show up to school with huge bruises and cuts on his face and actually missed quite a bit of school while he was healing up from several of the beatings. In fact, Derek was passing all of his classes before he started having to miss more and more time to heal. But, between the days spent at home with injuries and the days spent away from school because of suspensions for swearing and fighting, Derek was now failing everything, and his demeanor at school was clearly getting darker. Jean noticed this as well, and although obviously not a nurturing, caring sort of mother, she started trying to hide and protect her favorite son a little bit from his dad. Jean would much rather see one of her other boys take the abuse than Derek, especially since Derek was taking it almost daily, so she'd run interference for him on days where Bill was especially fired and liquored up – even going so far as to set Tony up on something he didn't do.

Unfortunately for Derek and Jean, she couldn't protect him on that day eight months after they moved in that forever changed their lives. That was the day that Bill found out that the boys had been keeping a portion of his money. Greg Thompson, one of the boy's customers from the community, couldn't get into the school that day so he went directly to the Morrison's house.

"Who the fuck are you?" Bill said when Greg came up and knocked on his door.

"Name's Greg," He said. "Are you Derek and Tony's dad? I'm looking to make a purchase."

"How do I know you're not a cop?"

"Don't your boys keep track of who they sell to? My last name's Thompson. I buy weed every couple of weeks. Look it up."

Bill didn't go in to look it up because there was nowhere to look. The boys did not keep track of who they sold to, but Bill recognized the name from hearing the boys talk about their regular customers. From now on he'd also definitely have his boys keep more detailed information on who they sell to and what they sell. He'd have to beat that info into their heads after school.

"Alright, how much you want?" Bill asked gruffly.

"I'll take half an ounce. Here's 125 bucks," Greg said pulling out six 20's and a 5.

"What the fuck is this? I don't make change. Go to the bank and come back with the 90 bucks even."

"90? You havin' some sorta sale? I don't got no coupons. Is it buy one, get one free day?" Greg said chuckling. "I've got another fiver in here if that's all ya want."

Greg exchanged the bills and handed Bill the 90 dollars as Bill gazed dumbfounded for a second. Then it hit him, and he instantly became irate. His boys were screwing him over. He grabbed the cash, tossed the weed at Greg, and slammed the door shut. It was only 10 AM, but Bill went immediately for his whiskey and stewed. As he sat there drinking all morning and early afternoon he became more and more heated. He was building himself up for an explosion as his rage was welling up inside of him. The boys were going to pay for this. How dare they steal from him!

Finally, at around 4:30, the boys and their mom came home. Tony was the first one through the door and, while talking to one of the twins, was greeted by a fist to the side of the head and immediately went down in the middle of the doorway. Bill dragged him inside and dropped him in the living room.

"Think you can steal my money?" Bill yelled, slurring his words and giving Tony a kick to the ribs.

The twins sprinted up the stairs to hideout in their bedroom, but Bill had no interest in them. Derek was a step behind Jean looking terrified. Bill threw Jean out of the way and grabbed Derek by the hair.

"You thought I wouldn't find out?" Bill fumed. "These are my drugs and my money. You don't get to keep any of it. I give you everything you need."

Bill threw a right hook to Derek's left eye and he went down as well. The boys had learned to go down easy, and then they were normally left alone once on the ground. Not today, however. Bill gave Derek a couple of kicks while he was on the ground, and then moved back over to Tony and sat down on top of him pinning his arms to the ground.

With his nose just inches from Tony's he growled, "Whose idea was this?"

Tony could smell the whiskey on his breath and was too scared to respond, but he turned his eyes and looked over at his brother Derek.

"That's what I thought. Always Mr. Smart Guy comin' up with these great ideas. Well, Mr. Smart Guy, now it's time to pay up," Bill said, giving one more quick punch to Tony's mouth before moving back to his brother.

Derek, realizing what was about to come, tried crawling away, but Bill grabbed him by the back of his pants and pulled him back.

"Where do you think you're going? It's time to pay the piper."

Bill lifted Derek up off the ground and gave him a shot to the gut. Derek was down again curled up in the fetal position, and Bill started kicking him. After two or three kicks Jean had seen enough.

"Stop it, Bill. That's enough," Jean yelled trying to grab onto Bill and pull him back.

"You just shut up, bitch. You probably knew about this the whole time." And he pushed her off and gave her a couple of kicks as well. The front door was still open, and Jean gave off a couple of terrifying screams; terrifying enough that the Kramer's next door had heard plenty and immediately called the cops.

Bill left Jean where she was, went back to Derek, and gave him a big boot to the face that broke his nose. Blood was now streaming out everywhere, but still that was no deterrent to Bill. If anything, Derek's wails of pain were just more incentive to keep at him.

Tony, meanwhile, had scrambled upstairs to his bedroom and was trying to stay quiet and out of the way while Derek was getting cursed at and spat on. He, like all of the Morrison boys, didn't care who was getting beat-up or how bad they were beaten as long as it wasn't him. Tony had no feelings of sympathy for his brother; it was every man for himself.

Jean had never seen Bill like this before. Sure there had been some beatings, but normally they would stop after a couple of blows. This just seemed to continue and drag on, and she was to the point of believing that Bill was going to kill them all. So she decided to do something about it. Quietly, while Bill was focused on Derek, she went into her room and took out the 9mm handgun that Bill always had loaded by the side of his bed. She hurried into the other room and fired off a shot into the wall to get Bill's attention.

Bill looked at her. "What the fuck do you think you're doing?"

"I've had enough of this Bill. We aren't going to live like this anymore. Let him go, now!" Jean didn't have a lot of experience with a gun, but she figured she could point it and shoot it effectively at this close range.

Bill dropped Derek onto the floor and said, "Alright, I'm done. Put the gun down."

"I don't think so. I don't think you'll ever be done," Jean said, keeping the gun pointed directly at Bill's chest. "We can't have you around anymore. There will always be more beating and more abuse. We don't need you around anymore. All you do is sit here at home and drink anyway."

"What are you going to do, shoot me?"

"Yes," Jean said, and just looked at him coldly.

At that moment Sheriff Aaron Nelson came through the door with his gun out and yelled "Police! Drop the gun!" Sheriff Nelson had been a county policeman for eight years now, but had never been involved in a situation like this before with a gun drawn. He had just been voted Sheriff of the county a couple of months ago and had felt confident in his abilities in that role until this very moment. The newness of this experience had him rattled, and he was noticeably fidgety and uneasy. Even his voice sounded tight when he spoke, like it was his words being spoken by someone else's mouth.

"No, I can't do that. Bill's going to have to die," Jean said lowering her gun to her side with an eerie calmness to her. "But first he's going to tell you about how he's been beating on his wife and his kids for all of these years. He's going to tell you the reason that this has to happen this way, and you're going to understand why he has to die."

Sheriff Nelson kept his gun trained on Jean, but started to notice Bill moving slowly towards a table that was next to the couch. "Hey, stand still," he yelled, "or I'll shoot!" He needed backup. He needed some assistance. A bead of sweat started rolling down the side of his face, and his mouth felt dry. The words that were coming out of his mouth didn't even seem like his own. It was like they were coming from someone else.

Just then, Derek staggered up from behind his mom. He was wobbly from the blows to the head and the blood running out of his nose, so the movement appeared sudden to the shaking Sheriff Nelson from the corner of his eye. Without completely processing what was going on, he just reacted. It was no more than a twitch, but it was a twitch that pulled the trigger. A twitch that would almost define him and affect his life. The bullet hit Jean directly through the heart, and she fell dead instantly - her red blood splattered all over her oldest son's shocked face.

Chapter 5

Richmond, VA

Life as a minor league baseball player is not one of expensive meals, five star hotels, and private jets. Instead it involves lots of McDonald's, Days Inn's, and long motor coach rides. It is not the glamour and glory of the big leagues. Rather, it's a grind; a grind with lots of time to just sit and think, especially for a starting pitcher. This is the aspect of baseball that Charlie likes the least. Since his last start on Saturday, he has endured a six hour Sunday afternoon double header, a six and a half hour bus ride to Altoona, three nights and games there, and now finally a five hour bus trip to Richmond. All of this was done without playing an inning of actual baseball himself.

Unfortunately for Charlie, this gives him lots of time to think and reflect – two things that he'd rather not be doing. The younger players use that time to play cards, sleep, listen to music, or watch TV. Sometimes Charlie joins the card games just to try and stay involved with his teammates, but he doesn't really enjoy it. Probably because he keeps losing money! Sleep is really not an option for Charlie, and listening to music and watching TV are not a big enough distraction from that thinking and reflecting thing that he was trying to avoid. So, without Karen and Timmy around he has learned to try and fill the endless time by reading anything he can find.

"Watcha reading now, Chuckster?" Dusty asked, charging into their hotel room a little bit intoxicated. Despite the fact that it was 1:30 AM and Charlie was pitching that day it was no surprise to see him awake at that hour. Dusty and Charlie had been rooming together on the road all season, and by now Dusty realized that Charlie just didn't really sleep.

"Been reading John Sandford lately," Charlie replied. "All his books take place back home in Minnesota. God's country."

"I'm sure that's some exciting reading about lakes and farms. Let me guess, they're mystery stories where they ask the burning Minnesota questions like 'Will the corn be knee high by the Fourth of July?' or 'How do I make the perfect hole in the ice to best fish?'" Dusty said, on a roll now. "Or, even better, I bet they are romance novels where the characters have to take off their parkas and ten layers of clothing so that they can have sex, and then quick throw them all back on so they don't freeze to death. Couldn't you find a more exciting state to read about like North Dakota or something?"

"We can't all be from the big city like you are, Mr. NYC. Your Minnesota knowledge has really improved, though. I must be a positive influence on you. You'll be all ready to go when the Twins call you up to the show. Hey, speaking of Minnesota, how about this hotel we're in. It's like something straight out of a Prince video with all the purple colors."

"A what? Who's Prince?"

"Never mind. I guess we still have some work to do on your Minnesota knowledge. How did the cards fall tonight?"

"Glad you finally asked! I thought we were gonna talk about the great white north forever for a second there."

"That's Alaska," Charlie interrupted.

"Whatever. Those states are right next to each other anyway, right? So anyway, Benny started drinking as soon as we rolled into town here tonight, and of course he starts talking. I'm goin' to the big leagues. You guys all suck. Blah, blah, blah. While he's mouthing off I'm sitting across from him setting the deck while a couple of the other guys keep him talking and distracted. Long story short, the Bonus Baby is out 400 bucks, and I'm gonna buy me and the boys a steak dinner tomorrow. Dumb shit might be a millionaire, but he'll end up in debt somehow. He sure ain't sittin' around reading wilderness novels about migrating deer like you are. Anyways, I've got a big day of chasing around your wild pitches tomorrow. Let's get some sleep. Try not to wake me up with any of your crazy man screams tonight, alright?"

"I'll do my best, Dusty."

For Charlie "getting some sleep" meant putting his book away and staring at the ceiling for a while as Benny snored away in the next bed. Tomorrow's start against the Flying Squirrels was an important one in Charlie's mind. Richmond knocked him around pretty good earlier in the season, and gave him one of his four losses on the year. It would be a good test of some of the adjustments that he's made, and he was looking forward to it more than a usual start. After this many years toiling in the minors Charlie has learned to use any extra motivation that he can find. More importantly for Charlie, Karen and Timmy would be in town tomorrow and he'd have at least one night where he could put his book away and have some enjoyment and happiness in his life.

Morning for Charlie comes around about four hours earlier than it does for Dusty. By this time of the year, Charlie has gotten good at quietly getting himself showered and ready and into the hotel lobby for a normally crappy continental breakfast. Game day has always been a favorite day of Charlie's, but it is for different reasons now than it used to be. Now, the baseball part of it doesn't matter much. He's just excited to see his family again. If his family could be with him all the time the baseball job wouldn't be so difficult for him. It's not that he doesn't still enjoy the game, he just misses them. He always brings his cell phone with him to breakfast, and gives Karen a call while he drinks his morning coffee.

"Hey, honey, all ready for the trip?" Charlie asked, not hiding his excitement.

"I think so. It will be another long one," Karen replied, not nearly as excited about the trip as Charlie is. After all Charlie doesn't have to be in the car for eight hours there and back all alone with a 3 year old.

"I know that it's tough making these trips, but I really do appreciate it. This should be the last one anyway, with school starting soon, right?"

"Yeah, I think so, except for Wednesday at Altoona of course. Unless we get rained out, the rest of your starts should be at home until my school year begins. Then I really won't see you. I'm not looking forward to that."

"Well, we'll worry about that when the time comes. I think of this being one big trip and forget that you really end up with two different drives. I'm sorry that you have to do that, but I really do like having you here," Charlie said, feeling guilty about putting his family through this. "When do you think you'll head out?"

"I think we'll leave once Timmy wakes up. I've got his DVD player and videos all ready to go. I just need to shower and get dressed."

"Alright, I'll let you get going. Love you!"

"Love you, too!"

The next nine hours were spent doing more of the same thing he'd been doing all week – waiting. More John Sandford, a little ESPN, and some time spent listening to Dusty talk about whatever topic happened to pop into his head.

Karen and Timmy arrived at the ballpark around 5:15 for the 7:00 PM game. After that long drive Karen needed a break, and Timmy needed to run, so Charlie would take Timmy out to the field while Karen watched from the dugout. For years Charlie would hardly speak to people on days that he was pitching, and like many starting pitchers you wouldn't want to be anywhere around him. But, like many other things from his early baseball days, those times were behind him. He let all of that go. That might contribute to why he couldn't zone out anymore in games. His priorities had changed and baseball just wasn't as important as it had been before.

Karen always enjoyed watching Charlie and Timmy running around the field. They'd throw a tennis ball around for a little while, wrestle in the grass, and sometimes play out in the warning track dirt. The hurt would leave Charlie's eyes for a little while, and she could tell that he was always at ease and like a kid again in those moments. While she was sitting there smiling to herself, Coach Scott sidled up alongside her.

"How's he doing, Karen?" Scott asked, knowing that Karen was the only one who truly could read Charlie. Scott was also one of the few people who knew some of the details of Charlie's troubled past.

"Well, he's still not sleeping, and he hates being out on the road. He sure is happy when Timmy is around, however."

"I agree with that. It's the first time I've seen him smile on the whole road trip. He's probably read three novels in the past four days alone. I'd like to think his happiness is because he's pitching tonight, but I know better. I'm not sure he could make it without you and Timmy coming to these games. He's definitely been throwing good ball for us lately."

"Coach, I know Charlie won't ask you this, but I need to know, is there any chance of him getting a September call-up here in a couple of weeks?"

"Honestly, I really don't know. If the Twins stay in the playoff race there's a greater possibility. If they fall off my guess is they'd go with some of the younger boys. But I tell ya what; if they ask me about it my answer will be an absolute yes. I know we'll have an organizational meeting sometime later on this month to discuss those decisions, and hopefully they'll listen to the old coot. It's hard to say whether they will or not. You know Karen, he's just been an amazing influence for us this year. I wish all of the boys were as professional about their business as he is."

"Thanks for being straightforward and honest with me Coach, I really do appreciate it. Good luck tonight."

The Twins were currently two games back in the division race tied with the Tigers in second. The Indians, fresh off a sweep of the Yankees, were now in first place in the division. Karen decided she needed to pay a little closer attention to how her hometown team was doing in the future.

About an hour before first pitch Karen rounded up Timmy and they made their way to their seats, and got Timmy his hot dog for supper. For a three year old, Timmy was amazing with his ability to entertain himself for long periods of time sitting relatively still. He'd had plenty of practice between the long drives and the three hour baseball games. Normally, Timmy would only make it through about the fifth inning before he'd fall asleep in his mom's arms. Tonight, however, Timmy made it through seven and a half innings because his dad threw a gem. His line was impressive: 7 and one-third innings, 3 hits, no runs, no walks, and 5 strikeouts. The game flew by in just over two hours, and the Rock Cats came out with a 2-0 shutout win.

"Hey Chuckster, that's the way to fling the baseball around!" Dusty said in the locker room afterwards. "It's too bad we weren't at home. The gun would've been registering at least 87 a couple of times tonight. I actually needed my mitt this game instead of just catching you with my bare hands. I haven't played in a game that was done that quickly since Little League. Hey, I gotta ask, you coming out with us tonight? Steak dinner, remember?"

"Nah, you know I have the family here," Charlie responded.

"I know, just wanted to let you know you're invited."

"Oh hey, you'll have the room to yourself tonight. I'll be staying with Karen and Timmy in their room."

"Uh oh," Dusty said with a big grin on his face and doing a little dance. "They better hide all the proper young ladies of Richmond if you know what I mean. Things are going to get a little bit craaaaazy in the purple palace of room 213. I might bring back 3 or 4 ladies. Maybe some dancers. It's on!"

"I'm sure, Dusty," Charlie replied, not believing one word of it. Dusty had a girlfriend named Megan back in

New Britain, and for all the talk of being a player there was no one more in love and faithful than Dusty. In fact, Charlie's being gone probably just meant more time to Skype with her that night.

A couple of seconds later Karen came walking in carrying Timmy who was amazingly still fast asleep - curled up in her arms. "Are you ready?" She asked, and handed Timmy over to Charlie.

"Yeah, just been listening to Dusty talk about the young ladies he's going to have up in our hotel room tonight. Right, big guy?" Charlie said with a smile on his face knowing exactly how to push Dusty's buttons.

"No. Never said anything like that," Dusty said, suddenly very serious and giving Charlie a death glare.

"Don't worry, Dusty, your playboy secrets are safe with me," Karen responded smiling, also knowing that Dusty wouldn't even look at another woman. Karen and Charlie would occasionally have Dusty and Megan over to their house for supper, and Charlie always thoroughly enjoyed it because all of a sudden Dusty became a quiet and proper young man, quite unlike the boisterous guy he was when with the boys.

The Becker's left the stadium and drove back to the hotel together, talking quietly about what Timmy had been up to over the past few days, while he slept in the back. On the way, Charlie drove through a McDonalds to grab a couple of late night cheeseburgers for his supper. His eating schedule was always a mess on nights that he pitched, and he unfortunately ended up eating a lot of junk. Luckily for Charlie he naturally burned a lot of calories.

When they got to the hotel Charlie managed to get Timmy into the double bed without him waking up, and wished that he could sleep like that. Karen, exhausted from the long day, fell asleep as soon as her head hit the pillow while Charlie watched some muted *SportsCenter*. It was a great day for Charlie, and because of it he even managed a couple hours of sleep that night without any big nightmares – for Charlie a huge success.

With the light of morning came another launch of the five day starting pitcher cycle. His routine started a little bit differently this morning as Timmy was up and ready to hit the hotel pool. Timmy and Charlie swam around together while Karen got the car packed up for another long road trip home that both she and Timmy were dreading. The traveling was wearing on Karen and she missed having Charlie around to help raise their son in the same way that he missed being around. By noon Karen and Timmy were back on the road again. Charlie was left alone once more and made his way to the fitness room to workout, trying to get lost in the cycle to make another four days go by as quickly as possible.

Chapter 6

Altoona, PA

During the long bus trips around the Eastern portion of the United States, Coach Don Scott likes to move around the bus and hold little meetings with his players. Sometimes he'd only get to three or four players depending on how much he had to go over with the rest of his coaching staff. On other days he'd nearly cover the entire squad. Don thought of them more as informal conversations than meetings, and he used them to try and keep a pulse on the heartbeat of his team. About halfway through the five hour trip to Altoona he took the opportunity to visit with Charlie a little bit.

"Hi Charlie," Scott said easing his way into a seat next to him on the team charter bus. "How are you feeling?"

"Feeling great, Skip," Charlie replied smiling. "My arm hasn't felt this strong in years. Not since before my surgery. You'd think with all the innings I've thrown that I'd be tiring out, but it's somehow going in the opposite direction. Hope it keeps up."

"Me too, but I meant how are you doing mentally?"

"I'm fine, Coach. Don't worry about that."

"Just want to make sure you're alright. You've really been a great addition to the team this year. I gotta be honest, when they told me that we were bringing in the infamous Charlie Becker at your age I wasn't very thrilled about it."

"I gotta be honest with you," Charlie said with a smirk, "I'd never heard of the not so infamous Don Scott! Luckily it turned out well for both of us."

"Yes it did. Listen, Charlie, I don't know what's going to come of next year or even next month, but if you'd ever like a coaching position someday I'd love to have you on my staff. I think you'd make a great pitching coach."

"Thanks, Skip, but I don't see that happening. I don't think I'm going to be ready to hang it up anytime soon, at least not until I either get my shot in the majors or no one will take me anymore. I just can't quit yet. Even if I did retire I couldn't coach professionally. I can't handle the time on the road away from home. I miss my family too much. Once I'm finally done I'm going to do something where I can see my kids every day. I want to be able to put Timmy to bed every night."

"I think that sounds like a wonderful idea, Charlie. You're a great father, and that's refreshing to see nowadays. I regret not being around more for my kids a lifetime ago. Just remember, being in the big leagues isn't everything. I've been there, and in a lot of ways life down here is better – better people, less stress, fewer egos. If you want to be home more, then just do it; be home more. Don't get hooked on some ideal big league life that might never happen for you."

"Alright, I'll give it some thought," Charlie said trying to put the subject to bed. "Anything else, Skip?"

"Yeah, actually there is. I want you to drive home after the game on Wednesday with your family."

"Are you sure, Skip? That's not team policy."

"Yeah, I'm sure. Enjoy the day off Thursday and we'll see you back at the ballpark on Friday."

"Thanks for doing that for me Skip, I really appreciate it."

"I'm not doing it for you. I'm doing it for that poor pregnant wife of yours that has to drive halfway around the world with only a three year old to keep her company. I can't even fathom what those car trips are like. That woman's a saint. Not sure what she's doing with a bum like you!" Scott said, letting out one of his body-shaking laughs that he was known for. He scanned the bus looking for someone else to talk to. "Guess I better go talk with Benny.

We'll see if I can get him off his cell phone long enough to talk to the senile ball coach that he can't wait to get rid of. I bet he's talking to his agent about ways to get off of this team right now."

With that, Don shuffled away leaving Charlie to his own thoughts again. He decided that at some point in the next couple of weeks, he'd allow himself to at least think about retirement from baseball a little more seriously. For now, however, he'd sit back and try to enjoy his book, and get lost in a different world. The important real life issues can wait for another day.

Charlie had nearly a photographic memory. It was a blessing, and at times, of course, a curse. For a pitcher it was a very useful ability to have, but for a man with something to forget it was a nightmare. On nights that he pitched he could reconstruct the details of the game and make decisions on how to handle those situations differently and to his advantage in the future. These reconstructions helped with Charlie's always active mind, and helped him be at ease when he couldn't sleep.

With a long drive home from Altoona ahead of him, it was a perfect time for him to go through his start from just a few hours ago while Karen and Timmy slept next to him. They were both exhausted, and both extremely grateful to have Charlie with them on the trip. Timmy was especially wound up when he realized that his dad was going to be taking him home, and he insisted that he was going to stay up the entire way. He was initially a ball of energy. He started making noises, sang some songs that he'd learned at Sunday school, and talked about some of the things that he'd been doing over the last few days. Ten minutes later, however, just like that, he was fast asleep.

Karen offered to stay up and keep Charlie company on the long trip, but Charlie insisted that she just get some rest. Karen didn't protest too much, and after about two hours of filling in Charlie on the details of her past few days she fell asleep as well. It had been a long week for her, too. So with about four hours to go before arriving in New Britain Charlie set the cruise control and let the reconstruction process begin.

Trouble started almost right out of the gate for Charlie. The first Altoona Curve batter took the first pitch and hit a line shot that happened to be pulled right into Byron Wells' glove at third, and knocked him backwards. Byron was playing in on the grass guarding against the bunt and he caught it more out of self-defense than anything. After throwing it around the horn it came back to Byron who walked it in towards the mound to Charlie.

"That thing about killed me!" Byron said with a smile, laughing at himself. "Next time you're going to throw a changeup and I'm in on the grass give me a little heads up or something."

Charlie, taking the ball back and rubbing it, replied, "Got some bad news for ya Wellsy, that was my heater. Better not be in on the grass too much tonight." With that Charlie gave Byron a smack on the butt and went back up on the hill.

Things only got worse from there. Not only was Charlie lacking velocity, but his pinpoint control also seemed to disappear on him. He walked the second batter on four straight pitches for his first walk in three games. Charlie could survive with no velocity by placing his pitches perfectly. If he couldn't locate his pitches and he couldn't blow it past anyone, than things were clearly going to be difficult. Luckily for Charlie the third batter, a first baseman that must have weighed 300 pounds, smoked a one hop groundball to Santiago at short which started a 6-4-3 double play to end the inning. One of the worst innings he'd thrown all season and there wasn't a single hit up on the board, he'd only faced three batters, and had thrown only six pitches. Baseball's a crazy game.

Going through the first inning in his mind helped Charlie discover two things. One was that he was missing inside to the right-handed hitters he was facing – possibly because he was opening up too early. The second is things were slightly up in the zone. He'd have to analyze a little bit more why he was missing to the right in his next bullpen sessions, but he was pretty certain the reason he was missing up was with his stride length. Charlie had a tendency to step too far forward with his right foot which kept his release point higher, and thus left his pitches up.

After that first half inning Coach Scott came up to Charlie right away. It was pretty unusual for him to visit after just the first inning, but he didn't need the home radar gun to let him know that Charlie didn't have it on this night.

"Give me the rundown, Becker."

"It could be a tough night tonight, Skip. I'll battle out there and do what I can, but you might want to have a short leash with me. I just don't feel right."

"I was afraid of that. At least with a day off tomorrow I have some arms I can use if we need to. Thanks for being upfront with me."

Most of the younger pitchers kept the way they were feeling on the mound to themselves. One thing that Coach Scott admired about Charlie was that he would always let you know if he was feeling well when he was throwing, or not. His honesty was refreshing compared to the hubris of some of the others that never wanted to admit that they were struggling, and never wanted to leave a game. They would tell Coach Scott that things were great, and the next thing you knew the team was in a hole that they couldn't get out of. Charlie's openness made Don's job a lot easier. With certain pitchers Don even had a set of signs for his catcher Dusty to give him when a pitcher was struggling out there.

This kept Dusty from being the bad guy, and also kept the rapport strong between his battery mates.

The next two innings were far from ideal, but Charlie survived them without too much damage inflicted. He allowed five hits, walked another batter, and threw nearly 60 pitches over those two innings, but he was fortunately bailed out by the aggressiveness of the Curve players. They were up there hacking away and they swung at some poor pitches. Most likely they smelled blood in the water and were trying for the kill. But with all that free swinging they only managed two runs and left four runners on base. They could have had another four walks if they'd just simply left their bats on their shoulders. When a pitcher is throwing in the mid 80's with little movement, however, it's tough to just let the pitch float on by.

In the fourth, the floodgates finally opened up. Charlie got the first batter of the inning out on a deep fly ball to the warning track, but it was unfortunately all over from there. The next six batters all got hits: a homerun, four singles, and a double; and that ended a disappointing evening for Charlie right there. His final numbers, some of his most dismal of the season, ended up being 3 and a third innings pitched, 6 runs, 11 hits, 2 walks, and no strikeouts. It was a disaster by anyone's standards, but especially for Charlie who had been pitching much better as of late. The loss dropped his record to 11-5 and saw his ERA rise up to a still very respectable 3.45.

There was a time when a game like that would make Charlie miserable. It would definitely bring about a long, late night of drinking and trying to forget. He'd never have gone back and reconstructed the game in detail like that in his mind years ago, but now the loss didn't really bring him any pain. If anything, Charlie was in a good mood knowing that he was on his way home for a day off and then a long home stand to enjoy with his family. He felt comforted in seeing his wife in the seat next to him and knowing that his son was sleeping peacefully behind him. It wasn't necessarily the baseball that tore him apart, but these long road trips away from his family. He also felt good about pinpointing one of the reasons for his struggles in the game, and was already getting prepared for his next start on Tuesday against Binghamton. Sometimes Charlie wondered what would have happened if he'd started this process ten years ago back when he had the kind of electric stuff that people raved about around the league. But unfortunately, as Charlie found out firsthand, and enjoyed repeatedly reminding his Double-A teammates, youth is wasted on the young.

Chapter 7

Stewartville, MN

Tony casually came strolling through the front door of the farm house carrying a couple of sacks with him like he was just getting back from a lazy Sunday evening trip to the grocery store. The sun was just starting to set on a day that seemed to start a lifetime ago. He entered to find his three brothers gathered in the living room so intently watching the TV that they didn't even notice him come in. All four of the brother's pictures were displayed on the TV screen, and the newscaster was discussing how federal agents would soon be on the scene to assist in the search and investigation.

"Hey, that's me!" Tony said, excitedly checking out his mug shot that was being broadcast throughout the entire area, and startling his brothers. "Don't you think that one of you might want to keep an eye on the fuckin' door? I coulda been the cops and you'd all be in deep shit."

"Where the fuck have you been? They're looking all over the tri-county area for us. You're lucky they didn't see you in that stolen van." Derek said, clearly frazzled from seeing the news coverage and frustrated that his younger brother hadn't run his plans through him.

"Oh, bullshit! I bet they don't even know about the stolen van yet. Anyway, I'm back and no harm done so no need to worry about it. We needed some stuff from Stacy's, and it was best for us to do it right away before things got too hot. Ya'll should be thanking me," Tony said, already a good way through the bottle of vodka that he'd grabbed.

"I think we could have made it one fucking night without the drugs or alcohol, Tony," Matt said, joining the conversation.

"That's not the stuff we needed, you dumb shit. They are just a nice added bonus, and I'm sure I won't see you turning any down tonight," Tony said, pushing one of the sacks at him. "Now let's all just calm down, have some drinks, shoot up some heroin, and start figuring some shit out. We've got lots of planning to do. Well, Derek's got lots of planning to do, and we've got lots of celebrating and clearing our minds to do."

"Derek's already been working on it while you were gone. We're gonna get up into Canada and hideaway," Matt said. "Tell him about it Derek."

"Yeah Derek," Tony said, feigning interest in a plan he knew they'd never carry out, "tell us about this great plan that's going to somehow get us off free and living like exotic millionaires up in a place that we've never been, doing something we've never done. I'm sure it's foolproof."

"Well, there are still some things to work out," Derek mumbled quietly.

"Of course there are things to work out! We're fucked. There's no way we get out of this without a lifetime spent in prison, and I'm not going back there. I'm done with Stillwater or any other state pen they want to shove us in. I just can't do it. Maybe you guys can, but I can't. For me, being in prison is the worst form of torture imaginable. I can't be caged up. Tell me honestly Derek. Chances we make it to Canada and somehow have a life worth living. Ten percent? Five percent? What?"

"It's not good, but what else are we going to do. There are no better ideas. It wasn't ever supposed to get to this point. We screwed up."

"I've got a better idea for you," Tony said, looking squarely in Derek's eyes. Somehow despite the fact that half of the vodka bottle was now gone Tony appeared extremely focused and alert. "Let's finish 'Operation Payback'."

Derek stood silent for a good ten seconds and just looked right back into Tony's squinty eyes processing things. A hundred different thoughts and ideas were running through his head, and he was searching for a reason to object, but nothing came to him. Tony was right. There was no way out of this except for prison, and Derek wasn't made for prison either. The twins were so lethargic and lazy and used to having people tell them what to do that they could probably make it in prison, but the older boys needed to be out and free. Derek's Canada plan was just something to give the twins some hope, but deep down he knew it wasn't going anywhere. They couldn't survive in Canada even if they did make it up there without getting nabbed on the way. It would only be a matter of time before they were caught. On the other hand, he had been looking for a way to finish his payback plan for years, and this might finally be his opportunity. His eyes narrowed and his expression grew darker. Maybe this was the way it was meant to be after all. It wasn't the way Derek expected this to turn out, but this might actually be better for him in the end. His life was already going nowhere fast.

"They're gonna need to know everything," Derek said looking over at the twins who were standing there dumbfounded not sure exactly what was going on. "And they're going to need to decide to participate on their own without pressure from us."

"I know. We probably should have just told them earlier anyway, and we can do it without them if we have to," Tony responded.

"We won't make it out alive, you know. The twins might, but we won't."

"I can handle that, and I know you can. We've been over this a million times before. Since it's all on the line and this is the end that means we can get the school now, too. Without the fear of prison we can get everyone. I can finally get my part of the operation taken care of as well."

Derek and Tony were now in their own conversation in their own world. The twins may as well not have even been there, and didn't understand what they were talking about anyway. The two older boys have been repeating this discussion for years, and whenever they went back to it the normal griping and fighting with each other that they otherwise did always vanished. Even the swearing disappeared. They would enter almost a trancelike zone where everything around them was gone. This was their dream. Their focus. Their everything. For nearly eight years they had hashed out in great detail what needed to be done, and there were always roadblocks along the way that kept them from accomplishing all of their goals. There had been plenty of progress, but Derek wasn't in it for progress. He had a final goal that needed to be met before he felt satisfied.

Certain parts of the plan were easy – like Greg Thompson. They took care of that big-mouthed loser right away. After what had happened to their mother the boys simply told Greg that they could no longer sell to him. They gave him a fake name and an isolated location to meet a new dealer up in Rochester, and when Greg showed up they beat him near to death and then shot him. Because of the hands-on, up close nature of that killing it was the most enjoyable for Tony. He would have just preferred to keep beating on him until he was completely gone, but Derek decided they needed to move on before someone else came along. They took his money and made it look like a mugging, and the cops hadn't shown any interest at all in the boys as suspects. But that was just a small part of the plan. Just a little piece to get their feet wet, check their mettle, and get ready for the more important parts. It was a nice test to see what they were made of, and they passed it with flying colors and felt damn good about it.

Starting the fire that killed the Kramer's next door who couldn't mind their own business was a little bit tougher. It was probably the old lady Kramer's fault that the cops were called, but the boys decided that the old man Kramer could have told her to leave it alone, so they both had to pay. Derek decided a fire would be the best choice to avoid getting caught on a double homicide. Two murders in a home could be complicated, but a house burned to the ground would hopefully cover some tracks. The detectives determined right away that it was arson, Derek wasn't smart enough to avoid that, but even though they did talk to the Morrison family this time, they never pinned anything on them. As long as Derek did the talking and Tony kept his mouth shut things seemed to work out alright. Plus, Bill

Morrison had no incentive to do anything to help the police out in any way, and the police knew that, so they stayed away from his place as much as they could.

The third portion of their payback plan was the part that Derek and Tony didn't know how well the twins would accept, even though they waited until the twins were older and essentially out of the house before they performed it. Finding out that your dad had been murdered by your two older brothers is not an easy thing for most people to hear, even if your dad was never really a father. In actuality, if anyone raised the twins after their mom died it was Derek. Derek often wondered if deep down the twins knew that things were a little bit fishy with the death of their father. After all, Bill Morrison was not exactly a big hunter. Sure, him getting drunk and accidentally shooting himself alone in the woods sounds like dad, but he really only hunted right by the house. Not far off in the deep woods where his body was found. He was too lazy to walk more than a couple of hundred feet away. The boys were questioned a little bit heavier on this one, but again they made it clear. Now the heat was on them a little bit, however, and things got more complicated. This added heat was a set-back for accomplishing part four – the final and most important part.

It was the final piece of the plan in Derek's mind anyway. Tony's anger and hatred spread further than Derek's did. Tony didn't feel the pain of losing his mom like Derek - he was never the favorite child. Tony just had anger for everyone that he perceived to ever do him wrong, and for Tony that definitely included many members of the school. He wanted the entire school staff to pay for the humiliations that were brought on him during his time at Spring Valley High School. Specifically, the principal and most of the teachers had done him wrong in his mind in some manner, and they should be paid back as well. Derek consistently tried to keep his brother focused on the murder of their mom, but Tony would always go back to the school. In the end, Derek just kept telling Tony that they would take care of the school last, and with the events of today that looked like a possibility, but really he had no previous interest in that. Derek actually kind of enjoyed his time at the school and the people there. Anyway, the school didn't kill his mom, these other people did. And, specifically, Sheriff Aaron Nelson did. It infuriated Derek that Sheriff Nelson was the one piece of his plan that hadn't been accomplished – that was the only piece that really mattered! He kicked himself regularly that he didn't just trust himself right off the bat and take care of Nelson immediately.

Part four would probably be finished by now if not for a couple of major screw-ups and setbacks. Derek determined that they needed to get a feel for Sheriff Nelson's regular activities so they knew his patterns and routines. Tony was put in charge of watching Sheriff Nelson and keeping a log of all of his activities. This was probably Derek's biggest mistake. He should have handled that himself. Not two days into the reconnaissance mission he was spotted by the Sheriff himself and arrested for trespassing. Because of Tony's inability to keep his mouth shut, a restraining order was placed on Tony and the other Morrison boys as well, and Nelson beefed up his security once he realized that he was a target. This trespassing was a violation of Tony's parole and Nelson made sure the book was thrown at him, so he was locked up for six months in the county jail. Just two weeks after he was released he got caught holding up that gas station, and was back behind bars for another ten months. By this point Derek had given up on ever finishing his mission without the boys either being killed or locked up for life. That did not mean, however, that he had given up on his mission. It just meant that the end result would really be the end. He would get his payback one way or the other even if it meant his own death.

As Derek revealed this all to the twins for the first time, he was simultaneously watching for a reaction from them. This is a lot of information to digest in a short period of time, and he really didn't know what to expect from them. He didn't get much visual input from the twins, however, who just sat there stone-faced and took it all in. They didn't even react when Derek told them about killing their dad, almost as if there was no emotional connection to him whatsoever. After Derek was done the silence continued for a good minute or two as the twins just looked at each other and weren't sure what to say or do. They were almost just waiting for Derek to tell them what to do next like trained dogs waiting for a command. The twins were not built for decision making, and were followers rather than leaders.

"Well, what do you think?" Derek said finally breaking the silence. "Do you have any questions? Are there any concerns? Are you guys in on finishing this thing? It's up to you. If you don't want any part of this, that's absolutely fine. There's no pressure from us."

Mike, who had hardly spoken since the van ride hours earlier after he'd been shot, said without emotion, "Of course we're fuckin' in." And that was the end of the discussion on that.

The rest of the night was spent in planning mode for Derek. The other three boys partied hard realizing it might possibly be the last party that they ever have. Might as well go out with a bang! Derek wouldn't touch the stuff when he was planning, and he had a lot of details to work out in a limited amount of time. He knew that it was up to him to make sure everything ran to perfection to help his dream became a reality, and he wasn't going to get any tactical help from his brothers – just possibly some criticism from Tony in the morning. After all, Tony would want the entire school blown up and every single person in it killed. No amount of violence or destruction was ever enough for Tony. Derek, on the other hand, didn't really want to see people killed that didn't deserve it. He couldn't help but remember the pain that he lived with, and still lives with, after his mother was killed undeservedly by that idiot Sheriff. No one should have to live with that sort of pain. He would let the boys have their fun tonight, and then go over the details later on in the morning. It would have to be an early afternoon operation to give the boys some recovery time, but that should be just fine. As long as it was performed before the three o'clock bell everything would work out great.

After the plan had been finalized around two AM, he stepped over his fallen brother's bodies sprawled along the floor and found the old lady's bed in the other room. It was a good plan, and he felt proud of it. Not great, because he'd end up losing his life with it, but he knew it would accomplish the greater goal of finally avenging his mom's death and that made him smile. Derek fell asleep quickly, feeling at peace knowing that this would be the last night of sleep that murderous bastard Aaron Nelson would have, and not giving one second of thought to the fact that it would be his own last night of sleep as well.

Chapter 8

New Britain, CT

The Minor League baseball season is not a sprint by any means, but instead is a grueling marathon. The endless steps put a lot of wear and tear on the body, mind, and spirit. There are key checkpoints along the way. The All-Star game at the midway point of mile 13 is one of them. Another is the passing of mile 20 and the trade deadline which occurred about 20 days ago – always an important date for any minor leaguer worried about his future with the current organization. And, once mile 25 is hit on a Sunday in mid-august, that finish line is in sight. It is as if a team-wide rejuvenation takes place and excitement builds. Plans start to develop for the offseason, and uncertainty reigns for many players. The questions come from all ends of the playing spectrum. Will I have my opportunity to make the big league team next year? Will I be promoted or demoted? Is this my last year in baseball?

Will I be traded? And, the most important question on six of the Rock Cats players' minds – will I be a September call-up?

On the first of September every season Major League clubs are allowed to expand their rosters from the normal 25 players to anyone that is currently on their 40 man roster. For teams that are far out of the pennant chase this flexibility gives them an opportunity to evaluate some of the younger kids at the big league level. They get a chance to see if they can handle big league life for a short period of time, and maybe rest some veterans.

For teams that are fighting for their playoff lives, this rule is a Godsend. Teams are allowed to bring up the extra pinch-runner they can use at ends of games. They can carry an extra back-up catcher for blow out games, or a relief pitcher to spare the bullpen. The Minor League players love the opportunity to get a cup of coffee in the Majors, and dream of performing so well that they earn a permanent place. The only people that don't necessarily care for it are the current Major Leaguers who are concerned about losing their spot to a youngster, and the general managers who have to decide whether it's worth it to bring a player up knowing they'll have a salary that will need to be paid.

The six Rock Cats who are on the 40 man roster all have a unique trait that could be beneficial to the Twins in a playoff run, but they all also have some competition at the Triple-A level that could keep them down. Dusty Timms is hoping to get called up as the emergency catcher. Jose

Santiago can play all of the infield positions deftly, and also has speed to pinch run. Benny Phillips is the young slugger whose big days are likely ahead of him. Clayton Kearns has been the Rock Cats most explosive starting pitcher this season despite a lack of control at times, and Bryce Hodge is the flame-throwing closer out of the bullpen. Finally, there is Charlie Becker – left-handed innings eater.

The six all realize that the length of time the Twins stay in the playoff race could be the determining factor in them being brought up or them being done for the summer, and it is often discussed among them. Currently the Twins are one game back of the Indians in the Central Division. The Tigers, losers of five straight, have fallen off the pace and appear to be headed in the wrong direction. So, with about 40 games remaining in the big league season it looks to be a two team race. To Benny Phillips this is bad news, as he's ready for the future to begin today. The other five all see their special role that they could play on a contending team, and are hoping for a tight race down to the end.

"Hey, big Chuckster, give me the *SportsCenter* scoop from last night," Dusty bellowed as he entered the Rock Cats home locker room with Clayton.

"Twins won. Indians lost. We're one game back," Charlie replied. Saturday night was drinking and dancing night for most of the Rock Cats so they'd get their Sunday morning scores from the man they knew would be at home and wide awake through most of the night.

[77]

"You hear that, Clayton, we're on the warpath hunting some Indians. Time to call up the cavalry. It's the Revolutionary War all over again baby, and I'm Daniel Boone," Dusty said, playfully pushing tomorrow's starting pitcher who came walking in with him.

"Dusty, you are a true student of history," Clayton deadpanned, continuing to his locker.

"Remember the Alamo!" Dusty shouted back to him.

"You cheating on me with another starting pitcher, Dusty?" Charlie said while finishing putting his uniform on.

"Well, Chuckster, Clayton is younger than you. Better looking than you. Funnier than you. And he takes me places on Saturday nights. Plus he's got that cool Texas accent thing going. What do you got to offer? Your expertise of the fish on the Mississippi River doesn't cut it."

"My wife bakes you cookies."

"True that. That's why I keep sleeping with you every night on the road. You do know that I just use you for your wife's awesome chocolate chip cookies, right? I hope that you don't take that personally and it doesn't cheapen things between us. Not that I worry about losing you. You're not gonna find a better roomie than Mr. Dusty Timms, that's for sure. Hey, let's have some fun with the big dog."

Dusty turned his attention to Benny Phillips who was also getting ready for the game. "Hey Benny, did you hear, Twins won again last night. When are they going to finally bring your monster bat up there and replace that first baseman they've got? They'd probably be 5 games up by now with you there, right?"

"Fuckin' idiots in the Twins front office. They've got that fat slob clogging up the infield up there when they have me down here just wasting away. Did you see that ball I hit yesterday? Must've went 450 feet. All wasted in front of a couple thousand loser fans. I need to see some real pitching. Not the scrubs down here in Double-A. They better not call up you losers and leave me down here just because I'm younger than you are and they're in a pennant race. I'd get them to the World Series if they'd just let me."

Once every week or so Dusty would feed Benny's ego and get him wound up tight. Dusty enjoyed the show, and he thought Benny actually hit better when he was fired up. He never failed to piss off several of his teammates in the process, but Dusty always just rolled with it. Sometimes, this would continue for 15 to 20 minutes, but fortunately Coach Scott hobbled in with an announcement this time.

"Alright, listen up," Coach Scott yelled in the locker room. "The Twins General Manager Dave Duerson will be around the locker room and even in the dugout some over the next couple of days, so make him feel at home and don't say or do anything stupid. His plan as of right now is to watch Monday and Tuesday night's games, and then leave after that. Any questions?"

Benny spoke up right away, "Is this the main guy who's going to make the final decision on who gets called-up?"

"I can't say for sure, but he will definitely play a big role in that decision. Everyone should be ready to perform." Seeing no other questions Coach Don Scott waddled out of the locker room leaving the boys to speculate on their own. This was just a distraction as far as Don was concerned. The last thing he wanted was some GM walking around second-guessing his decisions and telling him what to do and who to play. He just wanted to manage and win ballgames. He kept telling himself that at least it would only be for a couple of days and then life would go back to normal.

Once Coach Scott was gone Benny started back in again, "You boys hear that? After that GM gets one look at my smooth swing he'll be shipping me up to the majors immediately. So long suckers!" Benny grabbed his mitt and was confidently off to the field for pregame batting practice.

"Hey, Chuckster, you hear that? They're coming to see you and Clayton throw," Dusty said excitedly before realizing that Charlie looked pale. "Shouldn't you be doing back flips, what's up?"

"Dave Duerson and I have a history," Charlie replied vaguely.

"You strike out his dad in a game 40 years ago or something? Or did you sleep with his Grandma and not call her back?" Dusty responded, trying to keep the mood light.

"Nah, I don't really want to talk about it." And that was all Dusty got out of Charlie on that subject, but it took Charlie back in his mind to that disastrous night in the hotel room six years earlier. In a strange twist of fate, Dave Duerson happened to be the Phillies GM at that time, and didn't take too well to losing one of his bright, young pitching prospects that he had drafted to a needless injury caused by the bottle. Duerson released Charlie from the Phillies organization almost immediately, but not before first making it extremely difficult for Charlie to come up with another job by dragging his name through the mud. Duerson was a guy that was used to winning and getting what he wanted, and if someone interfered with that he didn't have much patience or feeling for him. Second chances were not likely to come from the stubborn Dave Duerson. Charlie was certain that Duerson did everything he could to keep Charlie out of the Minnesota Twins organization before the season started, but luckily Charlie had a few strong allies from the past that helped him earn a spot with New Britain. The Twins current manager, Gordon White, being the main and most powerful ally. But ever since the day he signed with the Twins it had always been Charlie's greatest fear that Duerson would be a roadblock to the majors for him. Now, it especially looked like that would be the case as he appeared to be a prominent member of this decision on the September call-ups. Charlie was just going to have to look so dominant on Tuesday that Duerson wouldn't have a choice but to bring him up. Because, fortunately for Charlie, if there was one truth about Dave Duerson it was that he wanted to win at all costs, and everything else came in a distant second – even his pride and long held grudges.

Time can move very slowly for Charlie, especially when he's at the ballpark and excited about a big upcoming event. When he's at home with his family time operates at a much more regular pace, but not when he's away. The pace of the game is not a problem on days that he's pitching – it's the other days that leave too much time for his restless mind to wander. To help with life at a snail's crawl Charlie has grown accustomed to sitting alongside his manager and charting pitches on days that he's not on the mound. That helps him twofold. One, it keeps him actively involved in the game and eats away the time. And two, he sees firsthand which pitches are effective against which hitters. So that's where Charlie was on Monday night as the Rock Cats were facing the Binghamton Mets in an Eastern Division matchup.

"Clayton's nervous, Skip. He's all over the place with all of his pitches," Charlie said, looking down at his clipboard.

"I know. Duerson came up and talked to him in the clubhouse right before the game was about to start, and I think it rattled him. I'm kinda wondering if Duerson did it on purpose to check him mentally."

Clayton Kearns was a big 21 year old right-hander from Odessa, Texas who hadn't been in the spotlight of a big game yet in his young baseball career. A football star at Permian High School, he turned down a scholarship offer from the University of Texas to take the guaranteed money that the Twins were offering for him to sign. It's tough to turn down that type of cash even with an extreme love of football. He had a bright future on the mound and had overpowering stuff at times, but had a known tendency to be wild as well. With a strict pitch count on him to preserve his arm that wildness meant that Clayton would often have difficulty making it past the fifth inning even when he was firing on all cylinders. It wasn't unusual for him to strike out the side and walk two others all in the same inning. Clayton had amazing natural ability, but he hadn't learned to do the little things necessary to become great. He pretty much ignored the mental part of the game, and didn't spend as much time in the weight room as he should.

When Duerson came walking up to him about an hour earlier Clayton knew exactly who it was before he even introduced himself. Not too often did a man come strolling into the New Britain locker room wearing an expensive suit and tie, and looking like he could be a member of the mafia. Duerson had a powerful voice, intimidating strong handshake, and a personality that practically screamed out 'Don't mess with me'. Dave's dad was a general manager as well and so he grew up with the game. Right out of college he started working for his dad, and so despite only being 46 years old he had seen a lot of professional baseball. He commanded the room when he entered, and had an innate ability to get his way. Clayton was appropriately blown away.

"Has Duerson talked to you yet?" Scott continued. "Don't be surprised if he jumps you tomorrow before your start as well."

"I wouldn't worry about that, Skip. I don't think Duerson is going to come near me. He wouldn't even look in my direction when he walked through the clubhouse this afternoon. Luckily, I'm too old to be psyched out anymore anyway," Charlie said with a grin.

"Oh, that's right. You two have a past. Well, use that as motivation then. Dammit, I've gotta go talk to Clayton on the mound. You got a joke for me to use out there?"

"Yeah, go up there and start calling him 'two rabbits'. Ask Dusty how two rabbit's stuff is out there, or something. Dusty will play along. He's good about that. When Clayton finally asks what you're talking about tell him 'you've got as much control as two rabbits on a first date out here so I thought the name was fitting'. Then just turn around and leave."

"That joke sucks, Becker. It'll work great. Thanks."

With that Coach Scott called time and slowly made his way out to the mound to talk to Clayton a bit. Charlie could see Clayton smiling as Scott wheeled around and walked away. Eventually Clayton relaxed and made it through the game without too much damage. Not exactly the showcase start that he wanted, but at least he showed enough of his ability to hopefully keep the twins interested in seeing him up north later in the year.

Bryce Hodge came out of the bullpen and cranked out some fastballs to finish up the win and pick up the save for the Rock Cats. Tomorrow would be a big day for Charlie and he went home excited about what the next day would bring for him in his pursuit of reaching that elusive next level.

Charlie was right that Duerson didn't come up and talk to him before the game, and showed no signs of wanting to communicate with him at all. That was fine with Charlie as he didn't really know what to say to him anyway, and it just helped him focus on the task at hand – the Binghamton Mets. He knew that he screwed up six years ago, but there wasn't anything he could do about that now. He was adamant with himself, however, that neither Dave Duerson nor his mistake in the past would affect him in his start today.

Charlie normally could tell after just one inning of pitching how the game was going to go. Sure, he was a master at making adjustments to his pitch selection in-game, but there were a lot of things that just couldn't be changed in the middle of a game or things came up that he had limited control over. After the first inning on Tuesday night, Charlie was feeling sky high. Charlie, being a left-handed pitcher, faces an abundance of right-handed batters every time out. The only lefties he tends to see are the absolute studs that don't sit out against anyone. So for him to have success it is essential that he handles the right-handed batters effectively, and for Charlie that normally means dropping his curveball down and in on their hands. When he is on his game this produces a lot of jammed groundballs to the left side of the diamond. Not only did he get that from the first two Mets hitters, but he also shattered both of their bats in the process. Both Santiago at short and Wells at third had to deal with shards of wood flying at them along with the baseball. Things got even better with the third hitter as Charlie struck him out on three curveballs all down and in that the Mets powerful slugger couldn't even catch a piece of.

On the way to take a seat on the bench Charlie walked by Coach Scott and winked at him. "Rest easy, Skip, no rabbits out here tonight."

"Call me crazy, Chuckster, but it almost looks like you're having a good time out here tonight," Dusty said moving next to him on the bench.

"No matter how long you've been doing something it always feels good when you can still do it effectively. Plus, it's fun getting outs and making hitters look stupid."

"I hear ya there!" Dusty said as the last out of the bottom of the first was made. "Let's go get some more."

For the next 7 innings that's exactly what Charlie did. He struck out a season high 9 batters and only allowed 2 hits without walking anyone. As he walked off the mound to end the eighth inning Coach Scott congratulated him and said that his night was done despite the fact that he'd only thrown 85 pitches. Scott informed Charlie that Duerson had let him know that he wanted to see Bryce Hodge one more time while he was there so Hodge was going to be called on to finish the game.

"Good work tonight," Dusty said to Charlie as they waited for the bottom of the eighth to begin. "Wish you could be out there to finish it."

"You know, I'd like to finish it as well, but I am wearing down a little bit and probably still need to have another start at this same level on Sunday if I want any chance of being called up so it might be good not to tax my arm anymore tonight. I don't know. Not my decision I guess."

"You handle it better than I would, Chuckster. I just might have unleashed the famous Timms guns on someone in that same situation."

"Age mellows you. Priorities change."

"I guess," Dusty said as Benny walked by to grab his bat and get ready to hit. "Maybe that's why I kind of feel bad for that poor bastard Benny."

For the last two nights up to this point Benny had been hitless. In fact, he'd hardly touched the ball. Eight times he'd gone up to bat, and seven times he'd struck out. He was clearly pressing and finished off his last strike out by slamming his helmet down and cursing up a storm.

"Let me try something" Charlie said and turned over to where Benny was waiting to hit. "Hey Benny, come here a second."

Benny came walking over but was clearly in no mood to talk. "What do you want?" he growled, upset about being disturbed.

"First pitch fastball Benny, guaranteed. He's going to challenge you. Be ready to turn on it. Trust me."

"Whatever. What the fuck do you know?" Benny said, walking up to the on-deck circle.

Sure enough, the first pitch came in at 93 MPH right down the middle and Benny got all of it. He pulled the thing 430 feet over the wall in left to up the Rock Cats lead to 6-0. As he was circling the bases Dusty just stood there wide-mouthed staring at Charlie.

"How in the world did you know that?" Dusty asked.

"I didn't. I just figured there was at least a 50/50 chance of a fastball coming, and so he might think about that a little bit and not about the million dollar suit sitting up in the crowd."

"You know you've just made a friend for life, right? You and Benny are gonna be tight now. I'm gonna lose my roomie for the next road trip after all, aren't I? Don't break up the dream team, Chuckster," Dusty said enjoying himself.

As Benny was coming into the dugout Charlie stood up with a big smile on his face and walked toward Benny to congratulate him.

"What the fuck are you smiling about?" Benny asked him before he got there. "I didn't need any of your fuckin' help. I already knew a fastball was coming."

As Benny continued to accept the congratulations Dusty grabbed Charlie from behind and said into Charlie's ear, "It was a nice try, but you can't get rid of me that easy, Chuckster. The dream team survives, baby!"

Chapter 9

Stewartville, MN

Derek decided to let the day of the big event start when his body told him it was time to start. There was no point in setting an alarm clock today. It turned out that his body got him up right around 9 AM. The sun was already well up in the morning sky, and it looked like a beautiful day outside – a great day for restitution. He rolled out of bed and made his way into the kitchen to get some coffee started. After rustling around the cabinets for a bit he eventually found everything he was looking for, and had the pot brewing. Good thing the old lady was a coffee drinker! He didn't think stopping at the gas station to pick up a cup would probably be a very prudent move. The thought made him smile. He was in a great mood this morning – not feeling the tension of the day at all.

Derek turned on the TV to check the latest updates on the bank robbery. He kept the volume down low to let his brothers sleep a bit longer. Fortunately there was still no news on the stolen van. In fact, it didn't sound like the cops had any new information whatsoever since last evening. But really, except for the van, what more was there to actually find? Besides the criminals, of course, and Derek knew they hadn't found them yet.

Derek took his cup of coffee out to the garage to search for a few supplies that they would need to make the mission successful. After about 15 minutes he found some rope, duct tape, and a hammer. Not the exact materials that he wanted, but they would be sufficient. He was sure the old lady would have a bible around the house somewhere that he'd be able to borrow. The bible would be a nice added touch. She wouldn't miss it.

After a little walk around the farm to enjoy the morning, Derek went back inside and made his way to the kitchen. He found some eggs and bacon in the fridge, and thought that would make a good breakfast so he started frying things up. Hopefully that would rouse his brothers. If not, then he'd need to start kicking them and get them going. Derek was excited and ready to get the mission started.

The bacon did the trick. The twins were first to come staggering into the kitchen looking like death warmed over, and started devouring the food immediately. Tony was a little slower getting into the kitchen, but he made it there eventually as well. Tony tended to drink most of his calories, but even he ate a bite or two this morning. He still managed to grab his Kahlua to mix half and half with his coffee. Derek was too excited to eat very much, but now that he had all of his brothers up and together he started going over the details of his plan. His brothers were always amazed by the creativeness and ingenuity of their oldest brother, and were extremely impressed with this plan and excited to get it started. Tony, of course, had a few issues he felt the need to discuss.

"Derek, there are at least 20 teachers in that school that need some payback."

"None of those teachers killed mom. I'm giving you an opportunity to pick a few for us to take out, but we don't need to take out the entire staff."

"They may not have killed mom, but they made my life miserable, and they need to pay."

"Tony, this is the way it has to be. We won't have the time or resources to get them all. We'll get the worst offenders. Just let me know who you want and we'll make it work. Some of the others will have their own scars to deal with when we're through."

"Alright. The two that we need to get for the plan are Mr. Marchant and Mrs. Johanson. Oh, and we need to get Dr. Little of course. I also wouldn't mind taking down Mr. B., Ms. Darcy, and Mr. Barber if we have time to get them in."

Mike, of all people, jumped in on that forcefully. "We're not getting Mr. B. He can be there as part of the plan, but we're not killing him."

Mr. B. was the football and baseball coach at the High School. For one year Mike played 9th grade football and felt almost like a normal kid. It was the best couple of months of Mike's life, and Mr. B. remained a father figure to him throughout his short time in High School. He was the only positive adult male influence that he ever had. Even after Mike started drifting away from sports and into other negative things Mr. B. and him remained close and would talk in the halls on most mornings. While other teachers would simply ignore him, Mr. B. would joke around with him.

"Ok, whatever," Tony conceded. "If we have the time and the opportunity at the end I'm going to take a couple more down, however. I'll stay away from Mr. B. though, Mike."

Tony decided not to argue about things, but he wasn't going to make any promises about anyone else surviving after the main mission had been taken care of. If Tony was going down he was going to take a few others down with him on the way out if he could. Derek didn't have to know all of the details on that. Tony had found that sometimes it was just easiest not to argue with his brothers and just do whatever he wanted later on without their permission. Like the trip to Stacy's for example. It normally worked out fine.

The boys had the TV on and watched the twelve o'clock news, but there weren't any other updates; just lots of video clips of police out patrolling the highways. Luckily for the Morrison's it was highly doubtful that the police would be covering the road that they would be travelling on.

By 1 PM the van was loaded up and the boys were ready to go. They decided there was no point in waiting around so they jumped in and headed down the old farm driveway and within seconds were cruising south on County Road 1 towards Spring Valley. Derek was back in the driver's seat where he always sat, and everyone else resumed their positions that they had after the bank heist. Derek had to be the one to drive since his face was the only one that wouldn't jump out and be memorable to anyone that saw it while driving by. There wasn't any talking as the van drove slowly down the road, never even approaching the 55 MPH speed limit for fear of being pulled over. Some tension was starting to fill the air, and each brother had their own stream of thoughts and memories running through their heads.

County road 1 runs parallel to the main highway, and doesn't cross any major roads along the way. The road to Spring Valley is a winding one. There are several dips and sharp turns that can wreak havoc on fast moving vehicles in the winter time. In fact, many of the locals only travel on it during the ice free seasons. There was very light traffic on the road as was to be expected on a weekday afternoon out in the country.

After a couple of miles they drove past the turnoff to Stacy's house, and Tony thought about all of the drugs that would end up going to waste there now that they wouldn't be around to distribute them. Maybe Tony would find a way to sneak out after the dust cleared somehow. He could make his way to Stacy's house, grab the drugs, steal her car and drive south selling the drugs at biker bars along the way. It was something to keep in the back of his mind anyway. Without his brothers with him he might be able to make a clean escape. He could always keep his gun on hand in case he was about to be caught. If his brothers ended up killed and he got away that's what he'd do.

As they approached the town of Spring Valley they came upon the school to the left. Derek pulled the van around to the parking lot in the back of the school. This was deemed by Derek the best point of entry into the school. Mr. Barber, the physical education teacher, would always take his classes outside on nice days and would leave the rear entrance door propped open so they wouldn't have to go all the way around the school to get back in. Derek assumed he would continue to do this, and he assumed correctly. This was always frowned upon by the administration as a security risk, but no one ever made it a big enough deal to convince Mr. Barber to stop doing it. And besides, Mr. Barber had been doing this for 30 years already and wasn't going to stop now without putting up a fight. He wasn't one to be easily scared or intimidated by the thought of an intruder.

Except for the back door issue Spring Valley High School is actually closed up pretty tightly with strong security procedures in place. After the Morrison boys left the school the administration realized that they had a serious drug issue, and tried to completely shut it down from the public. The days of being able to use the locker room as a drug exchange area were long gone as the outside back doors of the locker room were now bolted shut, and the only way in or out was through the main entrance and down a steep stairwell. Not ideal for a drug exchange, but pretty appropriate for what Derek had planned today.

The school also had put a lockdown system in place right before the older boys left school. If there was any threat from the outside community the teachers had been drilled to quickly close their locked classroom doors and gather all of the students into a corner of the classroom with the lights turned off. This procedure, although well intentioned, would also be useful to the Morrison's plan. The Morrison's would know exactly where everyone was located.

There was an element of timing involved in the plan which was made difficult because the Morrison boys did not know the exact bell schedule. Derek just figured they could wait it out in the van until the ideal moment arose – the moment when Mr. Barber would be taking his class in to shower 10 minutes before the end of class. Fortunately, Mr. Barber was out on the soccer field right now with his class so the wait shouldn't be too long. The boys would just wait for

Derek to give the word and be ready to pounce when the time came. Tony might outwardly question his older brother in the planning stages of a job, but when the execution time came he was a loyal follower of whatever his brother told him to do.

Sitting in the van waiting, Tony couldn't help but be taken back in his mind to a time in the not so distant past when he himself was outside on these very same soccer fields for gym class. It was one of many painful memories that he had that involved the school. It was definitely not the worst, but it was the most vivid, especially now that he could see the kids out there with Mr. Barber standing guard.

"Tony! Get your lazy butt moving!" Mr. Barber yelled at him as the sophomore students were doing their laps at the beginning of gym class.

"I am moving," Tony muttered under his breath and not increasing his speed one bit.

"OK class, we'll just stay out here and keep running all day since Tony doesn't seem to want to run."

"Come on, Tony, get moving," One of his athletic classmates Nick yelled at him.

"Fuck you!" Tony snarled back and kept inching along.

This continued on for a good 10 minutes while his classmates became more and more upset with him, and Tony became more and more obstinate.

Another five minutes passed and when Tony looked in Mr. Barber's direction he noticed that he wasn't there anymore. It was strange for him to just disappear like that in the middle of the class. That's when the surprise attack happened. Nick came up from running laps behind him and shoved him to the ground. He started kicking him and was joined by a couple of his friends who were cursing at him and having a great time with it. Where was Mr. Barber?

"I guess you're the one that's fucked," Nick said, and after a few minutes of the beating he continued on running.

About a minute later Mr. Barber was back.

"Tony, get up and keep running!" he yelled at him. "If I get over there you better be just about dead."

Mr. Barber walked on over to him slowly, and when he finally reached Tony he realized that he really was hurt. He asked Tony who did this, but Tony didn't tell him anything. He just seethed and blamed Mr. Barber for disappearing during class. Mr. Barber had an excuse for why he was called away, something about a message from the office, but Tony never believed it. He just swore that Mr. Barber was somehow involved and someday he would pay for this.

Tony was just starting to get irate and red in the face when Derek pulled him out of his daydream. "Alright, it's go time. They're heading in."

Tony saw the familiar gate of Mr. Barber moving his direction with his class of what looked like juniors and seniors mostly out ahead of him, and prepared himself for battle. Yeah, one way or another Mr. Barber was going to have to go down today whether his name is on the take-out list or not. They were all going to pay.

Chapter 10

Spring Valley, MN

Since his first day teaching in Spring Valley twenty years ago he had always been known only as Mr. B. It was not that his last name was that tough to say, it was just that Mr. Barber's name was too close to his, so he became Mr. B. to all of his students. Mr. B., along with being the varsity football and baseball coach, was also a favorite math teacher at the school. The lower ability students found Mr. B. easy to understand and listen to, and the higher end students always felt challenged by him. The athletes, of course, enjoyed being in his class as well because he would have a tendency to go off-topic and into the sports world in the middle of class. Mr. B.'s favorite classes were the Algebra ones. His mind worked very sequentially, and he loved laying out the methods to complete a problem. Geometry was just a little bit too abstract for him so he didn't enjoy it quite as much, but it was still math after all so it did bring him some joy.

Mr. B.'s classroom was plain. Not a lot of decorations or posters on the walls. He just didn't feel like his time was best spent doing a lot of that superficial stuff. Being a varsity coach of two sports as well as trying to raise two high school kids of his own made him a very busy man. There was hardly an evening where he didn't have a practice, open gym, weight room supervision, or game to attend. He also made it a priority to stay in shape so he would wake up every morning at 5 AM and jump on the treadmill for at least 40 minutes to start his day. Then, three days a week after school he lifted weights with his players, even during the football and baseball seasons. He was the starting quarterback at nearby Winona State University, a top area Division II school about an hour east of Spring Valley. One of Mr. B.'s main tenets that he preached all the time was a healthy mind, body, and spirit, and he tried to make sure that he possessed all three. He was probably in better physical condition now than he was even when he was at Winona State, and he was very proud of the shape that he was in.

Mr. B.'s freshman class was nearing the end of an Algebra I test on linear equations when he heard the unmistakable and startling sound of gunshots reverberating throughout the school.

[101]

"Everybody in the corner," he shouted while moving towards the door to close it. "Lockdown. This is not a drill."

The Morrison boys exploded out of the van, and Tony made a beeline to Mr. Barber. Five quick steps later, before Mr. Barber even knew what was going on, Tony hit him with the butt of his gun on the back of the head and Mr. Barber was down. An instant later, gunshots filled the air and Derek yelled, "Everybody on the ground. Now!"

They were a smooth, coordinated team. Each knew exactly where the others were going, and what they were going to be doing. They even knew what each other was thinking. They had the tightness and intuitiveness that only comes from being a family. They had been through the wars and battles together.

A few of the 18 kids that were in Mr. Barber's PE class let out some shrieks of fear and terror, but they were all smart enough to get on the ground immediately. Derek, Matt and Mike each grabbed two of the bigger boys, easily identifiable by their game day football jerseys, and tied their hands behind their back with the rope that they'd brought with them. It was a fortunate coincidence that it happened to be a football Friday, and the football kids were marked. The three Morrison boys did this expertly and quickly, and had the six kids tied up in less than a minute.

Tony, meanwhile, had Mr. Barber pinned to the ground and was thoroughly enjoying the moment. "Hi Mr. Barber," Tony hissed in his ear. "Remember me, motherfucker? Guess you wish you wouldn't have let those boys beat me up now, huh? Your time has come to pay up today, Mr. Barber."

Mr. Barber, feeling groggy from the blow to the head, just groaned and tried to get his bearings. He could smell the alcohol on Tony's breath, and eventually figured out who he was. This realization and knowledge of how crazy Tony is just terrified Mr. Barber more. If there was ever a former student of Mr. Barber's that he was concerned about coming back and doing something like this it was Tony Morrison. Tony stuck his knee into Mr. Barber's back and tied his hands together, took out the duct tape and slapped a piece of it over Mr. Barber's mouth.

"Alright, everyone on your feet and down into the boys locker room!" Derek yelled, moving them into a line. "Mike, move 'em down."

"You heard him, move!" Mike's voice boomed as he started pushing them inside. It was Mike's job to guard the hostages down in the locker room since he was still recovering from the bullet wound yesterday, and was still visibly in pain with each step that he took. Mike was not exactly excited about this task, but he knew his limitations, and didn't want to jeopardize the mission.

The other three boys ran into the school shooting up the inside walls along the hall. This elicited the desired response as over the loudspeaker they heard the call for a lockdown from the office secretary. Tony ran straight for those lower level offices while Matt and Derek got started on the first floor classrooms.

When Tony got to the main office door and found it locked he simply shot through the glass window, reached around to the door handle, and let himself in. Not exactly top of the line security there. Scanning the room slowly he saw the secretaries hiding behind their desks and the principal, Dr. Little, on the floor of his office locked in as well. Tony was hunting now, and was on full alert. He was pleased to find no one unexpected in the office today.

"Hey there, bitches. Tony's back. Bet you wouldn't ask me to take off my baseball cap now, would you," Tony said, letting out a loud, terrifying laugh and looking insane. He decided that his fun was going to start now and shot the first secretary under her desk. Derek wouldn't like that, but Derek wouldn't ever have to know. She had always been a nuisance to Tony in the past, and was just a mean old lady anyway.

The other secretary let out a scream and Derek slowly walked over to her and hissed, "I suggest you lay low and shut up or you're going to end up like your friend over there."

Tony made his way over to Dr. Robert Little's office, and shot through the glass there as well and let himself in. All of the doors in the school had these glass pieces in them, which were nice to look out of, but were not exactly secure if someone wanted to enter. There would be quite a bit of broken glass in the building by the time this day was over.

"Doctor, doctor, give me the news. I've got a bad case of hatin' you!" Tony started singing, and then laughing loudly at his little joke. "Dr. Dipshit, it's good to see you. Why don't you stand up?"

"What do you want?" Dr. Little said in a trembling voice.

"I want payback, of course, but I'll take care of asking the questions. You can just answer me. Stand up right now, doctor. Do you still make the kids call you doctor?"

Dr. Little stood up but didn't answer immediately, which didn't make Tony very happy.

"I asked you a question, Dr. Dipshit, and I suggest you answer it right away and honestly or there's gonna be a hole where your head sits."

"Yes, I do," Dr. Little responded.

"And, do you remember when you gave me detention a few years back when I just called you Little?"

Dr. Little nodded his head.

"Well, that wasn't really necessary was it? I wasn't being disrespectful, it just came out. Of course, that's just a minor thing, really. I didn't go to detention anyway so no skin off my back. You've got bigger sins than that though, don't you? Glad to see you got my blood stains out of your floor. We'll go through the terrible details downstairs in a bit. Come with me."

With that, Tony walked over and gave Dr. Little a blow to the side of the head as well. He took out the rope and duct tape and tied him up just like he had done with Mr. Barber. He was feeling like the plan was going perfectly until he heard Derek scream from down the hall, and realized he needed to speed things up a little bit.

The freshmen in the back corner of Mr. B.'s classroom had heard the gun shots nearby and Mr. B. was doing everything he could to try and keep them calm. Even though Mr. B.'s heart was racing as well, he knew it was essential to not show it to his young students that were all around him.

He could hear the pounding footsteps of a couple of people running by and then all of a sudden a loud sound of crashing glass and students screaming next door in Mr. Marchant's room.

He didn't hear any gunshots coming from Mr. Marchant's room so that was a positive, but it was clear that they were going to break into the classrooms and so Mr. B.

realized it was time for action. He couldn't just sit tight and not try to do something.

"Stay low and stay quiet," He said to his frightened students, and he started moving.

His classroom door was set inside the hallway walls so that a little nook was around the corner somewhat hidden from the entrance. He needed a weapon, and there just are not that many options available in a math classroom so he decided to use one of the hard chairs that he had in his room, and took it into the nook with him.

It didn't take long before a hammer came through the classroom doorway making a loud shattering noise that startled the frightened kids in the back and made them jump. Mr. B. quietly moved the chair over his head as he saw a hand coming through to unlock the door, and pull the door open.

Mr. B. had it set in his mind that he'd swing at the first glimpse of a body part coming through the doorway figuring correctly that it would be the gun hand. The chair came down right on the forearm of the invader and the gun dropped just out in front of him near the whiteboard. The man screamed more out of shock than any pain, but realized quickly that he needed that gun so he dove towards it almost instantly. Mr. B. jumped on top of the man, who he now recognized as his former student Derek Morrison, right as he was getting possession of the gun, and Mr. B. went straight for the gun hand. They both held on to the gun with both hands. Mr. B. positioned on top of Derek trying to throw his hands into the ground to dislodge the gun. Derek was strong, however, and so far was holding on tightly.

"Matt!" Derek yelled.

While wrestling along the front of the classroom banging into desks, Mr. B. saw Derek's brother appear out of the corner of his eye with a gun in his hand and tried to make sure that he positioned Derek's body between the shooter and his own. He figured he wouldn't shoot at him if there was a chance that his brother would also get clipped.

"Drop the gun, Derek!" Mr. B. grunted.

"Can't do that, Mr. B.," Derek said trying to rotate his body between the gun and Mr. B.

Matt just stood there at the entryway to the classroom not knowing what to do. He couldn't shoot at Mr. B. for fear of the bullet going into Derek's body as well, and didn't want to jump in the tussle as the gun was being flailed all over the place and was likely to go off at any second. Fortunately for Matt, Tony came running in at that moment and fired a round of bullets into the walls above the students sending pieces of plaster raining down on the student's heads, and sending out screams from them. There was never even an instant of indecision for Tony – he was a man of action.

"Get up, Mr. B., or your students die," Tony screamed.

"Alright, alright, don't shoot," Mr. B. finally said, realizing that the situation was lost and began crawling off of Derek.

"Smart decision, Mr. B. Always been a fighter, haven't ya," Tony said smiling. "This isn't a fight you can win, though. It's really not even your battle. You're just here to get a front row seat of the proceedings. Get on your knees with your hands behind your back."

Mr. B. reluctantly complied and Tony tied his hands together and slapped a piece of duct tape over his mouth to the horror of his students in the back of the classroom.

"You all don't move and none of you will get hurt. We don't care about you," Tony said to the whimpering students in the back of the room, and then turned his focus to his brother. "You alright, Derek?"

"Yeah, I might not be able to use my arm much but I'll be able to go on. We're just going to have to be more careful entering the other classrooms. It's my fault I wasn't expecting resistance. Let's get moving, we're falling behind. I'll take them to the locker room, you two get started upstairs. We only have time for one more set of rooms before the police start coming in. I'll be right up."

Tony and Matt ran into the hall and took off for the upper level of the school while Derek led Mr. B. out into the hallway with the gun pointed at his back. In the hallway he saw Dr. Little and Mr. Marchant sitting against the wall. Mr. Marchant had a streak of blood on the side of his face and Dr. Little just looked terrified and defeated. Derek got them up and led the three of them around the corner and towards the locker room stairs.

At the bottom of the stairs they took a turn to the left and came into the area in front of the chalkboard where the teams would gather for their pregame talks. Sitting there, backs against the chalkboard wall, Mr. B. saw Mr. Barber and six of the students tied up in the same way the three of them were. Mr. B.'s heart sank as he saw those six included the team's quarterback, #12, his son.

Chapter 11

Spring Valley, MN

Ms. Darcy's room is located directly above Mr. B.'s classroom, so the locked down students and Ms. Darcy didn't know exactly what was going on, but they could tell things were not sounding so good. They could hear the banging around, screams, and eventually the sound of bullets hitting the wall right below them, and the tension in her room was increasing as the concern about if or when these people would arrive up there was growing. Ms. Darcy decided she wasn't just going to sit around and wait for something to happen. She was going to act to hopefully save her kids.

Before hearing the bullets hit below Ms. Darcy had been doing everything she could to try and keep the mood light even though she was terrified herself. She talked confidently about them being safe, about the police being there any second now, and even tried joking about the fact that there wouldn't be a homework assignment today. She was just trying to help her kids in any way that she could, just like she always did.

This is Ms. Darcy's 9th year as an English teacher at Spring Valley High School, and the school is her life. She's not married, has no children of her own, and essentially lives at the school. She thinks of her students as her kids, and she attends every sporting event and activity possible. She has very high expectations for her students, and gives them the nurture and caring that many of them don't have at home - yet they need to succeed. Ms. Darcy's students almost always graduate and leave, but they often come back to see her and can frequently be found in her classroom getting help with their college work in the late evening hours. The only students that have difficulty with Ms. Darcy and do not like her are the ones that refuse to do anything at all and won't put in any effort. She has little patience for those students. Students similar to the Morrison boys.

So far Ms. Darcy hadn't heard anyone moving through the upstairs hallway, but she decided she wasn't going to wait for them to show up. It was time for action. She knew from the noise below that they were entering the classrooms and if the students stayed there they were going to be sitting ducks. For years she had joked with her students and other teachers about her big sheets that she uses to cover up her books on her bookshelves to keep the dust off. She'd always say that if there ever was a fire she was tying those things together and going out the second floor window. Now the joke was going to become a reality.

"Quick, Heather, help me tie these sheets together," Ms. Darcy said. "We're getting out of here. Boys, work together and see if we can move some of the heavy furniture and desks against the door. Start with that big bookcase. Work together. Phil, you're in charge, get them moving."

"How are we going to break the window?" Heather asked, knowing that the windows did not open up.

"Kirby Puckett's going to get us through," Ms. Darcy responded heading towards her desk where her signed Kirby Puckett baseball sat, "with a little help from the best softball player I've ever seen."

Heather, Mr. B.'s daughter, was already a nationally known softball pitcher even though she was only a sophomore in high school. She became famous in a *Sports Illustrated* article that detailed the time when she struck out every batter she faced for three straight games. Forty-five batters retired in a row without as much as a walk. She was already being recruited by all of the college softball powers, but really hadn't given that too much thought yet. She was just enjoying high school for now, and often didn't even look through the huge amount of recruiting letters that came in the mail. She was also fearless and bold, and Ms. Darcy had no hesitation in enlisting her help in a terrifying situation like this.

By the time the sheets were all tied together Ms. Darcy heard the first sound of footsteps running by outside her room, and a few seconds later the sound of glass breaking next door. Fortunately for them they didn't appear to be coming to her room first.

"OK, Heather, let her fly," Ms. Darcy said once the sheets were all tied together, and Heather wound up and tossed the first pitch straight through the glass. Ms. Darcy then took a chair and broke through the rest of the glass until there was nothing left and plenty of room for everyone to fit through. She then hung the sheets out the window, tied the other end firmly around the leg of her desk, and tossed the rest out the window.

"Alright, one at a time, let's get moving. Be careful with the glass at the top, but move quickly. When you get down, run immediately across the street to the Johnson's house. Greg, you go first and help catch the others at the bottom. The rest of you, keep moving and stacking the desks in front of the doorway."

The 24 students one at a time climbed out the window and down the sheets into Greg's arms at the bottom. Once out, they ran across the street to the Johnson's house where they could take cover. Heather and Ms. Darcy helped the other students out of the window, and everyone seemed to make it down without too much trouble. The whole process only took a couple of minutes. Ms. Darcy's biggest fear was that one of the kids that lacked confidence would freeze up and slow the whole process down, but fortunately that never happened.

"OK, Heather, go ahead," Ms. Darcy said, and at that very instant the glass shattered in her door window and a hand reached through. "Quickly!" She added, for the first time displaying a concerned tone. Heather quickly jumped up on the window ledge, grabbed the sheet, and flew down to the bottom.

The door opened up, but the intruder could not get very far as there was that huge bookcase as well as piles of desks in the way.

"Matt, Tony, come here." Ms. Darcy could hear the man calling out, looking for assistance. She looked down at Heather and as soon as she hit the ground yelled out to both of them to run, and she jumped out the window herself. Ms. Darcy, in her late 30's, was not in great physical shape by any means, but she could definitely slide down a rope and so down she went. She landed on the ground hard, but had the presence of mind to get up quickly, and she took off running without stopping or looking back. Ten seconds later she was across the road, into the house, and could finally breathe easy. She found her students, gave them all big hugs, started crying, and prayed together with them that the rest of the kids and teachers would make it out alive as well.

After dropping off the three teachers in the locker room Derek ran back up the locker room stairs and into the main hallway. He took a quick look out one of the first floor windows and was happy to see there weren't any police cars around yet, and he didn't hear any sirens coming. Fortunately the Fillmore County police station is in Preston, a good 15-20 miles east of Spring Valley. Still, Derek was very conscious of the clock and knew they had a limited amount of time left. He quickly bounded up to the upper level of classrooms and saw the two classroom doors busted open that Tony and Matt were supposed to handle. The fact that he didn't hear any noise of a struggle was a good sign, but he took the time to step into both of their rooms to check on things.

Matt was in the process of tying up Mrs. Johanson, one of the social studies teachers who was near retirement. Mrs. Johanson was in her mid-60's and she had given up on teaching at least 10 years ago if not more than that. She was now just putting in her time to help pay for her husband's medical bills, and she was just recycling the same material that she taught 30 years ago. Her kids were all gone, her husband was sick, and she was certifiably depressed. She wasn't even capable of putting up a physical struggle with Matt, and she didn't have any students in her room at this time so that arrest was a walk in the park. She might not have resisted even if she was physically able. Across the hall, Tony was sitting on the back of Mr. Thompson thoroughly enjoying the process with a huge, crazy smile on his face, but appeared alarmed when he saw Derek.

"Did you get Ms. Darcy already? I heard the glass break."

"No, I just got up here. I didn't break any glass. You sure it wasn't from Matt's room?"

"I'm pretty sure it wasn't. It came from the direction of Ms. Darcy's room," Tony said when it all of a sudden hit him. "Shit! She's going out the window. Get over there."

Derek grabbed the hammer from his pocket and took off quickly for Ms. Darcy's room. He slammed the hammer through the glass and quickly unlocked the door from the inside. Once he looked up after opening the door, however, he was shocked to see a huge bookcase standing right in front of him blocking the way. He lowered his shoulder into the bookcase and drove with his legs, but it didn't budge.

"Matt, Tony, come here," He yelled and tried looking over the top of the bookcase. He could see someone moving over by the window, but couldn't get a clear view around all the junk piled in his way. He heard her yelling something out the window, but couldn't make out exactly what it was.

Matt and Tony each came out of their rooms pushing their two prisoners out into the hallway and quickly ran to their brother's aid. Between the three of them they could slide the bookcase to the side enough for Derek to edge his way through, but the room was empty. He climbed over and around the piled up desks to make his way to the window, but he couldn't see anybody moving out of it. He could, however, make out the faint sound of police sirens coming in the distance. No time to worry about losing Ms. Darcy, they had to move. She wasn't that important anyway, and Derek actually kind of liked her. Derek climbed his way back out into the hallway where his brothers had the other two teachers secured and ready to be moved.

"She's gone. Nothing we can do about that," Derek said. "The police are coming. It's time to get them downstairs and start part two."

Chapter 12

Spring Valley, MN

The locker room was now as full as it was going to get. There were 18 students, six of which were tied up, and eight teachers. Of the 18 students, ten were girls and eight were boys. All 26 of the hostages were sitting on the floor lined up against the chalkboard wall. There wasn't a lot of room for them to be moving around, but they weren't going to be doing any moving anyway. Mike had been busy getting things lined up downstairs while keeping an eye on everyone. He had a stool set out which was facing the hostages, and was sitting on it with his gun in his lap right now keeping an eye on them while Derek and Tony whispered to each other.

"You, in the pink shirt, come here," Derek finally said to one of the young girls sitting there. Terrified, she stood up and slowly moved over to him.

"We're releasing you. You need to go straight to the police outside, let them know that we're in the locker room and that if they come down here the hostages will all be killed immediately. Tell them that we have some demands and we can communicate with them through the coaches' office phone that's down here," Derek said, and turned his attention to his brother. "Mike, walk her up and then stand guard at the bottom of the stairs ready to fire up towards the doorway if anyone tries to enter."

Derek then turned around to face the rest of the hostages, and turned on a big, cheesy smile like he was about to give a presentation in front of a bunch of businessmen. "Welcome! You are now all spectators in the Morrison courtroom proceedings. There are a few of you that have committed crimes against the Morrison family, and you will now have your day in court. Most of you are innocent of all crimes, and if you conduct yourselves in an appropriate manner you'll have nothing to worry about. We have no reason to harm those that have not harmed us. Those of you who are guilty of crimes will have to pay for them of course. That's the way justice works. Matt here, is the bailiff. I am the judge, and Tony over there is the executioner. I expect silence in my courtroom and if you violate my rule you will be held in contempt and will have to leave with Tony. Trust me you don't want to be held in contempt. It won't be a simple overnight stay in the county jail. I'm so confident in your ability to act appropriately that

I'll take the duct tape off. Fellas, you can remove the duct tape."

Matt and Tony went around and ripped the duct tape off of the mouths of those that were taped earlier, but they kept the hostages hands tied behind their backs with the rope. With every opportunity that Mr. B. had he was straining against the rope and moving his hands around in an attempt to loosen it. He felt like he was getting some movement, but now that there were three Morrison brothers within visual range it was getting tougher to keep it discrete and unnoticed. Mr. B.'s mind was racing trying to come up with a way out of this situation. He hadn't really had any major run-ins with the Morrison brothers when they were in school so he wasn't especially concerned for himself, but he did know that his good friend Dan Marchant had some previous difficulty with a couple of them. Mr. B. couldn't just sit there and watch him get executed, so he set his mind to doing everything he could to somehow free his hands.

"Bailiff, please bring Dr. Robert Little to the stand," Derek said, taking his seat on the end of one of the locker room benches so that he could see the hostages on his front, left side and the stool on his front, right.

Matt walked over to Dr. Little, tossed him over his shoulder like a rag doll and carried him to the stool and plopped him down on it violently. Matt went around to the other side of him, took out his knife and cut the rope freeing his hands. Matt then took the bible that they brought from the old lady's house and stuck it out in front of Dr. Little who just looked at it and then up at Matt with a confused look on his face. Matt gave him a quick slap to the face, grabbed his hand, and put it on the bible for him.

"Do you swear to tell the truth, the whole truth, and nothing but the truth so help you God?" Matt asked.

Again there was silence from Dr. Little which was clearly starting to frustrate the Morrison brothers. Tony took out his gun, stuck it to the side of Dr. Little head, and said "If you don't start participating in this trial I'm going to find you guilty right now and execute you right here in front of all of your students. Now, answer the fuckin' question."

"Yes," Dr. Little said quietly with tears starting to come to his eyes.

"That's better," Tony said, calm again. "I'll be asking the questions for this trial, Bobby, and I expect immediate and honest answers. And, since I was the one involved I'll know if you're telling the truth or not. Any lie will bring about a bullet to the kneecap. Got it?"

Dr. Little nodded his head.

"Great," Tony continued, "do you remember when you suspended me for five days my sophomore year?"

"I think so."

"And do you remember why you suspended me?"

"You were involved in a fight in the cafeteria. You jumped a student from behind and started hitting him out of the blue."

"Huh. Out of the blue, you say. That doesn't seem like something someone would do. It doesn't sound like something I would do. Why would a person do something like that? Did you ever ask me why I did that?"

"Not that I recall," Dr. Little said, starting to whimper between questions.

"You don't recall because you didn't ask. If you did I would have told you about how he had been harassing me for the previous four weeks and wouldn't stop. About how I talked to a couple of the teachers here about it, like Marchant and Johanson over there, and they did nothing about it. In fact, they made it seem like it was all my fault. Can you believe that? They were blaming the victim. Do you know about any of this?"

"No, not that I remember."

"And why didn't you know about it?"

"I probably didn't ask because it doesn't matter. You can't just beat on someone that you disagree with," Dr. Little said, with a little bit of courage starting to show.

"Did you even hear what I said? He was harassing me for four weeks!" Tony said starting to get angry again. He took a deep breath to try and control his rage for now, and then continued. "Alright, I'm going to let that go for now because you fucked up worse than just that. What did you do when you saw me finally getting some justice?"

"I pulled you off of him and took you to the office."

"We're gonna need a few more details than that, Bobby."

"I'm not sure exactly what you're looking for."

"OK, let me help you out. You jumped me with a full speed diving tackle and slammed my nose into the ground breaking it. Then you dragged me to your office with my nose bleeding the whole way there. Does any of that sound familiar?"

"I was just trying to break up a fight."

"Bullshit! You outweighed me by literally a hundred pounds back then. You could have easily lifted me off. After you broke my nose you could have given me some medical care instead of dragging me into the office. You didn't even give me any ice! You just let me sit there and bleed all over myself and all over the floor."

By now Tony was getting hot again and was just inches away from Dr. Little's face. Derek decided that this was enough. "OK, I think we've heard enough for the verdict. Matt?"

"Guilty."

"Tony?"

"Fucking Guilty."

"And I say guilty as well. Dr. Little, you have clearly neglected your responsibilities as a principal to care for your students and treat them appropriately. You are sentenced to death to pay for your crimes. This case is closed," Derek banged his hammer down on the bench like a gavel. "Tony, you can take the prisoner away."

Mr. B. watched helplessly as Tony stuck his gun into the back of Dr. Little and pushed him into the shower area in the back of the locker room. Mr. B. and Dr. Little had never been especially close, but to see a colleague go through something like this was horrendous. Dr. Little was crying along the way and could barely move one foot in front of the other. Once out of sight Mr. B. could still hear Dr. Little wailing loudly, apologizing profusely, and begging for mercy. Then all of a sudden with the loud, reverberating explosion of a gun, silence.

Chapter 13

Spring Valley, MN

Just as he was the first time he had contact with the Morrison brothers nearly eight years earlier, Sheriff Nelson was in over his head. Standing outside the locker room door with his Chief Deputy, Alan Myers, he wasn't sure exactly what to do. The school was in the process of being completely evacuated, except of course for those stuck in the locker room. He had found the dead secretary's body, but there was clearly nothing he could do to help her. She was gone long before he had arrived. After the young girl ran out, he at least knew where they were and that they weren't all dead. What he didn't know was whether he should call downstairs there or wait for the experts from the Cities to get here. Even by helicopter that was still at least 45 minutes away. Right as Sheriff Nelson made the commitment to wait it out he heard a shot fired below, and decided he couldn't just sit there and let people be killed so he called them up to try and negotiate.

"Hi, I've been waiting for your call," he heard Derek say on the other line.

"I heard a shot fired, is everyone alright down there?"

"Oh, they're just fine. We're having a great time. It's nice to hear your voice again Sheriff. Are you ready to listen to our demands? This small talk is fun and all, but we're kind of on a schedule here."

"OK, I don't know if I have the authority to give you what you want, but I can try. Go ahead."

"Don't worry, Sheriff, I'm certain you have the authority. The only question is if you have the balls. We want to speak with you, and only you, face to face. That's our demand. For us to negotiate our way out of here we feel it's necessary that you're here with us since you are someone that we are familiar with and can identify. To show you that we're willing to free all of the hostages eventually and are operating in good faith we'll release five of the high school girls in exchange for you. That's a pretty damn good deal. You'll be looking like a great negotiator getting a five for one deal like that. Of course, you'll need to send all of your officers back out of the hallway there and be lying unarmed and face down right outside the door. We'll bring the hostages out, and bring you in. Do we have a deal?"

Sheriff Nelson wasn't sure what to do. He didn't trust Derek one bit, but also knew how bad it would look if he had the opportunity to release five kids and didn't take it. He stood there dripping in sweat. Was he really ready to possibly sacrifice his own life for the lives of five others?

"I don't know that this is a good idea," Sheriff Nelson finally responded.

"Well, here's the situation Sheriff. You're either going to get the five kids out alive or I'm going to shoot them right now and you can have them dead. Now that won't make you look like a very good negotiator. These girls' parents probably won't think too much of you then. Time's wasting. You have five seconds to decide. Five, four, three."

"Ok, I'll do it, don't shoot," Nelson interrupted.

"Good. I thought eventually you'd come to your senses. I just wasn't sure how many I'd have to kill first. Be ready in five minutes," Derek said hanging up the phone on him.

Sheriff Nelson was by now dripping with sweat. It ran down his face which otherwise looked pale. He started removing his gun, and handed it shakily over to his Chief Deputy.

"Are you sure this is a good idea, boss?" Alan Myers asked.

"No, I'm not. I don't trust them one bit, but I don't really have a choice here," Nelson responded, wishing he'd have just waited for the cavalry to arrive from the Cities before calling down there. Maybe the Morrison's would have just sat it out if he hadn't called. "If you hear any more shots while I'm in there that probably means I'm dead, and you should call the Morrison's immediately and get everyone ready to move in. I'm worried that the hostages are all going to end up dead down there if we don't make a move on them. Remember, these guys are wanted for the bank robbery and murders in Rochester yesterday and are extremely dangerous. These are not stable individuals."

With that, Sheriff Nelson sent the rest of his police force out of the hallway with Alan Myers now in charge until the team from the Cities showed up. He laid face down in the hallway on the cold tile floor with only his thoughts and fears to keep him company for what was actually just a couple of minutes but seemed like an eternity. Finally, the door opened a crack and he could see an attractive young girl with a gun to her head. Behind the girl he could see the dark eyes of Derek Morrison who flashed a smile at the Sheriff when he realized that this wasn't a trap. Derek let the first girl go and four others were pushed out into the hallway followed by Tony.

"Get up," Derek said, pulling him off the ground and frisking him quickly. They led him in to the stairwell, and closed the door back up again. The loud bang of the door shutting was enough to make Nelson jump. He could see

[129]

Mike down at the bottom of the stairs with his gun aimed up at him. They took a couple steps down the stairs when Derek gave him a shove and he fell hard down the cement steps not stopping until he reached the bottom. Nothing broken, but he did bang his head hard on the floor and must have passed out for a second or two because when he looked up there were three Morrison boys standing over the top of him smiling. This was not looking like a very promising situation for him to be in. What little chance that the Morrison boys were going to negotiate seemed to be gone.

Derek once again lifted him up off the ground and this time carried him into the other room and set him down on the same stool that Dr. Little had previously occupied. He was now looking straight across from the 19 students and teachers that were left, most with their hands tied behind their backs. He saw his son's old football coach, Mr. B., tied up amongst the group, and he knew at least half of the other faces that were looking back at him. Aaron Nelson lived in Spring Valley with his family and was very active in the community, and so he had connections to quite a few people in town.

"What's going on? Why am I here on this stool?" Sheriff Nelson finally asked. "I thought I was down here to negotiate with you."

"Change of plans, Sheriff," Derek responded. "You've been accused of a crime against the Morrison boys, and today is your day in court. Can't you tell, this courtroom was built specifically for you? Without you, none of us would even be here. This is all about you. So now it's your chance to stand trial."

"That wasn't the deal, Derek. I'm here to negotiate the freeing of the hostages," Nelson said standing up. This brought a fist to the kidneys from Tony who brought the gun up to his head.

"Sit down and shut up. We're not here to mess around. When we ask you a question, you answer it. Otherwise, you sit quietly. It's really quite simple. Forget about all that negotiating shit. That's never going to happen. Do you understand?"

Sheriff Nelson nodded his head and gingerly sat back down on the chair. He was afraid something like this might happen since he knew of the Morrison's anger and hatred of him, and he hoped desperately that the state police would be showing up soon with a SWAT team. He decided that his best bet was to just do as they asked and try to delay things as much as possible. The longer things dragged out, the better chance he had to survive.

He was sworn in just like Dr. Little had been earlier, and played along with the whole charade. The only difference between Dr. Little's trial and the Sheriff's was that now Derek was asking the questions and Tony had taken the Judge's seat on the other side.

"Tell us about the night that you came to our house," Derek said.

"I got a call from dispatch saying there were screams being reported coming from inside your house. I was in the vicinity and was there in a matter of a couple minutes. I drove up, came up to the door, saw the gun out, and yelled for the suspect to drop the gun. The suspect did not drop the weapon but said that the other person in the house was going to die. There was then movement, and the suspect was shot."

"That's a pretty vague, cold version of events there Sheriff. Your suspect was my mom. You can refer to her as Jean from now on, even though you probably don't remember her name, you piece of shit. Where was Jean's gun when you shot her?"

"She had it in her hand."

"No shit, Sherlock. Of course it was in her hand. Where in her hand? Was she aiming at you? At my Dad? Where was it pointed?"

"They told me later on in a report that it was pointed towards the floor at the moment when she was shot."

"What do you mean, they told you later on?"

"The forensic team said it was pointed down when I was debriefed later."

"Didn't you know where the gun was pointed? You were there! You just fired at someone that had a gun pointed into the ground?"

"There was movement, and I just reacted. When someone has a gun you need to make split second decisions. If Jean had dropped the gun right away I obviously wouldn't have shot."

"So, you don't feel any remorse for murdering my mom?"

"Listen, I never want to kill anyone, but I acted with my best intentions. I'm sorry that she was killed, but it was not malicious. I don't want to see anyone killed and especially don't want to play any part in it happening."

"So, you admit to murdering my mom, then?"

"No. I shot her, but I did not murder her. She had a gun and I acted in self-defense."

"You must have been really worried about that shot ricocheting off the floor and hitting you. Doesn't sound like self-defense to me. And what do you do for a living today? Surely you're not still patrolling the streets after these events."

"As you know, I was cleared of all charges, and it was ruled that I acted appropriately. It was just a tragic situation."

"Well, they may have ruled that you acted appropriately, but now it's time for our verdict, and I say guilty as charged. You're a danger to society, and I can't believe that they let you continue to walk the streets with a weapon after you've already murdered an innocent person. How many more people would you need to kill before they take your badge? Tony and Matt?"

"Guilty."

"Guilty."

"There you have it members of the court. Finally Sheriff Nelson will pay for his heinous act of killing a person in cold blood. Tony, I'll handle this one. I've been waiting for this for years," Derek said, grabbing the Sheriff and taking him into the shower area.

When they got in there Sheriff Nelson saw the dead body of Dr. Little lying there executed on the floor and for the first time really understood what was about to happen. "Wait!" he said panicking, "We can work something out. We can get a deal set up where you get out free. I'm the Sheriff. I can make it happen. We can get you out before the SWAT team gets here. Whatever you want!"

"I want my mom back," Derek said, and fired the gun at his head killing him instantly.

Chapter 14

Spring Valley, MN

Chief Deputy Myers heard the gunshot downstairs, followed by a loud chorus of screams and instinctively thought that Nelson had just been killed. As directed by Sheriff Nelson he immediately got on the phone and tried to contact the locker room. The phone did not get picked up, however, and eventually went to a voicemail. He tried again and this time just got a busy signal, the phone apparently either left off the hook or unplugged.

Alan Myers had worked under Sheriff Nelson for the last five years and had never been involved in a hostage situation. This was just not something that happens in Fillmore County. Speeding tickets, domestic abuse reports, maybe some drug busts, those were the areas that Meyers had experience in. But Alan Myers was aggressive and bold in all of the decisions that he made as a cop and he wasn't about to change that now in the midst of a crisis. It was time to act, and Myers decided they were going in. He called everyone together, coordinated the effort and they got ready to move.

Hearing another man murdered may not be quite as devastating as actually seeing a man killed, but Mr. B. was having a tough time dealing with the fact that people he knew were getting picked off all around him. Looking around to the faces of the other hostages he could tell that they were having some difficulty as well, as there were white faces and tears in many of their eyes. Some of the kids were visibly shaking and whimpering. There was also an almost visual sheen of fear in each of their eyes, including his son's. This was trying for an adult to handle much less a teenage kid.

With the focus squarely on the interrogation of Sheriff Nelson, Mr. B. managed to almost get his hands free unnoticed. And, finally, when Derek and Nelson were in the shower room he got them loose. He decided he needed to wait for the right time, but he'd definitely pounce when the moment came. He wasn't going to let another innocent person die if he could possibly help it. The lives of those in this locker room would be forever affected as it was, and if it meant that he had to sacrifice himself he was willing to do that. Mr. B. figured they'd be coming in his direction to grab

Mr. Marchant who was sitting next to him soon, and that might end up being his best chance. He'd be ready.

When Derek returned from the showers he heard the phone ringing and went into the coaches' room and angrily pulled it out of the wall. There was nothing to talk about anymore with the police. They'd be coming in eventually and the shootout would begin. He actually hoped they'd come in soon. He probably could have talked to the police and convinced them to hold off, but what was the point in that.

Rather than feel the elation of finally eliminating Sheriff Nelson, Derek was actually feeling a hurtful sadness now. This was supposed to be his crowning achievement, his moment of relief and release, but he was instead remembering the loss of his mother now, and things were starting to be a lot less fun for him. He was just ready to be done. This mission of his, this plan, had always been the event to look forward to. This was the one thing in his life he could set his mind to when he was missing his mother, but now it was done and there really was nothing else for him to live for.

Tony, on the other hand, was ready for the next trial. In his mind the more people that were killed the better. His biggest disappointment was that he couldn't be the one to kill Sheriff Nelson himself. Not because he had any more hatred for Nelson than any of the others, but because he just enjoyed the act of killing, and was itching to do some more.

He had only been able to eliminate two people so far today personally, and he was ready for more. He picked up Mrs. Johanson and carried her over to the stool. He wanted to move quickly before they ran out of time. Now that Derek had stupidly ripped the phone out of the wall they wouldn't be able to stall for more time.

"Derek, let's go. Next fuckin' trial," Tony said to his brother.

Derek, in his own world, snapped back to the task at hand and quietly told Matt to swear Mrs. Johanson in.

Before Matt had an opportunity to swear her in, however, there was the deafening sound of the door being blown in, immediate gunfire, and a scream coming from Mike over by the entrance.

"I'm hit in the leg," Mike yelled, crawling around the corner after being shot for the second time in two days. "They're coming in. I'm going to need some help."

Derek and Matt immediately dropped what they were doing and ran to their brother's aid. They started firing up the stairwell, and so far the police weren't making any attempt to come down the stairs. They were just sticking their guns through the opening and firing down on them. The police had the positional advantage, but they also were the ones that had to make their way down. All the Morrison boys had to do was stay behind the corner and fire up the stairs intermittently. The problem for the Morrison's was that the bullets were starting to ricochet and were tearing up chunks of the wall which were then hitting them. It was only a matter of time before they'd be shot or have to move.

Tony, meanwhile, completely ignored the gunfire. He had business to take care of with some of the other teachers. He wanted to try at least two more, and was really hoping to have Mr. Barber on the stand as well. There was no way that was going to happen anymore. He had to move quickly and decided to just forget about the whole trial thing. They were all going to end up being guilty anyway. He might as well just speed up the entire process.

"No time left, you're guilty," he said, grabbing Mrs. Johanson and pulling her with him over towards the other teachers. Tony figured he could handle executing two at a time since they were still tied up, but any more than that might get difficult. He'd take care of two now, and then hopefully he'd have time to make a second trip. He knew who he wanted to grab right now. The question was who he was going to take with Mr. Barber on the next trip. He would decide on Mr. Thompson or Mr. B. after he got back. "You're guilty too, Mr. Marchant."

Right as Tony was about to snatch Dan Marchant, he heard Matt scream out from the other room. Tony turned for a second to see Matt crawling back into the locker room area with a bullet through his chest and blood pouring out of him. He was struggling to breath and there was a wheezing noise coming from him. Tony could tell almost instantly that he wasn't going to make it. Seeing his brother dying didn't really bother Tony. What did bother him was the knowledge that there would be one less person keeping the police at bay while he was taking care of business. Matt's screaming and crawling into the room was just the distraction that Mr. B. had been waiting for. He exploded off of the ground with a quick wrap-up tackle that Tony didn't see coming until it was too late. He pushed down on Tony's arms as he hurled his body at him, and tried to dislodge the gun from his grip. When Tony's body hit the floor with the full force of Mr. B.'s weight on top of him Tony let out a grunt and the gun went flying out of Tony's hand and rolled across the floor towards his son and the rest of the students.

With the surprise attack Mr. B. had gained the upper hand on Tony, and was slamming his head into the hard concrete locker room floor. Tony was not built for hand to hand combat, and wasn't able to really even get a hit in on Mr. B. The fight was over almost before it started, but Mr. B. knew his job wasn't done yet.

"Dad, come here, I'll kick the gun to you," his son yelled out. With his hands behind his back he couldn't grab it, but could send it in his dad's general direction with his feet. He had the gun positioned near his feet ready to go.

Tony's body was going limp and everything seemed to be in hand so Mr. B. moved off of him and stepped quickly over towards his son and grabbed the gun. He could hear the gunshots continuously pounding the walls right next door, and the whole place sounded like a warzone. He lifted the gun and had it pointed directly at Tony when Derek reentered the room, scrambling for cover. Derek saw the gun out and pointing at his brother and reacted. The shot caught Mr. B. square in the chest, his blood spraying and hitting his son.

"No, Dad!" He yelled, and ran to him, but his father was gone.

Chapter 15

New Britain, CT

"**D**ad!" Charlie Becker yelled from his bed around 3 AM on the Sunday morning of his next start. Charlie woke up from his dream sweating and hyperventilating, and was sitting straight up, wide eyed.

"It's ok, Charlie," Karen said rubbing his back. "Take some deep breaths. It's all over. I'm here."

Charlie always woke up from his reoccurring nightmare at the same exact time, right after his dad had been shot and he had been hit with his dad's blood. In fact, that's precisely where the memory of that terrible day 17 years ago ends for him. Even with his photographic memory the rest of the events of that day after that moment have been blocked out. The only way he knew anything else that happened after that was from talking with his friends and teachers later on.

Through conversations over the next few days Charlie was told that the twins were both shot and killed in the stairway. When the police took the hostages up through the stairs they walked them right past the twins' bodies which were riddled with bullet holes and their blood was all over the walls. One of the girls vomited while going past them at the sight of their mutilated bodies that had been literally torn to pieces.

The events that played out in the locker room after Charlie's dad had been shot still didn't make a whole lot of sense to him, even after hearing them several times from Mr. Marchant and others. Derek, after firing the deadly shot, just stood there and looked at Charlie who was splattered with blood and was hovering over his father. He didn't look towards his brother Tony who was in pain on the ground and in need of help, or his other brothers that were dying by the stairs, or even the cops that were making their way down the stairs, but just at Charlie – a kid that he didn't even know. Tony's gun had slid over near Derek's feet but he just ignored it and continued staring with a vacant expression on his face. Tony, who now had several of the football players on top of him trying to hold him down without the use of their hands, yelled at him to start firing, but instead of shooting any of the hostages or policemen Derek lifted the gun up to his head, mumbled something about being sorry to his mom, and with tears in his eyes shot himself.

Both guns were then on the floor by Derek's dead body, and a few seconds later the police came charging down the stairs and into the locker room to secure the area. Tony was put into handcuffs and was yelling the whole time for the police to shoot him. He kept screaming like a man insane about how he couldn't go to prison, and needed to be killed. Instead, as it turned out, a couple of months later he got sentenced to life in prison with no possibility for parole. As far as Charlie knew he was still alive and in prison today, but that was not something Charlie kept track of or really even cared about.

Mr. Marchant was overwhelmed with emotion knowing that he was just a matter of seconds away from being killed, and that instead Charlie's dad, his good friend, had taken his place. He stayed and consoled Charlie as best he could down in the locker room, and eventually helped him move up the stairs and out of the school to where his mother and sister were located.

"I'm sorry I woke you up, honey," Charlie said, regaining his composure and finally deciding to get out of bed.

"Where are you going?"

"I just need to get some water and calm down a bit. Go back to sleep, you have a big day tomorrow."

[144]

Charlie would be literally shaking after reliving that terrible moment, and going back to sleep right away was never an option for him. Sometimes he'd just lay there in bed to not worry Karen, but he just felt like he needed to get up today. It was always during these moments after the nightmare where it was difficult for him to resist getting a drink. Alcohol had been pretty much the only thing he could use to relax his body and help the terrible visions disappear. It was also during these moments that he thought the most about his dad, and how he'd feel like he would be letting him down if he walked away from the game without making it to the majors.

His dad was his coach all the way throughout his early life and not just his formal coach on his baseball teams. Baseball was always a part of the Becker household, with Heather and Ellen even joining in the games in the backyard with some of the neighborhood kids. There were dirt areas where the bases were located. The lawn just didn't stand a chance against all of the baseball that was played out there. One of Charlie's dad's favorite quotes was by his Minnesota baseball hero Harmon Killebrew's father who said that they were raising boys, not grass. Even when there weren't other kids to play with, Charlie's dad would take the baseball bat and send pop-ups out to Charlie and Heather who would chase them down. Every evening after supper, all spring, summer and fall, they'd be out there in their spacious backyard playing ball.

Sure his dad played and coached football as well, but baseball was the most talked about item around the Becker house, and the thing that drew the family together. They would sit around the house on a nice, summer night and watch the Twins games together as a family. His dad would always say that someday he'd be watching him playing there in the majors if he kept working at it. That was always the dream, and Charlie always had the desire and love of the game needed to keep pushing for it. Once his dad was killed, that desire to make the big leagues kept fueling him on, but he hadn't quite been able to make it to the top. Maybe if he kept pitching well this season could finally be his chance.

Fortunately for Charlie it appears as if the Twins are going to make the season relevant by staying right in the midst of the playoff chase. After their win last night on the west coast they have now drawn even with the Indians for first place in the Central Division with a little over a month left to be played in the Major League season. The Twins just received some bad news two days ago, however. One of their starting pitchers is going to be out for the rest of the season with a torn rotator cuff. Charlie had hoped that his outing on Tuesday night would be enough to convince the Twins to give him a shot, but they filled the spot in the rotation with one of the Triple-A pitchers instead. There was still time, however, as now that there was an injury there was one less pitcher in line ahead of him. His start in nine hours on an early Sunday afternoon would just have to be another good one.

A couple hours later Karen and Timmy came sleepily walking into the living room finding Charlie wide awake watching the morning news while sitting on the couch drinking some coffee.

"Good morning, Timmy," Charlie said cheerfully.

"Hi Dad, I want to watch cartoons."

"Sure, if you come over here and sit next to me for a little while. Are you all ready for the big flight to Minnesota tonight?"

"I put my toys in my backpack. Are you flying, too?"

"No, I have to stay here."

"Why?"

"I still have a couple of games left. It won't be too long, though."

"I want you to come, too, Dad," Timmy whined.

"I'm sorry buddy, I don't have a choice."

Karen and Timmy were taking the 5:00 PM flight from Hartford to Minneapolis after Charlie's game tonight. It was getting to be the end of August and Karen's in-service started on Wednesday. Karen already felt like she was behind since she hadn't been in her classroom all summer and planned on spending all day Monday and Tuesday there at school to make up for the missed time. Ellen would watch Timmy during that time and she was planning on picking them up from the airport tonight for the 100 mile drive south from Minneapolis to Spring Valley. Ellen had called three or four times in the last couple of days to work out all the details, and she was clearly excited about having her only grandchild back home with her soon. Sometimes it seemed like Charlie's traveling baseball schedule was harder on Ellen than anyone else, but Ellen did a good job of hiding that. It helped that Ellen still had her daughter Heather living in the area.

Karen came over with her cup of coffee in hand and sat next to Charlie and Timmy as well. "I'm not looking forward to being at home alone again, Charlie," Karen said.

"There's nothing I can do about it," Charlie replied defensively. "It won't be too long, anyway. The season ends here in two weeks."

"Yeah, the summer season ends in two weeks, and then when does the winter season start? The whole process is never-ending. I don't want to be home alone when our new baby is born."

"Mom will be around to help out."

"Listen Charlie, I know that Ellen is a huge help, but she's not you," Karen said getting up and moving into the kitchen. The time apart was never that terrible for Karen once she was in the middle of it, but the anticipation and dread in advance was always tough on her. That's when Karen and Charlie would argue the most, and it was mainly because Karen wanted him around. Charlie had learned to just try and listen and not escalate the argument.

Karen had started getting things packed up last night and she now continued on that task as Timmy's show finished up and Charlie turned the TV off to build some block towers with him. Their apartment was completely furnished so getting everything put away for the winter pretty much meant just getting their clothes and Timmy's toys packed up. Charlie's job for the next couple of weeks was to get everything that they couldn't pack in their bags for the flight stuffed into the car. He would be making the 20 hour drive west immediately after the season was over.

At about 10:00 AM it was time for Charlie to head to the ballpark to prepare for his start. He only had three scheduled starts left this season if he didn't get called up to the big leagues, and even then the odds of him starting a game there were probably not likely. He'd be up there for long relief if a starter was getting shelled to give them some innings. Not exactly glamour work. But, at least if he was up there that might keep him out of the winter leagues. Even the thought of being with the Twins didn't excite him like it used to, however, as that would add an extra month to his season and more days on the road. He was tired of being away, tired of the road and the travel, and he came to the ballpark already in a foul mood. The truth was his heart just wasn't in it. Events that occur in Charlie's everyday life affect him in the clubhouse and on the mound now. Not like previously when the events that took place there were his entire life.

The first three innings of the game passed by very similar to many other games that he'd pitched throughout his career. He was in and out of trouble, but managed to escape each time without allowing a run. The Akron Aeros, Cleveland's Double-A squad, had some strong bats but Charlie hadn't given up the big hit thus far. In the bottom of the third Benny Phillips hit a 2-run homer giving New Britain a 2-0 lead, and that's when things started getting interesting. After Benny hit the ball he stood there admiring his shot for a while, and the Akron pitcher did not appreciate that.

"Get moving!" He yelled at Benny.

"Fuck you! Did you see how far that thing went? Did that ball ever come down?" Benny responded back with a smile, and slowly made his way around the bases.

Dusty, standing on the on-deck circle, knew what was going to happen next. He was going to pay the price for Benny's idiocy. Sure enough, the first pitch thrown to Dusty was a 94 MPH fastball right at Dusty's head. Both benches rose up to the top step of their respective dugouts, but everyone stayed put except for Don Scott and the team trainer who came jogging out to check on Dusty.

"Dusty, are you alright?" Scott asked, looking down at him.

"I think so, Coach. Just need to jog over to first and that will shake the cobwebs out," Dusty said, getting up to his feet. But as Dusty began to run towards first he started wobbling backwards and almost fell down again. Scott and the trainer quickly grabbed his arms and held on to him.

"Whoa! Take it easy, Dusty. We're going to need to have that head looked at. I think you might have a concussion. Let's call it a day and get you checked out," Scott said.

Dusty, who never came out of a game for any reason, couldn't even argue about that, seeing as he couldn't walk straight. He nodded and the three of them began walking gingerly back to the dugout, and then back into the clubhouse as the rest of the team patted Dusty on the back and the umpire warned both benches that the next incident would result in automatic ejections.

Already in a poor state of mind to begin with, Charlie was now steaming mad. He immediately walked over to Benny and got right in his face.

"This is your fault, Benny. Next time you hit a homerun get your ass moving."

"Fuck you, old man, this isn't the 60's. Sit your ass back down and shut up."

Charlie's nose was about an inch away from Benny's now, and he was about to take a swing at him when Clayton Kearns grabbed him and pulled him away.

"Easy there, Charlie," Clayton said. "I'd love to see you knock the shit out of Benny and all, but you have some other business to take care of here first. We'll take care of Benny as a team later."

Charlie knew exactly what Clayton was talking about and relented. Benny started this whole mess, but the Akron pitcher was to blame as well. It's one thing to brush a player back in retaliation or maybe hit him in the small of the back. It's a whole other thing to throw at a player's head and risk permanently damaging or even killing them. Charlie knew precisely what he had to do, and although he didn't like it, he would do it. He needed to protect his teammates.

Unfortunately for Charlie the next batter up that inning was Akron's 6'4" 230 pound slugger Darnell Williams. The ball made a distinct sound coming off of Darnell's bat; almost like it was screaming for mercy. Charlie had heard that plea for help too often already this season. Darnell, the Indians first round draft choice two years ago, would probably be up with the Indians right now if not for an anger management problem. He was suspended earlier in the year for bumping an umpire, and had an extremely short fuse. That wasn't going to stop Charlie from doing what he knew he had to do.

Charlie's first pitch was an 87 MPH fastball that hit Darnell square in the back. Darnell hardly let the ball hit him before he jumped out of the batter's box, dropped his bat, and went screaming towards the mound. Charlie was not exactly a big fighter, but he did play football in High School and had a little experience with a bar fight or two back in his hazy, drinking days. Charlie was a quarterback, however, whereas Darnell was a defensive lineman. There was a definite size mismatch. Charlie knew that Darnell would be coming, and he wasn't about to back down, so he bent his knees and decided his best bet was to stay low, hope that Darnell came in high, and pray his teammates would come to the rescue quickly. He really only had to buy about 10 seconds of time and the benches would be emptied and out on the field.

That approach paid off as Darnell launched his massive body towards Charlie's chest. The instant Darnell left his feet Charlie ducked low and used his shoulders to push upward on the lower half of Darnell's body. Darnell flew head over heels and landed hard on his back. Darnell was momentarily stunned more than anything else, but eventually got to his feet. He moved back towards Charlie again, a bit slower this time, ready to throw a punch while Charlie was backpedaling with his fists up in a boxer's stance. But, by the time Darnell got close enough to Charlie to hit him he was surrounded by a mob of players from both teams and couldn't get a clean shot in. The sea of people grabbed and clutched at Charlie and Darnell and they didn't end up near each other for the rest of the scrum.

Clayton, meanwhile, found the Akron starting pitcher milling near the edge of the melee and went directly after him. Clayton wrestled him down to the ground and got a couple of quick shots in on him before the mob got to him and order was restored.

Clayton, Charlie, and manager Don Scott were all ejected from the game along with a couple of other Rock Cat and Akron players – including Darnell. Clayton was still pretty amped up as he and Charlie were walking back into the clubhouse.

"Charlie, that was a sweet move you put on Darnell out there, for an old guy."

"Thanks, just trying to stay alive," Charlie responded feeling a little bit better now. "I noticed you went after that little starting pitcher rather than come and save me from Darnell."

"You looked like you had it all under control," Clayton said smiling. "Plus, I knew Benny had your back."

"Yeah, as I'm trying to avoid Darnell I'm at the same time hoping that Benny doesn't sneak up behind me and sucker punch me in the ribs."

"That would be too much effort for Benny. He probably used the fight time as an opportunity to grab a hot dog or something. My guess is he never left the dugout. Both teams would want to hit him!"

As they walked into the home clubhouse they saw Dusty sitting there with a bag of ice on the side of his head. Dusty looked up when he heard them coming in and gave them a smile.

"Looks like all hell breaks loose as soon as I'm out of the game," Dusty said. "I must be a positive influence on you guys."

"You missed a good fight, Dusty. Charlie decided to pick on Darnell a little bit out there, and of course I had to take care of the guy that dropped you," Clayton said.

"Thanks fellas, I appreciate it."

"No problem, Dusty," Charlie said. "How's the head?"

"I should be fine. They just think I might have a slight concussion. I'll be back soon. Hey, you gonna come out with us tonight? Celebrate the big fight?"

"Nah, I need to take my family to the airport. Then I better get some stuff packed up and put away." With all the excitement of the game Charlie had momentarily forgotten that he'd be seeing his family off tonight. The thought instantly put him back in a sour mood again and his heart sank.

"Alright, if you change your mind give me a call."

"You just be careful out there with that messed up head of yours. Take it easy. No keg stands tonight." Charlie said and started getting undressed. He quickly showered and changed, and found his family standing outside the clubhouse door waiting for him.

"Are you alright?" Karen asked right away giving him a hug.

"I'm fine. He picked on the wrong guy." Charlie said.

"Yeah, you're such a tough guy," Karen responded sarcastically. "Don't do that anymore. You scared me. Let's get out of here so we can spend a little bit of time together before we have to go."

A couple of hours later Charlie drove his family to the airport in Hartford and helped them get checked in. Charlie hated airports as they almost always meant goodbyes to him now. He left feeling empty and hollow inside, and he arrived home where for the second time in two nights he felt the temptation of a drink. He decided he needed something to do so he set about packing up the apartment and getting everything put away. The team was heading out for a four game series in Harrisburg in the morning so he wouldn't be at home very much in the next two weeks anyway. He soon realized, now that the adrenaline had worn off, that he was a little bit sore from the scuffle earlier in the day, however, so he decided to sit back down on the couch and get some ice.

He used the time icing his back to think about what he was going to do with his future. Could he really just walk away from the game, or would the guilt of not reaching the goal that he and his dad had of making the majors tear him up inside? Would that feeling of disappointment be too much for him? These were questions that Charlie didn't know the answer to, but he had to figure out soon. What he did know was that right now he really missed his family and more than anything else just wanted to be home, and not getting ready for a long night and another long five hour road trip to Harrisburg.

Chapter 16

New Britain, CT

"Screw it," Charlie finally said to himself, "I need to get out of here." Maybe getting up and out of the apartment would help him loosen his back up some, and it definitely would help his ever-moving mind. Charlie picked up his cell phone and started dialing.

"Hello?" Came Dusty's tentative voice over the line.

"Dusty, where you at?"

"I'm, uh, sitting here on the couch with, ah, ice on my head."

"Really. Then what's that music I hear?"

"The, uh, TV. The loud volume helps clear my head."

"Shut up, Dusty, I'm not calling for the team and Megan's not here with me, so I don't know why you're lying, but you can stop. I'm just looking for something to do."

Dusty perked up at hearing that and went back to his normal loud, confident self. "Chuckster! Ready for a little fun tonight, huh? We're just out here at Dooley's playing a little pool, but we can hit up some dancing somewhere if you want."

"No, I don't want any dancing. Dooley's sounds great. I'll be right over."

Charlie hadn't set foot in a bar in years, but was glad to hear that it would be Dooley's that he was going into. He had been there a couple of times when he was playing against New Britain in his earlier years, and it had more of a restaurant feel than a bar atmosphere. The place would still have the stench of stale beer on the sticky floor, but there wouldn't be the deafening, thumping music or the violent dancing there. There was even a decent amount of lighting. Charlie figured that Dusty probably chose Dooley's to not be too big of a strain on his concussion.

"Chuckster," Dusty called out as he entered the bar, "we're over here."

Charlie saw that Dusty was joined with Clayton, Bryce Hodge, and unfortunately Benny. Apparently Dusty wasn't holding a grudge towards Benny, so he better let it go as well. There were only three other people in the entire place, making Dusty's location help pointless, but Charlie still appreciated the invitation. He was no longer in his element in this environment and walked tentatively over towards them. Charlie had avoided bars as a needless temptation. At this point in his life, however, spending some time in a bar wasn't going to drive him out of sobriety.

"What's he doing here?" Benny sneered, looking over at Charlie. Despite being only nineteen years old Benny had a beer in hand and didn't look like he had any difficulty obtaining it. Actually, Benny looked older and more mature than all of the others, except for Charlie of course.

"Shut the fuck up, Benny, or we'll steal your car and ditch you again," Clayton said viciously and then turned to Charlie. "Can I get you a drink, Charlie? You drink on me tonight!"

"No thanks, I don't drink anymore."

"Well, I'm going to get you a coke then," Clayton said and took off for the bar. Bryce and Benny were involved in a game of pool with some money on the line by the looks of things, so Charlie stood around watching next to Dusty.

"Clayton can't stop talking about you after that move you put on Darnell," Dusty said. "Apparently you're his new hero now."

"Huh, that's something I guess. How's your head?"

"It's fine as long as I don't move around too much. I'd like to play again tomorrow, but I'm not sure if they'll let me. Everyone worries so much about concussions now, it's crazy."

Over at the pool table Benny just sank the 8-ball and was doing a little celebratory dance while mocking Bryce a little bit. "You guys all suck," Benny said while scooping up the money that Dusty was holding. "I put down four dollars to every one of yours yet I still end up making a killing off of y'all. Who's next?"

"Don't look at me," Dusty said, "you've already cleaned me out?"

"I'm done," Clayton said, "I'm using the rest of my money on drinks tonight. Tonight is a celebration!"

Hodge jumped in, "What's the point in throwing my money away? I suck."

"What about you, old man. You up for a game? Maybe see if you can do better than the rest of these guys?" Benny asked.

"I don't normally gamble," Charlie said.

"What the fuck? You don't gamble; you don't drink; what do you do? Just sit around and watch your hair turn gray? You must be the most boring man alive. Come on, I'll give you five dollars for every one of yours. We'll call it the old man special."

"Alright, I guess. One game." Charlie actually took some pride in being called boring. After years of being the polar opposite of boring, he had grown up and realized that being boring had made his life substantially better.

"How much you want to play for, Becker? How about ten of your dollars for fifty of mine?"

"How much have you taken from the other boys so far tonight?"

"Ah, I wiped out Dusty's fifty bucks right away. Then I think I got seventy from Clayton after a couple of games. And now just took thirty from Hodgy. So that makes, what, 150 dollars, right?"

"OK, let's play for those 150 dollars then. I'll put down 30 for your 150. But this is it – one game and I'm done."

"Ohhh, for someone that doesn't gamble you're quite the big spender," Benny said smiling. "It's a deal. Give Dusty the cash and let's get it on. You want to break?"

"Nah, you go ahead."

While Benny racked the balls and prepared to break Charlie went around looking at the pool sticks. He was searching for one with just the right tip on it, and finally found one that seemed straight enough as well. He chalked the cue tip and watched Benny get started.

Benny struck the cue ball similar to the way he struck a baseball – hard. When he broke, the balls went flying all over the felt. He rolled in one of the striped balls and walked around the table confidently stalking his next victim. Benny wasn't his normal brash self while he was playing. He instead kept his focus on the game in front of him. After an easy shot on a ball hanging right next to a corner pocket, Benny had a tough angle to try and cut. He missed it just by a fraction and the ball hit off of the rail.

"Shit!" Benny yelled. Once his turn was done he was back to his old, obnoxious self again. "Hurry up and miss so I can get back to the table and finish your sorry ass off. Better not miss any shots because I'm not going to miss another."

Charlie casually walked over to the cue ball and surveyed the table. He found the shot he wanted, slowly guided the pool stick back, and smoothly pulled it forward - knocking the cue ball into the waiting solid ball which then rolled directly into a side pocket. The cue ball backtracked after making contact, like a yo-yo being pulled, and rolled towards the center of the table. Whereas Benny was focused and silent while playing, Charlie decided to have some fun while he was shooting.

"You see, Benny," Charlie started, lining up his next shot, "sometimes when you're playing pool, just like when you're playing baseball, you need to be able to assess your opponent, especially if you're trying to make some money off of him."

Charlie sank his second ball and continued the dialogue. "You look at me and you see an old guy that just looks boring to you and just stop assessing there." He paused for a second to knock in a bank shot. "What you should be thinking about is the old man's history. Maybe he hasn't always been so boring. Did he have a previous drinking problem? Why, yes he did." Another ball finds the pocket. "Did he spend an obscene amount of time in bars? Yes, on that one, too." Knocks in another. The boys watching were now starting to hoot and holler with every shot that Charlie made. "What do people do in bars, besides drink of course? They play pool."

"Now, take an alcoholic who's a fairly athletic guy, if I say so myself, and take the booze out of his hands and what do you have left?" Two balls pocketed at once this time in an incredible shot that left the others really whooping it up.

"You have a pretty darn good pool player. 8 ball, corner pocket, no eyes." With that, Charlie closed his eyes and calmly finished the game off. Dusty, Clayton, and Bryce were now going ballistic – high fiving each other and having a great time. Charlie simply gave a smile and accepted some congratulations from his teammates while Benny stewed.

"Here's the money, Chuckster," Dusty said, handing him the wad of cash.

"Just give me my thirty back and you guys split the rest back up. Everyone leaves here a winner tonight," Charlie said.

Benny, not able to handle the embarrassment of losing and the harassment that he was receiving from his teammates stormed out of the bar while delivering a slew of expletives. This just caused the other boys to bust up laughing some more. They didn't necessarily mind spending some time hanging out with Benny, but they always loved it when the big money bags ran into a little taste of his own medicine. They were also still a little pissed at him for getting Dusty hit.

"There goes our sober sister," Bryce said, and they all broke out in laughter again.

For a couple of hours Charlie gave his racing mind a pit-stop. While the others began the journey towards intoxication, Charlie sipped on a couple of cokes, sat back, and enjoyed listening to Clayton describing and acting out the move he put on Darnell earlier.

After driving the boys home Charlie returned to his quiet apartment and tried to get some sleep. He reflected some more on his family, on his teammates, on his life, on God. He eventually decided that everything was going to be alright and drifted off into sleep unaware of the looming disaster.

Chapter 17

Rochester, MN and Harrisburg, PA

In the 1990's and early turn of the century, Rochester, Minnesota was a consistent top three finisher on the "best places to live" list conducted annually by *Money Magazine*. Although a great honor, this brought quite a few people and quite a bit of trouble to the previously peaceful city. A pipeline developed between Chicago and Rochester, with many low income people moving to the Rochester area looking for a better life, but bringing the drug use and gangs along with them. Throw in the population coming in from war-torn Somalia, and Rochester was becoming a more and more volatile place.

The divide between the haves and have-nots is also splitting up the city. The doctors at the Mayo Clinic and the technicians from IBM are sending their kids to the private schools or sending them to the lily white neighboring communities, while the immigrants and poor are slowly bringing down the public schools. Gang violence at the schools and in the community is steadily increasing and the weapons of choice have gradually escalated from fists to knives to guns. Still, despite the growth, Rochester is only hovering around 100,000 people and doesn't have the tremendous major crime issues that the Twin Cities does.

It's the type of community that Heather Becker enjoys being a police officer in. This is Heather's 9th year on the Rochester Police Department force, and she's only had to draw her gun a couple of times. Most of the work that she's done has involved drug use and petty theft cases, and she's well known throughout the community as there's not an abundance of female cops on the force, and definitely none as attractive as Heather. This is a fact that her partner and boyfriend of two years, Kenny Bridges, reminds her of frequently when they're out on patrol. Kenny has dark hair and dark eyes that women find attractive, but he's not a magnet to the opposite sex like Heather is.

"I thought that guy was going to lean through the window and kiss you when you pulled him over," Kenny said after a traffic stop minutes earlier.

"I did too, that's why I gave him a ticket," Heather responded smiling back.

"You know, you're too beautiful to be a cop, don't you? Someday one of these guys is going to actually lean in and do it."

"I hope they do. They'll be missing a couple of teeth afterwards."

Heather didn't put a lot of extra effort into her looks – didn't wear much makeup, dressed modestly, and spent very little time on her hair. She just had a natural beauty that seemed to be enhanced by her police uniform. Heather wasn't just the most attractive female officer in the department - she was also the toughest. She had taken down several male suspects twice her size without a problem, and actually relished the opportunity to fight more than a lot of the male officers did. After four years of playing softball on a full scholarship for the University of Minnesota she joined the RPD that next year and has been an integral part of it since. Heather had decided after losing her dad that joining the police force was her calling. She felt like she could fight crime in a way that would hopefully prevent others from suffering in the same way that she and her family had suffered. As more and more came out about the Morrison's past she felt like if the police department had done more to crack down on them earlier, the events in her school would have never happened. She also wished the police would have made a forced entry into the locker room earlier, and not waited trying to negotiate. Maybe Dad would still be around, then.

"Did you get a chance to spend some time with your nephew yesterday?" Kenny asked.

"Sure did! It's so much fun having him back around again. I can't wait to have some kids of my own."

"I can't wait to make some kids with you. Wanna start tonight?" Kenny said grinning at her.

"I wanna start when you put your money where your mouth is and buy me a ring," Heather shot back.

Kenny and Heather had been talking about marriage for months now, but Heather was waiting for Kenny to propose, and he hadn't yet. Heather didn't know it but Kenny actually had the ring in his pocket right now and was waiting for the right moment to ask her. Maybe he should take her out to dinner tonight somewhere nice and get it done. Better see how the day goes first before deciding for sure. He was hoping they could have a short engagement and be married within the next couple of months.

Kenny was pretty much part of the Becker family by now anyway. His family was from Alaska, and so he had spent all of his holidays with the Becker's for the past four years, even before they were dating each other and were just partners. Their relationship grew somewhat cautiously as it was frowned upon in the department for officers, especially partners, to date, but the more time they spent together the more they realized that they had a chemistry and attraction to each other that they'd never experienced before. Even now with their relationship out in the open they still kept things pretty quiet when they were involved with the job in any manner.

Kenny didn't plan on being a police officer, it just sort of happened. He was majoring in Biology with plans of heading back to Alaska with his degree in hand when fate intervened. There he was, minding his own business at the local Wal-Mart, when a man came running by carrying a purse with a woman yelling behind him. Kenny just instinctively went running after him. Kenny caught him from behind, held the victim down, and waited for law enforcement to arrive. The woman was extremely grateful and Kenny felt like he'd done something to benefit society. Something more than a biology degree could bring. From that point on he was hooked.

"Hey, why don't you come over to my mom's house tomorrow afternoon?" Heather asked while they were driving along. "Karen will be at school so it will just be my mom and Timmy. We can hang out there for a little bit and then maybe go see a movie or something like that."

"Sure, sounds like fun," Kenny replied. "I bet you're planning on us going to a good horror film, right?"

"Very funny, you know the movies I like."

"We might need to check the listings first. There's a pretty good chance that we've already seen all the chick flicks that have ever been made. Matthew McConaughey needs to get to work! He's been slacking lately."

"Don't even go there. Leave my man Matt alone. We have enough real drama and horror in our work world. No reason to experience any more when we're off work."

Their conversation was broken up by a call coming from dispatch telling of gunshots coming from Southeast Rochester, just a couple of blocks down from where they currently were located. Like a flipped switch their tone went immediately from conversational to business-like and they hit the lights and siren and were off. They were the first police to arrive in what looked like a war in the middle of the day. Two groups of gang members were firing at each other. One group was shooting from behind a couple of vehicles in the middle of the street, and the other group from inside a neighborhood house.

As Heather and Kenny sped in, the two cars that were in the street quickly took off down the road in the other direction. Kenny hurriedly called in the license plate numbers, parked the car, and informed dispatch that it appeared by their colors that they were members of the Shotgun Crips. They might have taken off after the vehicles, but as the vehicles were driving away the people inside the house ignored the fleeing vehicles and without provocation redirected their fire towards the lone police car.

"We're taking fire, and need assistance now!" Kenny yelled into the radio.

Heather and Kenny had both jumped out of the driver's side door away from the house and were pinned back behind the cop car. The car was getting torn to shreds and the two of them really didn't have anything that they could do besides just sit tight. Finally the gunfire let up enough for Heather to glance around the car tire and fire off a couple of shots towards the house.

"It's the Somali Bloods," Heather loudly yelled over the gunfire to her partner.

That was probably the reason they were taking fire. The Somali Bloods had been having an especially difficult time with the cops lately. One of their own was shot in the back by a policeman a couple days ago. All the Bloods needed to hear was that he was shot in the back, and they were dead set on revenge. Never mind the fact that he was shot in the back as he was firing upon another police officer in a different direction. That piece didn't seem to sink in with the Bloods who didn't really care about the specifics.

This was not encouraging news for Kenny and Heather for another reason. The Somali people that had moved into Rochester were very familiar with weapons and shooting. The life that they were leaving in Somalia was a terrible one filled with guns and violence from the moment that they were born until the day they moved away. These guys weren't just firing randomly and hoping for the best. They had accuracy and precision in their shooting ability.

"We're in trouble here," Heather yelled over to Kenny. "We need to keep getting a few shots in or we're not going to make it before the others show up. On the count of three, let's do it. One, two, three."

They each turned around opposite sides of the car and began firing at the house. This seemed to slow the pace of the bullets coming at them, but it still continued. The Bloods were using three levels of the house to fire out of and there was no way for the cops to stop them all despite the fact that both Kenny and Heather were very accurate shots. They were just shooting at a vicinity rather than a person.

After about 20 seconds Kenny turned to Heather and saw her not moving. He went over to her and pulled her further behind the car to see that she'd been shot in the head. He hadn't even heard or seen it happen with all the commotion. The bullet may have ricocheted because it entered the side of the head but didn't appear to have exited and she was breathing, conscious, and seemed to be responsive. Still, the situation was dire and she needed immediate assistance.

"Officer down!" He yelled desperately into the radio. "Get here, now!"

A few seconds passed before the first backup police car showed up, and by the time two others had arrived the shooting had stopped. The Somali's were trying to make an escape through the back door and into the alley. The ambulance came just a few seconds behind the police cars as the Mayo Clinic is not far away, and Heather was quickly put into the ambulance and rushed to the Intensive Care Unit with Officer Bridges by her side. A short trip, but an eternity for Kenny.

Charlie was just arriving at Metro Bank Park, home of the Harrisburg Senators, with his teammates for the Wednesday night game when his cell phone vibrated and Karen's number appeared on it. It was abnormal for Karen to call this close to game time so Charlie had an immediately sensation that something was not right.

"What happened, Karen?" Charlie worriedly began the conversation.

"It's your sister Charlie; she's been shot in the head. She's in the ICU right now, and your mom is on her way over there. They didn't give her too many details over the phone, but Heather is breathing on her own and Kenny is there with her. Kenny's going to try and keep us informed if he finds anything out, but it doesn't sound very good. I'm so sorry, honey."

Charlie stood there in the entryway to the stadium, and just stopped to take in the horrible news. Charlie had always been worried about something like this happening with his little sister as a police officer, and now that it did happen he was just stunned and in shock. His legs felt weak and he let himself slide down the wall and sat leaning against it trying to figure out the questions that he should be asking. Even though Charlie's life had been filled with disaster, it didn't help him prepare for something this terrifying.

"Is she going to make it?" Charlie finally choked out.

"They really didn't say yet. It seems like they are hopeful. I wish I had more details for you."

"Is mom ok to be driving up there?"

"Dan and Sarah Marchant are taking her up there and then they're going to stay with her for a while. Once Timmy goes to bed tonight they're going to come over here and stay with him while I drive up and spend some time with Ellen and Heather."

"What about Kenny? Was he there when it happened? Is he alright?"

"Yeah, they were out on patrol. He didn't say if he had any injuries or not. I'm sure that he'll be up there at the hospital with Heather as well."

"OK, I'm coming home right now. I'll talk to Coach Scott, but I'm sure it will be fine. I'll start making some calls to find a flight, and then I'll try and rent a car in the Cities and go straight to the hospital. I'll call with the details later. Please call or text me right away if you hear anything."

Charlie hung up and sat there with his head between his knees trying to collect himself. His world around him was spinning. He knew he needed to move, but his whole body was frozen in fear. He was back in the locker room, helpless and watching without knowing what to do. Horrible memories from the past filled his head. He heard the music from his dad's funeral. Smelled the food from the meal afterwards. But now he saw his sister being the one taken away. How could this happen?

When he finally looked up he saw Coach Scott standing there waiting for him. As the last one off the bus, Coach Scott saw Charlie drop down and knew that something terrible must have happened so he waited around for Charlie to get done with his conversation before approaching him. He knew that Charlie had been through enough in his life and had an immediate feeling of concern for him.

"What do you need, Charlie?" Scott asked putting his hand down on his shoulder.

"It's... it's my sister – she's been shot. She's a police officer. I need to fly home and see her and help out my mom."

"No problem. You get on the phone and get a flight set up right now. I'll get the bus driver to take you to the airport. Take the time you need. Don't worry about being here. We'll take care of getting your stuff from your room."

"I'll probably have to miss my start on Friday. I don't think I'll be able to make it back in two days."

"Charlie, I don't expect you to be back in two days. In fact, if you are back in two days I'll just send you back away again. Take your time. If you need the rest of the season we can even make that work."

"Thanks, Skip, I'll be in contact with you."

Charlie quickly called the airlines while Coach Scott talked to the bus driver about getting him to the airport. The fact that Charlie could at least do something helped ease his mind a little bit, and kept him from the terrible thoughts in his head. The next thing Charlie knew he was on an airplane heading back towards Minneapolis to see his sister. He had just a couple of days ago desperately wanted to go home, but not like this. He knew that it was irrational to blame himself for this, but still that's what he did.

It's barely over a two hour flight from Harrisburg to Minneapolis, but the time seemed like an eternity, especially since he was without the use of his cell phone and any kind of updates. As he taxied in to the Lindberg terminal he prayed that when his cell phone was turned on there wouldn't be any desperate text messages about his sister being gone. He held it in his hand and waited for a good 20 seconds before finally exhaling with the realization that there wasn't any more bad news coming over his cell phone.

Practically shaking, he began walking off the plane and did the only thing he could think of that might help – he prayed.

Chapter 18

Rochester, MN

The Mayo Clinic in downtown Rochester is a massive establishment that operates two hospitals and is a known leader in medical research. "Mother Mayo", as it's sometimes called in the area, is a non-profit organization that was recently named the #3 hospital in the United States by *US News & World Report*. This is a ranking that those working there steadfastly believe should be a couple numbers better. Presidents and royalty from all over the world fly in to tiny Rochester Airport to receive treatment from some of the leading experts in various medical fields.

Heather Becker was taken to Saint Marys Hospital via ambulance following her gunshot injury. Saint Marys emergency department sees nearly 75,000 patients each year, and has 200 ICU beds – the largest Intensive Care Unit in the nation. One of the best places to be in America when dealing with an injury like Heather's is right where she currently is.

Charlie made the 75 mile drive from the airport to Saint Marys hospital down Highway 52 in a little under an hour. He drove a bit too fast probably, but he figured if he was pulled over the police would give him a break once he shared his story. Charlie spent much of the drive on his cell phone taking turns talking to Kenny, Ellen, and Karen. Charlie parked quickly underground and ran through the parking garage towards the emergency room entrance. He ran up the stairs and rushed into the waiting area where the others were sitting together visiting in hushed tones.

"Hi Charlie," Ellen said through her tears as he approached, giving him a big hug.

"Hi Mom, have we heard anything new?"

"They were just in here a second ago and gave us some information. It sounds hopeful," Karen said trying to keep things as positive as possible. "They've put Heather in a medically induced coma to give her brain time to heal and the swelling to reduce. Everyone keeps telling us what a good doctor we have so hopefully that's true and they're not just saying that to make me feel better. One of the nurses said we'll be able to go in there and see her soon."

Kenny, who was pacing back and forth with his police uniform still on, had dried blood on him and looked like a wreck. He had seen other cops injured in the line of duty, but this was the first time that someone close to him had been hurt this badly and he was having a tough time handling it. Kenny's whole life here in Minnesota, both work and personal, involved Heather. Charlie thought he should try and include him in the conversation to try and distract him a little bit. If anyone understood the dangers of time to think about disasters it was Charlie.

"Kenny, was she conscious at all after being hit?"

"Yeah, she was responding to simple commands in the ambulance and they said that was a very encouraging sign. I hope she's ok."

"You know, Kenny, there's nobody tougher than Heather. She's like her dad that way. If anyone can make it through something like this, it's her."

"I know. It's just, I wish she didn't have to go through it."

They sat there in silence for a while just waiting when eventually a nurse came by and said they could go into Heather's room.

"Remember," the nurse said, "she's in a coma and won't respond to you, but I'd still encourage you to talk and communicate with her."

They entered the room to find Heather attached to several different monitors with her head wrapped, and a peaceful look on her face. Considering she'd been shot in the head and was in a coma she actually looked quite comfortable and at ease. They stood around the outside of her bed and engaged in some small talk towards Heather for a couple of minutes before the doctor came in.

"I thought I should come in and give you an update personally," said Dr. William McGuire, Chief Neurologist at the Mayo Clinic. "She's really doing quite well considering she has a bullet lodged in her head. I'm actually very encouraged. We are fortunate that the bullet penetrated just one side of her brain, and the fact that she's been responsive is a very good sign. Do you have any questions for me?"

"What's the next step then, Doctor?" Charlie asked.

"We'll watch her swelling closely, and when it recedes far enough we'll take her in to surgery to remove some skull fragments to prevent infection."

"How long will that take before she can have the surgery?" asked Ellen.

"It all depends on how quickly the swelling goes down. It could be a day or two or it could be a couple of weeks. We'll just have to see how she heals."

"Is there any possibility that my daughter will be the same person she was before this happened?"

"It will be a fight, but yes, she could be. She might have a few memory difficulties, but I think there's a very real chance that she can almost fully recover. I don't want you to get your hopes up too much, however. It could go the other way as well. We're going to have to see. We'll know better after we do the surgery."

"Thanks, Doctor. I'm sure we'll have some other questions eventually as we take everything in," Charlie said, allowing the Doctor to continue on with his work.

"Just write any questions that you have down and I'll do my best to be around to answer them," Dr. McGuire said as he was making his way to the door. "If you need anything, all you have to do is hit this button which will contact the Nurse's station."

It was getting pretty late by the time Dr. McGuire left, and they decided that it wouldn't make sense for all of them to stay there at the hospital with Heather all night long. Ellen wasn't going anywhere, but she encouraged the others to go home and get some rest and eventually they all did just that.

Over the next couple of days there wasn't much change in Heather's condition. Ellen stayed by Heather's side at all times. Charlie had been at the hospital during the days with Ellen, but would go home at night to sleep, while Kenny and Karen were in and out when they could be there. Finally Friday night Charlie convinced his mom that she needed to go home and get a good night's sleep. He'd stay there with Heather that night. While Charlie was there he talked to her about his life, baseball, Timmy, and their Dad.

It was not the type of conversations that Charlie would typically have, but with Heather lying there in a coma it was somehow easy and cathartic for him.

The swelling slowly made its way down, and by Saturday the doctors decided that they could bring her out of her coma and perform the surgery. This was the key moment in the recovery process. If the surgery went well and Heather came out of it awake and responsive the likelihood of a near full recovery would be strong. If she was slow to regain consciousness and didn't respond well there was a chance that Heather would never quite be the same. The whole family, except for Timmy who was staying with the Marchant's, was back at the hospital waiting around again, and the tension was thick.

"How long have they been in there, now?" Ellen finally asked.

"It's been just over three hours now, I think," Charlie responded. "Remember, they said it would take some time. It's better that they go slow and do a thorough job. I'm sure they'll let us know as soon as they can."

Charlie was just as nervous as his mother was, but tried to downplay it to be strong for her. After Ellen lost her husband her level of anxiety had increased substantially, especially towards her kids. She became very protective of them, and eventually turned to some medication to help her relax. Charlie was unaware of that, but he instinctively knew he had to be strong for her, and try to convince her that there wasn't anything abnormal about the wait. Finally, a half hour later, Dr. McGuire approached them.

"Good news. Everything went great," he said with a smile.

"Thank you, God," Ellen said with her eyes shut.

"We're not out of the woods, yet, however. We're going to have to keep an eye on her and see how she reacts when she wakes up. She might wake up and it would be like she had just been sleeping or she might wake up very confused and disoriented, and possibly not be able to speak or know who any of you are. Once she awakens we'll know what life will be like for her. You can come see her now. She should be waking up at any moment, and I think it would be good if you were all there with her when that happens."

"Thanks, Doctor," Charlie said as they anxiously walked into the recovery room with him.

When they arrived in the recovery room Heather was already starting to move around a little bit, but they let her take her time and come back on her own. Eventually her eyes opened and she looked around the room at her family. Kenny walked right up to her bed with tears in his eyes.

"Listen Heather. Before you say anything, I've wanted to say this to you for a couple of weeks now, but just haven't been able to, and I need to say it before you say anything. I need you to know that I'll be here with you forever, no matter what happens. Even if you don't know who I am or can't say my name, I need you to know that I'll be here for you," Kenny said, dropping to one knee next to her bed. "Heather Becker, will you marry me?"

Charlie, over on the other side of the room, held his breath as he waited for a response from Heather who was looking the opposite way towards Kenny who was still down on his knee. Was she trying to comprehend the question? Could she speak? Charlie couldn't tell exactly what was going on from where he was standing. Finally, after what seemed like a lifetime of silence Heather looked up over at Charlie with a smile and a tear running down her cheek.

"That depends," Heather finally said, "have you asked permission from my big brother yet?"

Chapter 19

Minneapolis, MN

"Testing. Testing. Can you guys hear me on this contraption?" Don Scott leaned forward and yelled forcefully into the computer screen.

"We can hear you just fine, Don," Dave Duerson said frowning. "You don't have to lean close to the monitor and you can just use your regular volume. No reason to yell."

"Alright. Never done anything like this before." Scott responded, still too loudly and still leaning forward.

Mondays are often off-days for both the Major League and Minor League clubs, and the last Monday of the Minor League season was always a day full of meetings for club officials in Minneapolis. This was already Dave Duerson's fourth meeting of the day, and even for a man used to attending meetings he wanted this one to be done quickly and his patience was wearing thin.

With the Twins now in a dead heat for first place in the AL Central with the Indians it was clear that the goal would be to win now. There was no playing for next year or worrying about the future. Everything was being done to help the Twins make the playoffs this season and compete for a championship.

Don Scott had just minutes ago gotten off the bus after a four and a half hour trip to Reading, PA for a three game set against the league leading Reading Phillies. He knew that Duerson was waiting for him up in the Cities, but he didn't hurry. In fact, if anything he moved slower. Don worked on his own schedule. One of his technologically advanced coaches, Ray Jones, had set up the computer for him and had him online in his hotel room. Ray was clearly more nervous and intimidated by Duerson, and was doing everything he could to hurry Coach Scott along while Duerson was barking at him on his cell phone. Scott had been around too long to care, and he had all evening just to sit around with nothing else to do anyway.

"Alright, let's get this done," Duerson said. "I've got Coach White here with me, and we're just going to go through your players that are on our 40 man roster, and discuss each of them with you. We have a pretty good idea what we're going to do and this little meeting might not change much, but we are interested in hearing your opinion on them and their mental makeup specifically."

"Sounds good," Scott replied without leaning forward this time. "How ya doing there, Gordon? The problem with holding this meeting over this machine is that you can't buy me some of that expensive scotch that you like so much."

"I think it's your turn to buy there, Donny," Gordon White said laughing. "Have you ever bought once?"

"Oh, I buy all the time. I think your memory is getting a little fuzzy now that you're getting old like me. Anyway, I don't make the big Major League dollars like your sorry ass does."

Gordon and Don had spent quite a bit of time together over the years. They managed against each other several times in the minors, and had now been working together in the Twins organization for the past three seasons. They had similar managerial styles and got along great with each other. Duerson, on the other hand, didn't get along well with anyone and interrupted as soon as he got the chance.

"Alright, let's get down to business." Duerson said, in no mood for wasting any time with small talk. "Let's start with Santiago. Give us your thoughts on him, Don."

"Well, the kid can't hit a lick. Won't drive the ball out of the infield with any sort of regularity. He's not a bad bunter, and slaps the ball on the ground pretty well to try and take advantage of his speed. He's the quickest guy we've got, so if you need a runner from us he would be your man. Absolutely great defensive infielder. He gets anything hit even remotely in his direction. So, if you need a backup infielder with speed, that would be him. But if you're looking for someone to hit, you better look elsewhere. I don't think he'll ever hit in the majors."

"That was our thinking, as well. We're going to go with Sanchez over in AAA for that spot because he does hit the ball a little better and matches his speed. Even though he's an outfielder we feel like he'll meet our needs."

"We aren't going to replace either of our middle infielders defensively anyway," Gordon added. "They're not going to get pinch hit for, and they won't come out of the game so his defensive prowess won't help us. He's someone we might want to look to trade down the road, actually. I don't see him in our long term plans unless we have injury issues."

"I agree," Duerson said. "Let's worry about that another day, however. I'm more concerned about right now. So we agree that it's a no-go on Santiago. What about Benny Phillips? The boy sure hit the ball a long ways when I was out there. He's got a great build."

"Gordon, would he likely be in the everyday lineup if you brought him up? Or would he just pinch-hit in certain spots?" Scott asked.

"He wouldn't be in the everyday lineup. He'd be used as a possible late innings pinch hitter against lefties. We probably would hit for Simms at third against a lefty, pinch run with Sanchez and then leave him for Cummings in right who would move to third for the last few innings. I don't think Phillips would hardly even see the field unless we're in a blowout situation."

"Then I wouldn't take him. Kid thinks he's the best thing since sliced bread, and would just be pissing and moaning every time that he wasn't in the lineup. He definitely wouldn't be happy to be taken out for a pinch runner either. He complained all season long down here with us. He needs to mature a little bit first, in my opinion. I'd get him started in our fall league down in Venezuela. He has the natural ability, but to put it bluntly, he's a jerk."

"I'm not sure I agree with that." Duerson said. "If we put him up here with the veterans that we have they will keep him in line. He has the type of power that could win a game or two down the stretch. We're here to win now, and I think he could help us do that. I say we take him. Gordon, I'll leave it up to you as the tie-breaker on this one."

"One thing I really like about our team this year is our team chemistry. The guys genuinely like each other and I don't want to do anything to potentially ruin that. If a veteran coach like Don had difficulty with him, than I don't want to mess with him. They even had a veteran pitcher on their team this year. I could just use Monson in a late game pinch hitting situation and probably get the same results. Let's send him down south, and see if we can work on his attitude and maybe he can be ready in a year or two."

"OK," Duerson said, "I don't agree with you two, but I'll let you make the call this time. Tell us about Dusty Timms, Don."

"Love that kid. He'll do whatever you want him to do. He's not going to ever hit great for you, but he'll take pitches, and can lay down a good bunt. Most importantly, he calls a really good game and would be an ideal third catcher for you guys. Shoot, he might have been better than that back-up catcher you guys have up there this year."

"Great! I'm relieved to hear that," Gordon responded. "We were going to have to take him no matter what you said because of Hiller's leg injury, but it's nice knowing that he is someone who will be good to have around. We'll possibly even be using him once a week or so to give our starting catcher a rest."

Duerson continued, "Alright, let's move to the pitching staff. Bryce Hodge? I liked his movement when I saw him pitch."

"That kid is just crazy enough to be a really good reliever. I'd bring him up if you need another bullpen arm. He throws the ball hard, and the pressure of the situation won't bother him."

"We do need a bullpen arm. He might not pitch much, but our bullpen has been overworked badly this year," Gordon said. "I just can't get enough innings out of our starters. So, let's bring him up."

"Alright, that's settled then," Duerson said. "That leaves us with our starting pitcher decision. With all the injuries we have had this season we don't have anybody in AAA that we would even consider calling up anymore. So all we have left are your two arms there in New Britain. Tell us about Kearns and Becker."

"Well, Clayton's got a nice, strong arm, but has some serious control issues. If you're interested in getting some innings out of a starter I'd definitely go with Becker."

"The pitcher we take won't be starting, unless we have another injury – in which case we're really screwed. This will be emergency mop-up work in the pen only," said Gordon.

"Regardless of the role, I'd still go with Charlie. He's a steady influence, a good character guy, and he's smart enough to be a manager someday if he wanted. I don't know if I've ever managed a player who was more prepared to be a professional ballplayer. Clayton's going to be something special if he can fix his control issues, but he's not there yet. It's a no brainer in my opinion."

"I disagree with you, Don." Duerson responded. "I think he is ready, and can do the job. I even think Clayton could handle starting right now at the big league level. He looked steady enough when I saw him throw the other day. I don't think Becker will ever be ready mentally or physically to handle it."

"With all due respect, that's bullshit, Dave," Gordon said. "I worked with Charlie four years ago in the minors and there aren't many pitchers more prepared mentally than Charlie Becker. He may not have the arm anymore, but he's mentally there and I'd trust him in a tough spot. I agree with Don."

"Where's he at right now, Don, and when was his last start?" Duerson asked, already knowing the answer to both questions.

"He's in Rochester. His sister is a police officer who was shot in the line of duty. He's on leave to be with her and his family. Charlie last pitched a week ago Sunday."

"Has he called you and let you know what's going on?"

"No, I haven't had any conversations with him since he left, and I wouldn't expect a call in a situation like this. I told him that with something this serious he should take his time and not hurry back."

"So, he hasn't thrown in eight days now, and we don't know when he'll be back. His last start only went three innings, and he could be out another eight, ten days, who knows. We can't take that kind of risk. I'm going to go with Clayton here. He's the one in our long term plans, and I think he's ready to show what he can do. I think a taste of the big leagues will be good motivation for him."

"That's the wrong decision, Dave," Coach Scott said, putting himself out on a limb and making one final attempt to change Duerson's mind. "I think you should at least consider taking both of them then."

"I hear your objection, and I hear you too Gordon, but this is what we're going to do. I can't take the risk, and I feel like Becker is too big of a risk. If he had continued to be with the team and made his scheduled start I think I could convince myself to give him a shot, but with him being gone I can't do it."

"Alright, you're the boss. Do you want me to tell the boys now?"

"No, wait until your season is over. I'd rather them stay focused on playing as hard as possible down there, and I definitely don't want the ones not coming up knowing about it. Tell them after their game on Sunday, and we'll get them up here in Minneapolis for the start of the Toronto series next Tuesday. With all of the games that have been cancelled because of the rain lately we shouldn't need any of them urgently before that point, but if we do I'll let you know."

Just like that, without any notice, Duerson cut the signal and they were gone. Don Scott cursed under his breath at that idiot Duerson. Here he had an opportunity to give the man who deserved a shot his chance and he wasn't going to do it for his own stubborn reasons. It's not like Charlie was off on a vacation on a beach somewhere. He was already dreading having the conversation with Charlie about him not being called up. Maybe when Charlie called him to let him know he'd be rejoining the team he'd just tell Charlie to stay there with his family for the rest of the season. He eventually decided that he'd worry about that later. For now, he needed a drink.

Chapter 20

Rochester, MN

"How are you feeling today, little sister?" Charlie asked as he walked into Heather's recovery room at the hospital.

"I'm doing pretty good. I have a bit of a headache off and on, which I might just have to deal with now. I wish they'd let me get out of this bed and go home, but other than that everything's fine. Three days seems like plenty of time to recover from a surgery. I want to get out of here."

"Heather, you were shot in the head, give it some time."

"Ah, it was just a glancing shot. No big deal. How's everybody at home?"

"They're doing a lot better now that they aren't so worried about you. If you wouldn't be going around getting shot up everybody's life would be great. Timmy wanted to say hi."

"You should have brought him. He can teach me how to use all these buttons on this bed. I bet he'd figure that out quicker than I could. Bring him with next time."

"OK, I'll do that. I didn't want him to bother you. Have you and Kenny figured out when the big day is going to be yet?"

"Not yet. Poor guy's up to his eyeballs in paperwork from our little adventure. My head just hurts too much to handle the stress of helping out with that," Heather said sarcastically while tilting her head back and touching her forward with the back of her hand.

"Kenny actually believes that?" Charlie said laughing.

"Well, he might not, but I think he's too scared to argue with the lady that has a bullet in her head."

"Anything else you need around here to make things easier for you?"

"No, I'm good. All I need is a way out of here. Why don't you go on home for a little while and spend some time with Timmy. I'm probably going to take a little nap here now since they keep waking me up in the middle of the night to make sure I'm still not a vegetable."

"Alright. I'll see you tomorrow then. Don't turn into a vegetable overnight, please."

"OK, I won't. Thanks for stopping in, Charlie."

Amazingly Heather seemed like her normal self again less than a week after being shot. The body can do incredible things, especially when a person has the toughness and perseverance that Heather has. There was no doubt that Heather would do everything she possibly could in therapy and fight to get back up and running as soon as possible. She wasn't one to enjoy lying around. She needed to be active and doing something all the time.

It was almost 4:00 PM when Charlie pulled out of the Saint Marys parking garage and gave Karen a call. Karen should be off of work by now, and hopefully had Timmy picked up from the Marchant's house. Without Ellen around as much as usual, Timmy had been spending quite a bit of time over there with Dan and Sarah, and he thoroughly enjoyed every minute of it. Dan and Sarah were almost like another set of grandparents to Timmy.

"How was Timmy's afternoon?" Charlie asked over his cell phone on the drive back home to Spring Valley. Charlie had dropped him off over there after lunch to see Heather and take care of a couple little things in Rochester.

"It was so good that they don't want it to end. Timmy wanted to stay and play and the Marchant's weren't going to let him go, so we're all going over there for supper tonight. Hope that's alright."

"Sounds good to me. We should really be having them over, though, for all they've done for us over the past few days."

"I know, and I made that argument, but Sarah just told me to hush up and come on over. She's not someone that you can really argue with."

"Alright, I'll be home in about 15 minutes and we can head over there together. See you soon."

The Marchant's had been a huge support for the whole Becker family since the day their dad had been shot. Dan had tried to fill the role as a father figure as best he could during the couple years of high school that they had left. Then, after high school was over, he attended almost all of their college athletic events with Ellen. He would do the driving and that way Ellen didn't have to go by herself. Sarah would often come along – more for the socialization than the actual sporting events.

Both of the Becker kids decided not to go very far away for college, but instead stayed close to their mom after high school. Charlie ended up following in his dad's footsteps and attended his dad's alma mater, Winona State, where he was a star pitcher right away as a freshman. By the time Charlie had graduated he had set pitching records that will probably never be broken again. Heather decided to go up north to the University of Minnesota in Minneapolis where she was good enough to earn an invitation to try out for the Olympic team, but just came up short of making it. Both Becker's were given full ride scholarships, and both could have played at more prestigious universities but that wasn't as important as staying close to home after all that had happened to them. They were always a close knit family, but the three of them rallied around each other and became even closer.

Sarah Marchant had always been a very good friend of Ellen's, and now she was becoming friends with Karen as well despite the age difference. Sarah had retired from her job working at the bank, and was always willing and excited about watching Timmy whenever Ellen couldn't do it. Both Dan and Sarah had just turned 60 and were starting to show some of the signs of age. Dan, however, still ran every day and would frequently win his age group in the different races that he participated in.

As Karen and Charlie were pulling into the Marchant's driveway they could see Timmy and Dan playing football in the back yard and so they went around back to see them.

"Who's winning?" Charlie asked as Timmy came running up to them.

"I'm winning. I'm too fast for Dan," Timmy said. "He can't catch me. Try and catch me too, Dad."

Charlie joined in the chasing after Timmy and would every once in a while catch him enough to strip the ball loose and yell out fumble and then wrestle with him trying to get the ball. Dan decided to take a break and talk to Karen.

"Your boy is the spitting image of Charlie. You know that right?"

"Yeah, that's what everybody says. I've resigned myself to the fact that he's going to look like his dad and not much like his mom."

"Maybe things will be different for number two coming here soon," Dan said, gently touching her belly. "How are you feeling?"

"I'm still feeling pretty good. We'll have to see how tired I am when school starts here in a week."

"Mom, I'm thirsty," Timmy said running over with the football.

"Let's go inside," Dan responded. "I bet Sarah's got something good to drink inside for us."

The smell that greeted them as they entered the house was like a small taste of heaven. Roast beef, mashed potatoes, stuffing, gravy, apple pie – this wasn't just a supper, this was a full blown feast.

"What's going on here?" Charlie yelled towards the kitchen. "You don't have to spend your whole day cooking for us, Sarah."

"Oh, it didn't take me all day. It's not a big deal at all. I like having a family to cook for now that my boys are all grown up and gone."

"Well, it smells great. I can't wait to eat."

Charlie walked into the kitchen and was about to grab a roll until Sarah slapped his hand away.

"We'll be ready soon. In fact, I was just about to call you all in. You can go ahead and grab a place to sit there at the table."

They sat down at the kitchen table and enjoyed a long, delicious meal. Most of the conversation related to Heather and how she was recovering. The Marchant's hadn't been up there to see her since Sunday and they were amazed at the progress that they were hearing about from Charlie. They decided that they'd have to make a drive up there and visit Heather tomorrow in the afternoon sometime.

When dinner was done and the table was all cleared off Sarah invited Timmy and Karen into the living room. She turned on the TV so Timmy could watch some cartoons while she and Karen talked about the upcoming school year and some of the students that Karen would have in her class this year. Sarah knew quite a few of the families in the community and so she knew a relative of almost every name that Karen listed off. Dan had another plan for him and Charlie.

"Hey Charlie, let's go out and throw the baseball around some before we eat our dessert. I don't get a chance to play catch with a professional baseball player very often, and I need to create some space for the pie," Dan said with a smile.

"I don't know, Mr. Marchant. Let's just sit inside and talk to the ladies some."

"Ah, forget that. They aren't going to talk about anything that I want to hear about. Humor an old man, let's play some catch. My boys are too grown up and cool to play catch with their dad anymore, and I want to loosen my arm up some."

"I didn't bring my glove here with me. I'm not going to catch your blazing heat with my bare hands."

"That's alright, you can borrow one of mine."

"I'm left-handed, remember?"

"Don't worry, Charlie, I have one of those around here somewhere, too."

"You just happen to have a left-handed glove lying around your house? Somehow I don't believe that."

"Well, here it is," Dan said grabbing the glove that was already sitting out right next to his on the table. "Let's go play some ball."

Dan took Charlie out to the yard and they started throwing lightly back and forth with each other. Charlie couldn't remember the last time he just picked up a ball to toss it around when he wasn't at a ballpark getting paid to do it, and he kind of enjoyed it. It was a nice, warm evening and it reminded Charlie of the days playing baseball about this same time of the day with his dad in the yard.

"You throw the ball pretty well for an old guy, Mr. Marchant," Charlie said, taking a couple of steps back and throwing it with a little more pop.

"Charlie, you know you don't have to call me Mr. Marchant anymore. My name's Dan. You can call me that. You're 30 some years old now for Pete's sake. This isn't 10th grade American History class."

"You might as well be asking me to call my mom, Ellen. I've been calling you Mr. Marchant since I was eight years old when you were assisting my dad with the football team, and then all through those exciting, unforgettable social studies classes. I can't just change like that now."

"Alright, fine, as long as you cut the sarcasm. Did you know that your dad used to do the same thing? I think it helped him so he didn't slip up and call me Dan in front of the kids. He wanted to stay professional."

"No, I didn't know that, but now that I think about it I do remember him calling you Mr. Marchant as well. Huh, that's funny."

"You know, you and him are alike in a lot of ways. I can see a lot of him in you, and then a lot of Timmy in you. The way you interact with Timmy reminds me of the way he interacted with you. You were very important to him, and he was very proud of you."

"Thanks, Mr. Marchant. I know he always pushed me to be my best athletically and was proud when I succeeded."

"It's not just athletically, Charlie. I hope you realize that. You know the proudest I think I ever saw him was after you were in the high school play your sophomore year. He went on and on about that for weeks."

"I didn't know that. I kind of assumed that he thought of my doing that stuff as a distraction from sports."

"Sports weren't everything to your dad, Charlie. Yes, he wanted you to be successful in athletics, but they weren't everything – he wanted you to be happy more than anything else. That was the big thing. He wouldn't care if you made it to the majors or not. He wanted you to be happy." He paused for a second. "Are you happy, Charlie?"

"When I'm with my family I'm happy. I'm happy today. It's just tough sometimes. It's tough being away from home. It's tough remembering things from the past, but I'm making it."

"I know it's not easy. It's tough for me and I only experienced a portion of what you have." Dan said, rubbing the ball in his hands now and just talking. "You know I had a lot of guilt after that day. I always thought that I should have done more – that your dad was a better man than me and it should have been me that was killed, not him. Why didn't I free my hands like he did? I drank a lot those first few years. You may not have realized it because you were so busy with sports, but I was a mess. Eventually I figured out that I was letting that event kill me as well. I decided that I would become the teacher and coach that your dad was, and not just put in my time. I decided to become a better person – to quit drinking and start living life. I decided to be happy. That's what your dad would have done, and it's what he would have wanted out of us. Think about that, Charlie. Think about how you can be happy."

"Alright, I'll do that Mr. Marchant," Charlie said, his eyes starting to get a little damp.

"Well, enough about that. Let's get inside and get some of that apple pie. I've had to smell that thing all day," Dan said grabbing Charlie's shoulder and leading the way back in the house.

"That sounds great, Mr. Marchant," Charlie responded as he wiped his eyes and entered the house. "I can never thank you enough for everything you and Sarah have done for us."

"Ah, no problem, we haven't done that much. You can just thank me by playing catch with me every once in a while and making sure I get an extra big piece of that pie tonight."

Chapter 21

Spring Valley, MN

Once Timmy had fallen asleep that night, Karen and Charlie sat next to each other outside on the back deck and enjoyed a nice, warm late-August evening. Charlie had a glass of iced tea that he was sipping on while Karen sat there with her eyes closed just enjoying the night. Iced tea had become Charlie's drink of choice since he abandoned all alcohol. Karen hated the stuff.

"This is nice being able to sit out here together," Karen said.

"Yeah, it was a fun day today all around. It sure is relaxing being at home again."

"It's nice having you here. It feels like we're a normal family again when you're here with us. When do you think you'll have to head back to New Britain?"

"I don't know. Pretty soon I guess. The season ends in five days so I should probably get back before Sunday. Maybe I'll get one more start in. I'll go see how Heather is doing tomorrow and then if she's still improving maybe head back to Connecticut for the weekend, and then spend Labor Day driving back here."

"Have you talked to Coach Scott, yet?"

"No, I'll need to give him a call pretty soon I guess. Maybe tomorrow. I'll wait until after I see Heather."

"They should have some information for you on who's getting called up and what they're going to do with you this fall pretty soon, right?"

"My guess is they'll wait and let us know after our last game on Sunday," Charlie said. "I've been thinking a lot about next season lately, Karen, and I can't do this anymore. I'm going to retire after this season whether they call me up or not."

This was a pretty big shock for Karen. She had talked with him about retiring, but she never really took the possibility seriously. He seemed so committed to baseball that she just didn't see it happening anytime soon.

"Are you sure about that, Charlie? You know I'd love to have you at home, but I don't want you to do it unless you're sure. Maybe you should wait and think about it a little bit more."

"No, I'm certain. I've been thinking about it plenty. That's all I do is think. Even just knowing that I'll be gone this weekend is depressing to me, much less thinking about being away all fall and winter again. I want to be here when our new baby is born. I want to be around to see you and Timmy every day. I want to be able to see my sister and mom on a regular basis. It's time for me to be done."

Karen walked over towards Charlie and wrapped her arms around him. She wasn't sure exactly what to say so she just snuggled up with him and started thinking about the logistics of the decision.

"Is there anything you need to take care of with this?"

"I'll wait and tell the Twins organization once the season is over. If they call me up I'll tell them in a month, and if they don't I'll tell them on Sunday after the game I guess. They won't be too shook up about it. Other than that I think I have everything set. Let's worry about that later. For now, let's just enjoy the evening."

Almost as soon as Charlie had made this decision he was starting to have second thoughts. He had assumed that when the decision would finally be made he would feel some sense of relief, but that hadn't come yet. Would it ever come? Would there ever be peace? Maybe he needed one more game with New Britain for some closure. He hoped that was the case. Charlie lay in bed and thought about his life and the decisions he had made along the way. Sleep did not come any easier with this decision made, but at least there were no nightmares on this night.

The next day Charlie and Timmy drove up to Rochester together to visit Heather at the hospital. It had been a week since she was shot, and the recovery was going as well as possibly could be hoped for. The doctors were amazed with Heather and with how well the recovery process was going. Kenny had just left 15 minutes earlier and Ellen wouldn't be coming until later on in the afternoon so Heather appreciated having Charlie and Timmy around for some company.

"Hey Timmy, come on and jump on the bed here with me and we'll find something fun to watch on TV," Heather said, sliding over on the bed and turning on the television.

Timmy jumped right in, cuddled up with Heather, and went into his own little cartoon world while Charlie and Heather talked.

"Heather, there's something I want to tell you, and I'm not sure how you're going to take it. I've decided that this will be my last year playing baseball. I want to be at home more often than I am now, and I'd like to hopefully get a teaching job somewhere in the area eventually."

"Well, it's about time," Heather responded excitedly.

"What do you mean? You're not disappointed that I'm quitting the game? You don't think that I'd be letting Dad down since I didn't make it to the big leagues?"

"What are you talking about? Dad wouldn't want you to keep doing something you didn't want to do. Sure he loved baseball but he loved us more than any kind of sport. Anyway, I quit playing softball like 10 years ago so obviously if anyone quit it was me."

"Well, you didn't have the opportunities to continue playing softball like I did with baseball."

"Charlie, when I didn't make the Olympic team they still wanted me to work out with the team, and they told me that I'd likely be a part of the team in time if I stuck with it. I had plenty of opportunity. I just chose something different. I wanted to be a police officer and help people just like you'd help people as a teacher. You shouldn't feel bad about choosing something different. You're actually choosing something beneficial to society and something that your own dad did. If it was good enough for him it's good enough for you."

"Thanks, Heather. You're a good little sister."

"You're a pretty good big brother yourself. But I've got an important question for you."

"Sure, shoot."

"What in the world are you still doing here in Rochester? Go back and finish this season off. Don't be using me as an excuse to hang around here. Your manager is going to think I'm some kind of wimp that's keeping you away from the team. I'm fine. No offense, but get outta here. I'll see you when the season is over."

Timmy and Charlie hung around the hospital for about an hour before Ellen came in. Timmy would have stayed there all day as long as the cartoons kept rolling, but Charlie didn't like him sitting in front of the TV for very long periods of time so they said their goodbyes and drove home. On the way Charlie gave Coach Scott a call.

"Hey Charlie, how's your sister doing?" Don Scott said after Charlie said hello.

"She's actually doing really well. She was shot in the head, but somehow the bullet must have hit just in the right spot because it looks like she's going to come out ok."

"Wow! That sounds great. I've been worried about you here."

"Sorry, I probably should have given you a call earlier and filled you in."

"Nah that's fine, I'm sure you've got enough other things going on around there."

"Well, anyway, I'm planning on catching a flight back to Connecticut tomorrow night so I'll be there for the final home stand this weekend."

"Are you sure about that, Charlie? We can manage just fine here without you. I don't want you to feel any pressure about hurrying back. You can just stay with your family and call it a season."

"That's ok. I'm sure. I need to finish the year. If I didn't know any better I'd think you didn't want me back," Charlie said, laughing.

"Well, the jokes have been a lot funnier around here now that you're gone. But, seriously, I'm glad to have you back. How is your arm feeling? Will you be ready to pitch with the time off that you've had? It's been close to two weeks since your last start, and that one only went three innings."

"Don't worry about me, I'll be ready. I even threw a little session last evening with an old coach," Charlie said, exaggerating the game of catch with Dan to help convince Scott that he'd be ready. "My arm feels great."

"Alright. I'll plan on starting you on Sunday for the afternoon finale. I'm throwing Clayton on Saturday so hopefully it will be a good way to finish our season on a high note."

"Sounds great. I'll see you Friday afternoon at the ballpark then."

"There's something else, Charlie, before you go. I'm not supposed to tell you this, but I think you should know before you make the trip. The Twins have made their decision and they aren't going to call you up this year. I tried to convince them that they should, but Duerson wouldn't listen. I'm sorry. I know that was important to you." After a pause Scott continued. "If that changes your decision and you'd rather just stay at home I'd understand."

"No, I'm coming back. It's not a big deal," Charlie said somewhat casually.

"Really? I expected you to be pissed. Shoot, I'd have been pissed. What's up?"

"I've come to accept that getting to the big leagues is not the most important thing. Sure, I would have loved it, but I can live contentedly without it. I'll see you soon Skip."

"OK. Have a good flight. Tell your sister to duck next time the bullets start flying."

"I'll do that," Charlie said hanging up the phone.

Charlie actually did feel a little bit of disappointment that he didn't get called up, but he didn't want it to show. He had it in the back of his head that maybe he'd get one shot before he retired. He wasn't lying when he said that he could be content without it, however. At least, he hoped he could be content without it. Part of him was happy to know that he could start living his regular life after the weekend, yet the other part still longed to complete the goal – to finish the dream. It was a tug-of-war that played out in Charlie's heart. The happiness of today versus the pain of yesterday. Charlie was glad to hear, however, that he'd get one more start before the season was done. Maybe that would be a way for him to get closure on baseball and help him come to terms with this really being the end.

Charlie decided to concentrate on the joy for now and worry about the pain later. He smiled back at Timmy in the backseat who was just looking out the window.

"Hey, Timmy, you know what? Let's get some ice cream."

"Yeah!"

Chapter 22

New Britain, CT

When Charlie woke up on Sunday morning he was ready to go. He had spent much of the previous two days on the phone talking to Heather, Karen, Timmy, and anyone else that happened to be visiting Heather at the hospital. Everything still seemed to be going well in Minnesota, and they were even talking about letting Heather go home in a couple days as long as she had someone with her at all times that could check on her when she was sleeping. Charlie was sure that Ellen would happily take that role on.

Charlie wasn't always able to make it to church on Sundays during the season. The team was out of town half the time, and then when they were home they normally had afternoon games on Sundays. Charlie liked to arrive early for them if he was scheduled to start to help himself get mentally prepared. Karen and Timmy would make it to church nearly every Sunday during the summer and they actually started to become pretty good friends with a couple of the families that would sit around them. Charlie had attended service probably four times over the course of the summer. Karen convinced him over the phone the night before that it would be important for him to go to say thanks to God for Heather's recovery and also to let some of their friends from church know what had happened. He didn't like going by himself, and he didn't want to come into the clubhouse at the last minute, but eventually he begrudgingly promised her that he'd attend. The church was just a couple blocks from their apartment and although it wasn't quite like being at home it was still a very nice church with good people. As he was walking in he felt good about being there and was grateful that his wife convinced him to go.

Charlie went to the back of the church where the Becker's always sat and quietly said hello to a couple of familiar people around him. While he was checking the church bulletin to see if there was communion today he could tell that someone was staring down at him from the aisle so he looked up.

"Surprise!" Timmy yelled a little bit too loudly for the worship hall of a church. Charlie just sat there in surprise looking up at Karen who was holding Timmy and had a big smile on her face.

"What's going on?" He finally spat out, eventually standing up and giving his wife a hug.

"Timmy and I couldn't miss your last start so we got an early morning flight in and got a ride straight to the church. Thanks for listening to me and going to church this morning. You'd have been in trouble if you weren't here!"

"When do you have to fly back?" Charlie asked, still trying to process what was happening.

"Well, that's the other thing," Karen said with a twinkle in her eyes. "We don't have a return flight. We're going to drive back home with you."

"How's that going to work? Don't you need to be back for school? That's an awful long drive for Timmy to make, isn't it?"

"We can leave after the game today, go halfway, and then stay at a hotel somewhere. Maybe get Timmy a little swimming pool time. If we do the rest of the trip tomorrow I'll still be able to get into school tomorrow night to finish getting ready for the start of school on Tuesday. Labor Day helped us out there. Don't worry about things so much. Everything will work out fine."

"Now, be quiet," Karen continued over the sound of the organ. "Church is starting."

The last time that Charlie faced the Altoona Curve a month ago things did not go well to say the least. He was out by the fourth inning, and it had been one of his worst starts of the year. For some pitchers having to face a team that had knocked them around earlier in the year would be a daunting task that they wouldn't look forward to. Charlie, on the other hand, relished the idea of getting some payback from an earlier pounding. He was excited about the chance to face Altoona one more time before his career was over. He always had an irrational, strange kind of dislike for Altoona. What the heck is a "Curve" anyway?

"Hey Chuckster," Dusty yelled over to him in the locker room, "Are you going to try and set the record for hits allowed again today? You remember what happened last time when we were in Altooooona, right? You were spraying gas all over that fire. That was ugly."

"You know, Dusty, some catchers actually give their pitchers encouragement before a start. Some are even supportive."

"What are you talking about? I am giving you encouragement. I'm encouraging you to not get shelled again."

"Thanks, Dusty."

"No problem, Chuckster. My middle name is support. Hey, Coach is going to meet with us after the game today. You think we'll be taking a trip to the Twin Cities together?"

"I don't know, Dusty," Charlie said lying. "We'll have to see I guess. I'll be going to Minnesota either way."

"Yeah, you're probably just excited to get back home for Caribou hunting season."

"Deer hunting, Dusty, not caribou. Is that bump on the head still affecting you?"

"Caribou, Deer, same thing. Either way you're just killing Rudolph," Dusty said heading out to the field with an extra spring in his step.

Charlie just shook his head and laughed. One thing that he'd miss about playing baseball was the characters that filled the locker room. It didn't matter what team he was playing on the locker rooms always had the same people. There was always a comedian, always a young rookie, and almost always an asshole along with several other strong personalities. He'd have a tough time saying that any of these guys were really, truly his friend, however. After each season is done a whole new cast of characters appears that fills the familiar roles. He wondered if he'd see those same personality types and camaraderie in the teaching profession, but figured he probably wouldn't since there's not the same down time in education as there is in getting paid to play ball. They also didn't have 10 day road trips in the teaching world to help with getting to know each other. But he imagined that what was lacking in intense time together for a few months would be offset by the relationships formed over years. At least his dad seemed to form strong friendships when he was teaching.

In the blink of an eye Charlie was standing on the mound, toeing the rubber, ready to make his last professional start. This wasn't exactly the way he envisioned his final appearance. There were maybe 2,000 people in the stands today, and lots of empty seats. Labor Day weekend had driven many fans out of town on mini vacations, and with the Rock Cats out of playoff contention there wasn't anything riding on this game. A cloudy, dreary looking day didn't help put people in the seats, either. For Charlie, none of that mattered. He was just happy that his family was here one more time to see him pitch. He saw them sitting in their familiar seats behind the dugout, gave them a smile, and quickly went to work.

In the bottom of the sixth inning while the Rock Cats were batting Charlie finally noticed something. No one was sitting anywhere near him or talking to him. Coach Scott, who always checked in with him by now, hadn't said a word to him. Charlie looked up at the scoreboard and saw the 1-0 lead when it hit him. He hadn't allowed a hit yet. Not only that, but he hadn't allowed a base runner either. He was in the middle of a perfect game.

"Hey, Dusty, come here," Charlie called over to the other end of the bench where Dusty was sitting.

Dusty just ignored him and looked the other direction. Charlie sat there and laughed to himself. He was never big into superstitions, yet he was always amused with how superstitious baseball players were. Can't talk to the man with the no-hitter going for fear of jinxing him!

"What about you, Clayton? Want to talk to the old man?"

Clayton didn't even stay in the dugout when he heard Charlie talking to him. He made a quick exit for the bullpen without even glancing in Charlie's direction.

The seventh and eighth innings passed quickly and Charlie still hadn't allowed a runner on base. There was a definite murmur that was spreading throughout the meager crowd, and the applause for each out was increasing in intensity. Charlie had never thrown a no-hitter before, much less a perfect game, but it had also never really been a goal of his. Still, now that he was this close he was excited about the prospects of getting one. This would be a fitting end for him. He took a second and looked around at the crowd. He saw Karen and Timmy on their feet and gave them a smile. For once he actually enjoyed not being in the zone and tuning out everything around him. He was happy that he could share this moment with his family. This would be an event he could tell Timmy about when Timmy was older.

The leadoff batter in the ninth inning had grounded out to Santiago at short in both of his first two at bats, and

Charlie was going to try and jam him inside to get him to ground to short again. Sure enough, the very first pitch was a slider inside that produced a slow dribbler over to Santiago that he scooped up and gunned over to Benny at first for the first out. Baseball can be so much fun for Charlie when everything is working perfectly for him. Two outs to go.

Up next was the eighth batter in the lineup who decided his approach was going to be to take a couple of pitches. The next thing Charlie knew it was a 3-1 count and he was in danger of walking him. He didn't want to just lay one in there because he wanted the no-hitter, but he also didn't want to walk him since a perfect game would be even better. He decided he would go with the pitch he had the most command over today, his fastball, and try to paint the outside corner with it. He put it in precisely the exact spot he wanted, and the umpire gave him the strike call to run the count full.

Charlie stepped off the mound and took a deep breath. He just needed to duplicate that pitch one more time. As soon as Charlie released the pitch, however, he knew it was trouble. Instead of going for the outside portion of the plate Charlie left it right down the middle, and the Altoona batter crushed the ball to the warning track where Jenkins in left field somehow made a fantastic diving catch to preserve the perfect game. Twenty-six batters up and twenty-six batters down. All he needed was one more and it would be finished.

After that amazing catch Charlie felt that this perfect game was destined to happen. This was the end, and he was going to go out on top. His and his father's dream of making the big leagues wouldn't come to fruition, but he'd leave baseball with a bang. His dad was probably looking down on him watching him right now and smiling. He could leave feeling proud of this baseball career knowing he accomplished something that few before him ever have.

The ninth batter for Altoona was their shortstop. He was a little guy, probably not more than about 5'6" tall and Charlie had struck him out twice already this game by using his curveball down and in. He went right back to that pitch and immediately got two strikes on him. He was one strike away, and he was having a tough time remaining calm out there on the mound. Whereas a few minutes ago Charlie was feeling good about seeing and hearing everything around him, he now wished that he could go back in that zone and block everything else around him out. The crowd was on their feet and producing more noise than Charlie thought possible for so few people. His mind was racing. His heart was pounding. He was thinking about Timmy seeing his dad doing something special, about his own dad looking down on him, about this being the end. Possibly the final pitch.

He took a step off the mound, rubbed the baseball some more, and finally toed the rubber again to try and throw one more perfect curveball down and in. He felt a shaking in his hand that he hadn't experienced in a game before. He looked in towards Dusty, saw the sign that he wanted, nodded his head, and like he'd done a million times before wound up and let the ball fly. But, just like with the last batter, this pitch did not end up where he wanted it. The ball was left up in the zone and right over the heart of the plate. The Altoona hitter turned on it and hit it right down the line towards the foul pole. Everything moved in slow motion for Charlie as the ball hung in the air and Charlie tried to will it to go foul. Charlie even leaned his body trying to convince that ball to hook foul, but instead it bounced right off the foul pole. Fair ball. Home run. Tie game. Just like that he lost the perfect game, no-hitter, shutout, and win all in one fell swoop. His heart sank as he watched the Altoona batter cross home plate. This wasn't the way it was supposed to end. This couldn't happen. He felt the weight of the world back on his shoulders again, and stood in shock over what just happened. Once again Charlie was so close to doing something important and just couldn't finish it. All of the feelings of excitement and joy that he had been experiencing earlier all turned into a wave of devastation.

The few people in the crowd gave Charlie a big ovation, but he didn't hear it now. He caught a new ball that Dusty threw out to him and tried to concentrate on the next batter, but his focus was gone. He just felt regret and sadness. Four balls later the next batter walked. Then another home run and Coach Scott was on his way out to the mound calling for a new pitcher from the bullpen.

"That was a fantastic game pitched, Charlie. One of the best I've ever seen," Scott said, trying to give Charlie some encouragement.

Charlie didn't respond. He just handed the ball to Coach Scott and walked slowly off the mound with his head down. Each step toward the dugout was a struggle, as if he were pulling his feet of deep mud. Again the crowd gave him another round of applause and Charlie heard this one, but Charlie didn't think they should be cheering for a pitcher that was losing a 3-1 ballgame. He didn't even look up in the stands at Karen and Timmy. Charlie stayed in the dugout without talking to anyone until the game ended in a disappointing loss 15 minutes later.

The loss didn't really affect any of the other Rock Cat players. This was the last game in a long season, and they were just happy to be done and off to other things. Charlie tried to put on a positive face in the clubhouse, but didn't feel like talking too much with anyone so he tried to change quickly and keep things brief.

Coach Scott was individually calling players into his office to let them know if they'd be sent up to the majors or not. Charlie already knew his fate, and wasn't going to wait around to talk to Scott about it again. He'd give Coach Scott a call in a few days and thank him for everything that he did for him this season. His dad always stressed to him the importance of thanking his coaches after a season had ended when he was younger, and he continued doing that throughout his baseball career. He did wait around long enough to hear that Dusty, Clayton and Bryce had all been called up and he congratulated them. He truly did feel happy for them as they were good kids that loved the game and deserved to be part of a major league team. They were teammates that Charlie could see himself actually staying in touch with through the years.

As he left the locker room for the last time, he did get one final smile in as he heard Benny yelling through Coach Scott's office walls, "What do you mean they're not calling me up? What kind of fucked up shit is this! I'm the best player on this team, and they're not calling me up? What a waste of a summer!" Walking out of the stadium, the sound of Benny's fading screams would be the last sounds of his ordinary and unremarkable minor league baseball career.

Chapter 23

Spring Valley, MN

The middle of September in Spring Valley can be an interesting place as far as the weather is concerned. One day it will be 95 degrees with high humidity and people are left wishing the community swimming pool were still open, and the next day there can be a freeze warning for the overnight and everyone is covering up their plants with sheets. This September a whole new character entered the world of September weather. Her name is Linda. Poor Linda had already been cursed throughout the New Orleans area when she came ashore ten days earlier and devastated a region still recovering from her bigger, meaner sister Katrina who showed up a few years earlier. Now the residents of Spring Valley had joined in the cursing of Linda, despite the fact that the torrential rains that they'd been having for the past six days probably had very little to do with the aftermath of Hurricane Linda, and more to do with a low front that seemed to be hovering in the area. Everyone likes to have a scapegoat however, and nobody names a low front after all, so Linda assumed that roll.

"Linda is screwing up all my plans," Dan Marchant said to Charlie as they stood looking out of his classroom window towards the football field. Water was rushing swiftly out of the nearby gutter.

"What's the plan? Back in the gym again?" Charlie asked. "Running some more dummy offense?"

"I guess so. The field is already a big pit of mud. I don't want to make it any worse before our game tomorrow night. Maybe we'll just spend a little extra time in the weight room today."

Dan Marchant took over the varsity football coaching position for Charlie's dad after he passed away out of a sense of duty more than anything else. The school had a strong football tradition under Charlie's dad. Marchant's plan was to just finish out the season to give the kids a little continuity after the disaster, but he couldn't leave Charlie with a new coach his senior year so he stayed on. He had retired in his mind at least a hundred times since then, but something had always drawn him back. Normally it was the kids. It wasn't the parents or the old, former football playing community members - that's for damn sure.

He led the team to a state championship with Charlie as his quarterback when Charlie was a senior, and got a second state title five years ago adjusting his offensive scheme and using a pounding running game. He also had been through three seasons where the team hadn't won a single game, and sometimes those seasons felt like the most rewarding ones, even if the people in the town thought they needed to win all the time and at any cost and were very vocal in that opinion. In a small community like Spring Valley it is tough to keep a consistently winning program. When a class comes through with only ten boys in it, for example, winning can be extremely difficult. But, when you have a high caliber athlete like Charlie, winning becomes pretty easy if the coaching staff is doing the correct things and adjusting appropriately to the personnel.

They were in the process of making another offensive adjustment with a talented, young quarterback. "How's Alex looking?" Marchant asked Charlie.

"He has a really strong arm. He likes to fire them in there to me when we're tossing the ball around to show off that thing. Every once in a while I need to let one fly at him to show off my cannon and remind him who's in charge here," Charlie said smiling. "I'm still working on his footwork. It's a little sloppy at times. As you know, he's also pretty soft yet, but I think that will develop eventually. After all, he's still only a sophomore."

Charlie had volunteered to help out with the young quarterback since he was back in town for the fall. Marchant approached him with the idea of him being the volunteer

Quarterbacks Coach right away when Charlie got back home. Even though he was a little reluctant at first he was glad now that he had accepted the invitation. He would bring Timmy into Karen's classroom after her kids had gone to the busses, and then stayed for a couple of hours for practice every day. He enjoyed working with Mr. Marchant and Alex was a good kid that listened well to him. He was a left-handed thrower just like Charlie had been so it was a natural fit for them. The team was undefeated after three games this season, and didn't expect too big of a challenge with winless Chatfield coming into town tomorrow night.

"How are you handling life without baseball?"

"It's nice being home with my family," Charlie responded, not wanting to get into the way that he really felt. In actuality, the couple of weeks since his last game had been pretty tough on Charlie. In his mind he kept seeing that ball hit the foul pole and ruin his perfect game. It was, similar to making the majors, another piece of unfinished business in Charlie's life, and he would have been lying if he said it didn't bother him - so he just didn't talk about it. Sure, he enjoyed being home with his family and he knew he couldn't handle going back for another season, but he was again questioning whether he made the right choice to retire when he showed that he could perform so well. He had been pretty dominant the last month or so of the season. Maybe he could have achieved his goal of making the majors if he had given it one more season. He knew that wasn't an option anymore, however, and he eventually would just have to learn to let it go and live with it but for now it still stung. The game of Tug-of-war was still being played.

"And how's Heather feeling?" Marchant asked as they walked together towards the gym.

"She's doing great. She wants to get back to work already, but they won't let her yet. She just can't handle sitting around. She's been over at our house a lot during the day while Kenny and Karen are working. Timmy just loves her."

Just as they were arriving at the gym Charlie's cell phone rang. "I should probably take this," Charlie said. "I'll be in before the start of practice."

"Hello?" Charlie said into his phone.

"Chuckster!" Dusty yelled over the other end. "You didn't tell me the Minnesota weather was going to be so crappy. You need to quit doing that Norwegian rain dance down there. I feel like I should be building an ark or something. Noah must have been from Minnesota. Is this why you guys have so many lakes here?"

Charlie just laughed. "Haven't you heard? It's all Linda's fault."

"Who? I don't know any Linda's. Does she do a rain dance or something?"

"Never mind. What's up?"

"Well, because of all of this fuckin' rain we keep getting rained out. We play thirteen games in the last eleven days of the season! Which normally would piss me off, but it works out good this time because they're running out of pitchers. Clayton's going to start the first game of the double header on Saturday, and they're going to have me catch it since I worked with him all year."

"That's great, Dusty, congratulations."

"Thanks. I've been wondering if I'd ever get off the bench and into some real action in a game where we weren't already up or down by 10 runs, and now it looks like I will. We have another double header already scheduled for the last Saturday of the season as well so I'm hoping to see some action there too."

"Nice. How's Clayton handling it?"

"Ah, you know him, he's a nervous wreck. Did you see when he came out of the bullpen last week? His first pitch bounced ten feet in front of the plate. Dude needs to calm down a little bit. Those Texans eat too much spicy food."

"What are you talking about?"

"That spicy food. Makes 'em jumpy and nervous. Everyone knows that, Chuckster. You've gotta get off the farm more. Anyway, I'm gonna take him out for some good

English food and get him to relax. Maybe go to the *Olive Garden*. Breadsticks – now that's a calming food."

"Dusty, I don't know where to start..."

"Listen, Chuckster, I'm calling to tell you that you should come up here on Saturday. Bring that hot wife and kid of yours and enjoy the game. Maybe stop in the locker room before the game and talk to Clayton a little bit. Calm him down. He'd appreciate that."

"I'll think about it, Dusty. Can't say for sure right now. Thanks for the invitation, though."

"Alright. Think about it. Later."

Charlie had for the most part avoided watching the Twins play since his season ended, and had turned all of his attention and focus to the football team. He wished his former teammates well, but it was a little too painful to watch a game on TV and he hadn't even thought about attending a live game. On the other hand, he had never watched a baseball game with Timmy at a stadium before. He might really enjoy that. Have to give it some thought. Maybe see what Karen thinks.

As soon as he walked in his home front door after practice he heard Timmy playing in his bedroom and headed in that direction. "Hey, buddy," Charlie said, squatting down beside him. "What are you doing?"

"These guys are firemen. This is their fire truck. See Dad, he has a hat."

"Hmmm. I don't think firemen wear baseball hats."

"Yes they do," Timmy snapped back. Over the past month or two Timmy had stopped wanting to be corrected in any way and thought he was right about everything.

"OK, your fireman can wear them," Charlie said trying to avoid an argument. "What do the firemen do?"

"They drive in this fire truck and save the animals when they are in trouble."

"That sounds like a good job."

"I'm going to be a fireman when I grow up. Or maybe a baseball player. Or both."

After hearing that Charlie decided then that he'd let Timmy choose if they were to go to the baseball game or not. Timmy had been to so many games over the summer that maybe he'd rather just stay at home and not see any more.

"Timmy, would you like to go to the Twins game on Saturday with me?"

"Will you be playing?"

"No, I'd sit in the stands with you."

"The whole time?"

"Yes, the whole time."

At that point Karen came walking into the room and Timmy exploded. "Mom, we're going to a Twins game. And Daddy is sitting with us. Not in the field. With us!"

"Really, your dad said that without asking me about it, huh?" Karen said giving Charlie a stern look. "I think that sounds like a lot of fun. I need to talk to daddy some, you keep playing."

Karen brought Charlie into the kitchen, and Charlie knew he was in trouble before they got there. "Listen, Karen, I was just trying to get a feel for what Timmy would think. I wasn't planning on asking him without talking to you first."

"Well, I guess your plan didn't work out so well, did it," she said coolly. "I've been to hundreds of your games, and I don't mind when you're pitching, but to go to a game where you're not pitching is not what I want to be doing on my days off. You should have talked to me about it first."

"We can tell Timmy that we can't go."

"No, we can't," she said, just getting angrier. "We're going. You can't promise him something like that and then turn around and take it from him."

"What if just Timmy and I went?"

"I hardly get to see Timmy now that school's started, and I don't want to be away from him for an entire day. You see how much time I put into teaching. I miss him. I'm coming, I'm just not happy about it."

"Hey, I've got an idea," Charlie said scrambling. "Why don't we go up early on Saturday and spend some time at the Mall of America. We can even park there and take the light rail over to Target Field. In fact, you can stay and shop later and then you won't have to sit through the entire game."

"You always use that Mall of America trick against me, and it always works. It's not working this time. I'm still angry." But, Karen softened just a bit and said, "OK, let's do that."

Chapter 24

Minneapolis, MN

The Twins were now three games up on the Indians in the Central Division. It looked like their playoff chances were pretty strong, but there was still plenty of time left. Especially with a rare five game series with the Indians looming to finish the season, thanks to all the rain. Still, if they held that lead for another five days the Indians would have to win four out of five games at Target Field just to tie and that wasn't too likely. These upcoming five days wouldn't be easy, however. Three games in the next two days against the Eastern Division leading Boston Red Sox and then a long flight down to Texas for three more against the Western Division leading Rangers.

Target Field has been the home of the Twins since April of 2010. It's a beautiful stadium that seats just under 40,000 fans. The Twins players love the more spacious clubhouse and nicer amenities that come with a new stadium, but for Charlie it just wasn't quite the same as the cozy, old Metrodome with which he'd grown up. Some of Charlie's favorite memories were attending games there at the Dome with his Mom, Dad and sister. Since Charlie's dad was a teacher they would go see several different games over the course of the summer when school was over, always sitting up in the upper deck cheap seats and waving their Homer Hankies. A contributing reason for Charlie's love of baseball was the joy and excitement that came with the 1987 and 1991 World Series victories. Charlie was in elementary and middle school during those times, and Twins fever permeated everyone and everything. Although he couldn't physically attend any of the playoff games he felt like he was there when watching it on TV and even felt like he was part of the team. Even today Charlie knows all of the important stats from those seasons, and counts meeting Kent Hrbek as one of his favorite baseball moments.

The mood in the clubhouse seemed pretty upbeat as Charlie and Timmy strolled in. Charlie marveled at the differences of the locker room at the old Metrodome versus this glamorous place. He had gotten a chance to be in the Metrodome locker room with both his football and baseball teams at the high school state tournament level, and he always thought of the locker rooms there as kind of old, decrepit changing areas. This place was all about luxury with nice, spacious lockers and lots of comfortable chairs and TV's. Charlie was greeted almost immediately upon entering by the Twins current manager, and a former coach of his in the minors, Gordon White. Gordon stands 6'2" tall and is a towering presence. He has a huge smile that contrasts his brilliantly white teeth against his night black face. He commands the respect of his players yet still has an easygoing, strong working relationship with them. Gordon was Charlie's manager during his three month stint with the Triple-A Toledo Mud Hens in the Detroit Tigers organization. Charlie had been traded to Toledo halfway through the season for essentially a bag of balls. Toledo's staff had been decimated with injuries and they needed an arm to eat innings, so that was Charlie's role. He didn't pitch particularly well that season, but he took the ball every fifth day and managed to go at least five innings in every start which earned the respect of his manager.

"Hey Charlie, good to see you!" Gordon said enthusiastically shaking his hand and flashing those white teeth of his. "Who's this big guy?"

"Hi Skip. This is my boy, Timmy," Charlie responded as Timmy was shyly clinging on to his leg.

"He looks like he's going to be a ballplayer to me. Have you seen Don Scott around here yet?"

"No, I haven't. I didn't think he'd even be here. Do the Double-A managers normally work with the team after their season is over?"

"Well, not usually. But when we decided to start Clayton and have Dusty catch him we gave Scott a call and asked him if he could help us out by working as an additional bench coach. We figured it would be good to have him around since he's worked with them all summer. Plus, he owes me money."

"Good luck getting that back," Charlie joked.

"Well, I gotta get ready. Nice seeing you, Charlie. Come on back any time."

Charlie and Timmy made the rounds saying hello to some of the other players that Charlie had played with over the years. Nearly half of the team had at one point in their careers played with or against Charlie along their twisting journeys to the majors. Charlie wouldn't really say he was exactly friends with any of them. In fact, the two he was probably closest to were Clayton and Dusty, and that closeness was really more of a mentorship than a friendship.

"Chuckster!" Dusty yelled from the other side of the locker room. "Come on over here."

"Hey Dusty. Glad to see that being in the big leagues hasn't quieted you down any."

"I don't know what you're talking about, Chuckster. Hey there, T-money."

"Hi Uncle Dusty," Timmy said back to him. Dusty was one of the few non-family members that Timmy felt comfortable with and did not shy away from. "Where's Aunt Megan?"

"She's not allowed in here. Men only."

"Can I be in here? I'm only a kid," Timmy said sounding concerned now. Timmy had a tendency to be nervous that he was doing something wrong and was always trying to please everyone.

"Don't worry about it T-money. You're my good luck charm. They wouldn't mess with Dusty's good luck charm. Plus, with those guns of yours you look like a man more than a boy now anyway," Dusty said holding out his fist for a pound. After Timmy knocked knuckles with Dusty they both pushed their hands back and spread their fingers out in a choreographed move that they'd done many times before and made an exploding sound.

"Where's Clayton at?" Charlie asked, looking around the locker room.

"Ah, they've got him going over some scouting report stuff for like the tenth time. Just clogging up his brain with junk that's only going to make him more nervous, if you ask me. You're probably not going to get a chance to talk with him, and that's what he really needs – just to calm down a bit. Stupid pitching coach thinks he knows what's best for Clayton after knowing him for two weeks."

"Oh, he'll be fine," Charlie said. "After all, he's got you calling the pitches for him."

"Damn right, Chuckster, you're finally learning something. They just better not get him so messed up in the head that he starts shaking me off all the time. I might have to walk out there and beat his butt in front of 40,000 people. That would sure be embarrassing for him."

"Sounds like a plan. Well, I guess we better get to our seats. Good luck!"

Before they got out of the locker room, however, Don Scott came waddling in and stopped them. "Charlie, Timmy, hold up a second."

"Hey Skip, looks like you got your call up to the big leagues."

"Yeah, but I'm not really sure why I'm here. I told the pitching coach to just leave Clayton alone, but he's not listening to the old man. I'm gonna have to tell Gordon that he's messing Clayton up. Gordon will still listen to me. He's the only one here that really wants me around. If I'd have known they weren't going to let me handle Clayton I wouldn't have come."

"Gordon just brought you here because you owe him money," Charlie said.

"Did he tell you that bullsh, I mean bologna?" Scott said cleaning up his language for Timmy and shaking his head. "What have you been up to since the season ended?"

"I'm helping out our local high school football team. They're coached by my old high school coach. I'm working with the quarterback some; tossing the old pigskin around. And then, of course, spending the day with my boy here," Charlie said, rubbing Timmy's head.

"Sounds like a good time. Thanks for coming to the game. Will you be around afterwards?"

"No, we've gotta get home. I'll stay in touch, though. Good luck today, Skip."

"Thanks, we'll need it. I'm more nervous for today than any game all season. Probably because I don't have any control over it yet I feel somehow responsible. See you later."

Timmy and Charlie found their seats and after a little bit Karen joined them. "Did you have any fun in the locker room, Timmy?"

"Yeah, I got to see Uncle Dusty. He's funny," Timmy replied.

"He is funny, isn't he? I hope he has a good game tonight."

"Me, too," Charlie said.

"Me, three," Timmy replied with his favorite joke that he'd been reusing as often as possible lately.

Charlie could tell just from watching Clayton warm up before the first inning that his body language was not looking good, and that it might be a rough start. His worst fears were confirmed almost immediately. Clayton walked the first hitter on four straight fastballs all up in the zone. Clayton was trying to do too much and although he had his speed up the control was horrendous. Clayton caught a break as the second hitter laid down a bunt on a pitch that was also way up in the zone. Dusty was catlike springing up from his crouched position and firing a bullet to first to just nip the runner.

Clayton was in a 3-0 count on the third hitter when Dusty came out to the mound for what was already his second visit this inning. Charlie could tell that he was just trying to calm him down and give him encouragement more than anything else. The next pitch, however, was way outside and now there were two runners on. Clayton had thrown nine pitches, and eight of them were balls.

He was now to the point where he was just trying to groove the ball right down the middle to get strikes, and this is where the vaunted Red Sox lineup exploded. Two doubles and a triple later the Twins were down 4-0 and there still was only one out. Clayton was clearly hanging his head and defeated and after another walk he was pulled from the game after facing only seven hitters and getting just one batter out.

Before the first inning was over the Twins were down 7-0 and didn't threaten the rest of the game, eventually losing 13-2, and also losing another precious game on the Indians in the standings. Not only that, but their heavily overworked bullpen also had to put in eight plus innings of work with another game coming up in just a few hours.

Charlie and his family only stayed for the first few innings to watch Dusty get a couple of at bats before deciding to get home before it got too late. On a positive, Dusty did collect a couple of singles in the game and Timmy was pretty excited about that. But, overall, Charlie's first experience at Target Field was a monumental disappointment that left him once again missing the good old days of the loud, decrepit Metrodome.

Chapter 25

Minneapolis, MN

"Ah, shit! We're fucked," Dave Duerson yelled rubbing his face anxiously with his hands. "Could we have had a worse scenario play out? What a messed up chain of events."

"It'll be all right, Dave. Don't worry so much," Gordon White responded, still in his baseball uniform despite the fact that the Thursday night game had been over two hours earlier. He was eating his supper, a 1:00 AM hotdog and a coke.

"You need to start worrying more! We're all going to end up fired over this. What fucking terrible luck we've had."

Just 48 hours earlier things were setting up pretty well for the Twins. They finished the Red Sox series by salvaging a win on Sunday to keep from being swept. Their number two pitcher, Javier Suarez, threw a great game for his 17th win on the season. The Indians also lost on Sunday so the Twins increased their lead in the division back up to 2.5 games.

The next day the positives continued when, down in Texas, the Twins ace Jonas Kline pitched five innings of four run ball. That was just enough for the bullpen to hold down a 6-5 victory. Cleveland had an off day on Monday so the Twins were now 3 games up with just seven left to play. Everything was looking rosy. Then, the unthinkable and unlikely happened. It rained in Arlington in September. And, not just a passing shower, a downpour that would force a double header for the next day. Now the Twins would be looking at seven games in five days, all against playoff caliber teams. Still, with a 3 game lead, there wasn't exactly a nervous wringing of hands.

As Duerson and White sat in the hotel room with the rain streaming down on Tuesday evening they watched the Indians play the Tigers on TV and worked out a couple of different pitching rotation plans for the next seven days. They'd have their 4th and 5th starters going in the double header tomorrow. Then their top three pitchers would throw the first three games of the Cleveland series. They'd scrape together the last two games with the bullpen, Clayton, and possibly their 4 and 5 could give a few innings on Sunday on short rest if it were absolutely necessary. Hopefully they'd clinch before Saturday and then they could save Jonas for the first playoff game.

[251]

"I'm a little concerned about Clayton," Gordon said. "He has not looked good at all, and seems very rattled right now."

"I know. I know. Hopefully by the time we'll need him on Sunday we'll have the division wrapped up," Duerson responded.

"I might try and use him for an inning tomorrow if the situation presents itself. Hopefully in a non-pressure situation where he can just be relaxed out there and collect himself."

"That's a good idea, Gordon. See if you can work that out," Duerson said as the Tigers wrapped up a big 5-2 win against the Indians. The Twins were now 3.5 games up and, with a sweep of the double header tomorrow, might have at least a tie for the division locked up. Then maybe a couple days later they could rest their regulars and get ready for the playoffs.

The next day Gordon worked Clayton into one of the games, alright, just not in the way that was intended. In the first game the Twins starter only made it through two innings before being pulled due to his ineffectiveness. The bullpen was forced to eat up the remaining innings which they did very poorly. A blowout 18-5 loss is not exactly what the Twins were looking for in a first game of a double header.

The results of the second game may have actually been worse. After 11 innings the score was tied 8-8 and the bullpen had already thrown 12 innings on the day. After the 16th inning ended the only pitcher left available was Clayton Kearns. Clayton proceeded to end the game quickly in the bottom of the 17th inning when he came out and walked four straight batters. The Twins had essentially played three baseball games in one day (26 innings), and with the Indians winning their game the division lead had quickly dwindled down to 2 games. After 12 long hours at the ballpark the day wasn't done as the team still needed to catch a flight back home that night for the big series starting the next day. The Tribe, with an afternoon game, would be sitting in Minneapolis relaxing for eight hours before the Twins chartered flight hit the runway.

The misery continued through the first game of the Cleveland series on Thursday. The bullpen was forced into action for five more innings and another loss sunk the division lead down to just one game with four games to play. They had lost two and a half games from their lead in less than 48 hours. Most worrisome was the bullpen issue. They'd now thrown 21 plus innings in just two days. So now Gordon sat in his office with Dave trying to convince him that his crazy idea was really their best option.

"Dave, I can't pitch Clayton unless we have the division locked up. He can't come into any more games that we have any possibility of winning. He's just not an option," Gordon said, finishing off his hot dog.

"I know, you're right. His confidence is shot, and the minute he walks his first batter our fans are going to boo the shit out of him. They might not even wait that long to start booing. Shoot, even I'd boo him if I were a fan. He's been responsible for two key losses already."

"He can be an emergency starter for Sunday if we're in the playoffs by then, but I can't count on him for Saturday, not even in relief."

"Is there any way we can string together the bullpen to cover a game?" Duerson asked.

"Probably not anymore. A week ago we could have. There's a possibility that if Javier can go late into the game tomorrow and Jonas can pitch all of the first game on Saturday that we could get five innings out of the bullpen for the second game. But even that's going to be pushing it. With the way Cleveland's been hitting the last couple of games we can't rely on that option. We need another arm."

"What about one of the two starters from yesterday coming back on short rest? Neither one of them went all that long," Duerson said, scrambling for ideas and even knowing as he was saying them that they were terrible ideas.

"That would only be two days' rest. Three days we could maybe try, but not two days. And even then, those two haven't exactly been lighting the world on fire lately."

"You know, what we are going to do is crazy, don't you? This is unheard of. We're going to be the fucking laughingstock of the league."

"We still just need to win two out of four games. Just need a split. We have our two best pitchers throwing the next two days. All they have to do is their typical job and we'll be just fine. No one will remember this mess."

"Yeah, and if we don't win this will follow us around forever. The thing that no one will remember is the rain. All they'll remember is the blown lead and the lack of pitching options available, and maybe the fucking stupid GM and manager."

"Well, I guess we'll need to make sure we win then. We win tomorrow night with Javy. He's been throwing well lately. Win the first game Saturday with Jonas. He's making ten million bucks this year; it's time for him to earn it. And then we can burn the youngsters' arms into the ground for the last two games which won't matter. We'll get into a short playoff series with Javier and Jonas ready to roll. Have confidence, Dave. Things could be a lot worse."

"Alright," Dave said, once again rubbing his face. "I guess we don't have a choice. I agree that your plan is the best one that we have. Get Don Scott back on the phone and fill him in. We'll want him back in the dugout again. Check with Scott to make sure he's still been throwing and will be ready to go. I can't believe I'm left again counting on fucking Charlie Becker."

"Hello?" Don Scott's groggy voice mumbled sleepily over the phone.

"You sleeping, Don?" Gordon said enthusiastically on the other end and knowing that he'd probably been sleeping for quite a while.

"I'm 75 years old. It's 1:30 AM. I've been sleeping for 5 hours, Gordon."

"Huh," Gordon said enjoying himself. "Well, I guess it's almost time to wake up then, eh?"

"Are you drunk?" Scott asked still half asleep.

"No, I'm not drunk. I just had to talk to you. This is kind of urgent so wake yourself up."

"I told you I don't owe you any money," Scott said still mumbling into his pillow.

Gordon laughed. "It's not about the money. It's about Charlie Becker. Now wake up."

That was enough to at least spark Scott's curiosity so he sat up on the edge of the bed. "Alright, I'm awake. What's up?"

"As you're probably aware we've got ourselves in a little bit of a situation here. Did you stay up and watch the game tonight?"

"Well, I started watching. Then my eyes got tired from watching you walk out to the mound to change pitchers every five minutes so I went to sleep. I take it that it didn't end well?"

"No, we got pounded again. Our bullpen is shot, Don. We're barely hanging on."

"At least the season is almost over," Scott said yawning. "Just get to the playoffs and ride your two stud horses long into the games. What does this have to do with Charlie Becker? You want him to come in and talk with Clayton and Hodge a little bit?"

"Not exactly. Has Charlie still been throwing since the season ended? How's his arm been?"

Scott, in his still sleepy state, wasn't sure what Gordon was talking about. Why did he care if Charlie had been throwing? Of course Charlie hadn't been throwing. He's retired, Scott thought. Then, all of a sudden it hit him and he bolted upright onto his feet wide awake. At least, as much as a man Scott's age can bolt. He realized that he never told the Twins management that Charlie had retired. He went from a dazed, confused expression to a smile.

"Ah, yeah, he's been throwing. He just told me on Saturday at the game that he's been working out with a high school team and throwing with them. He's working with his old coach from high school," Scott said, stretching the truth as far as he possibly could without lying and not mentioning that it was a football he'd been throwing. After working with Charlie all season long Scott had all of the confidence in the world in him and knew that if he were given a shot that he'd produce, even if he hadn't been throwing the last three weeks. Actually, he already did that once after his sister had been shot and he pitched the best game of his life. Plus, at this moment his loyalty was more to Charlie than to the Twins.

"Alright, well here's the thing. I need you to give Charlie a call right away tomorrow morning. Have him up here to the offices by noon and we'll work out all the administrative details that we need done. Let him know that he'll be starting the second game of the double header on Saturday."

"Whoa. Whoa. What? He's starting Saturday?" Scott said, shocked for the second time in the conversation. "I thought he'd maybe see some action out of the bullpen in a blowout or something."

"We don't have anyone else to use, and we'd rather start with the experienced starter and then use the bullpen like we normally use them. It's not ideal, but it's what we've got."

"OK. I'll let him know in the morning. Maybe it's good that he only has one day to think about it. This is quite a responsibility we're putting on his shoulders."

"Thanks Don. Hey, one more thing. We'd like to have you here with us this weekend as well. You can give us some insight with Charlie on Saturday and then perhaps we'll need to use Clayton some on Sunday if we've clinched. Can you do that?"

"Sure. But under one condition. If I'm up there with you I need some say in what happens. You need to let me work with Charlie and Clayton and leave the pitching coach out of it. The guy's already screwed Clayton up. The only coaches I want talking to them are you and me. Sound good?"

"Yeah, we can do that. I'll make sure that happens."

"Great. I have a feeling this is going to work out well for you guys."

"I hope so, or I'll be looking for a new job."

"Hello?" Charlie said over his cell phone at 7:00 AM sharp. It was pretty early for someone to be calling, but Charlie had already been up for over an hour.

"Hi Charlie, this is Don. How are you doing?" It wasn't too early for Scott. He'd been looking at the clock every few minutes since he got up at 5:45 waiting for it to be late enough in the morning for him to call without waking everyone up.

"I'm doing good. I wasn't expecting to hear from you. What's up?" Charlie wasn't very big on small talk, especially when he was curious about something. Charlie thought it was pretty strange for Coach Scott to be calling him, especially right away in the morning.

"I'm going to be back with the Twins here this weekend and I was hoping you could come up and watch a couple of the games. Clayton's going to get another start on Sunday possibly, and I've made sure that the pitching coach doesn't say a word to him. I'd like for you to maybe talk to him some. Also, Dusty will be starting a game or two this weekend. So, can you make it up?"

After Scott had hung up with Gordon he couldn't get back asleep for a while, so instead he just stared at the ceiling for an hour or so thinking about how he'd tell Charlie. He eventually decided to have some fun with it. After all, this was a lot of excitement for an old geezer.

"I'm not sure I can make it up there, Skip. It's kind of a busy weekend. We have a big football game tonight and Karen has some things that she wants to get done before the new baby arrives. I can talk to her about it, but I can't say for sure." Charlie didn't really feel like going up to another game. It just left him feeling kind of empty that he never was a part of a major league club. Anyway, Charlie was certain that Karen didn't want to spend another weekend watching baseball.

"Well, what about the second game of the double header tomorrow? That would be a really good game for you to be at."

"Why? Is that when Clayton's going to pitch? The Twins might have it clinched by then anyway. Just need to win the next two. That game might not even matter."

"True, it might not matter, but it could," Scott said. "And, no, Clayton's not starting that game. They're going to go in a different direction."

"Are they going to use the bullpen? They're not going to try to start Bryce Hodge, are they? Has he ever even started a game before?"

"Naw, they're not crazy enough to try and start Bryce. They're going with some rookie to try and save their bullpen."

"Who's that?" Charlie asked not really all that interested. He had made himself busy picking up some of Timmy's toys while they were talking on the phone and he'd already decided that he wouldn't be going to the games this weekend.

"Some kid with a rubber arm that likes to throw a bunch of slow stuff. Charlie Becker's his name."

Charlie stopped what he was doing and tried to process what he'd just heard. Coach Scott wasn't really one to joke around about something like this, but this was just a little too ridiculous to be true.

"Very funny, Skip," Charlie eventually said.

"I'm not joking, Charlie. They want you to start the second game of the double header tomorrow against the Indians. Gordon called me up around 1:30 this morning and told me to call you right away when you'd be up. They want you over at Target Field by noon today to get the paperwork and stuff taken care of."

"They want me to pitch tomorrow?" Charlie asked incredulously. "I haven't thrown in like three weeks."

"Oh, you'll be great. You didn't throw when your sister was in the hospital and that went pretty darn good. You've been throwing for 30 some years, a couple days off don't make a difference. Ah, just don't mention that three weeks off thing to anybody up in Minneapolis."

"I, uh, I mean..." Charlie sputtered not sure what he should be saying or doing.

"Charlie, relax. You've done it. You've made the majors. Now take a deep breath and get your ass up here by noon. I'll see you sometime this afternoon."

Charlie hung up the phone and just stood there. He had been waiting for a call like this for ten years and now that it came at the most unexpected of times he wasn't sure what he should do. He thought about all of the people he needed to contact and things he needed to do and decided that it would be best for him to get busy and just not think too much right now. But, before he went into his bedroom to get some things packed up, he stopped for a second, took a deep breath, looked up at the ceiling, and quietly said, "We did it, Dad."

Chapter 26

Minneapolis, MN

The two hour drive to the Twin Cities is one that Charlie has done hundreds of times in his life, but it never quite seemed as peaceful and serene as it did today. The orange and yellow colors of fall gave a whole new life to the landscape, and the sun reappearing in the sky after a long absence felt soothing through the car window. It wasn't the beauty of the terrain that left him feeling this way, however, it was the pure emotional high that he currently was on.

Highway 52 runs in and out of little farming communities on its winding way north. Quite a few people commute from the Rochester area all the way up to the Cities for work, but most of that traffic had already come and gone by the time Charlie was on the road. Even the congested rush hour traffic that normally drove him crazy wouldn't have bothered Charlie today, however. His mind was still racing from the incredible news, and he was still a little bit in shock over the whole incredible thing.

After hanging up with Don Scott this morning, he got on the phone and made a couple of quick calls. He called up Karen, who liked to get to school early, and shared the good news with her. Then he got a hold of his mom and Heather and they said they'd be glad to keep an eye on Timmy for the day. A quick throwing together of a suitcase of clothes and one last call to Mr. Marchant to tell him that he wouldn't be at the game tonight and Charlie was soon on the road. He decided he'd get up there early and get everything taken care of and in order so that he'd have time to find a hotel to stay at tonight with his family. They could have just stayed at home, but Karen figured that with the extra salary he'd be getting for being called up they should stay the night at a fancy hotel and enjoy this special time. Plus, with the four games in three days that were coming up Charlie would be plenty busy without four hours of driving each day on top of it. Karen and Timmy were going to drive up together after school was over and then meet him at the hotel after the game tonight.

Charlie spent the late morning and early afternoon getting everything done at Target Field. He had some forms that needed signing in the offices. He needed to get his uniform sized down in the locker room area. And then it was quickly over to the five star Graves 601 hotel in downtown Minneapolis for check-in, and a bite to eat. Before he knew it, it was time to get back to the stadium to get dressed for the 7:05 PM start time, and out to the field to shag a few fly balls during batting practice.

"Hey, hey, they're putting the band back together!" Dusty said boisterously, seeing Charlie in the locker room. "Who's taking care of the chickens, pigs, and donkeys on the farm while you're up here?"

"Dusty, sometimes I'm not really sure if you're being serious or if you're joking."

"Thanks, Chuckster," Dusty replied, taking that as a compliment. "Are you the starting right tackle for the Vikings now?"

"Huh?" Charlie said, continuing to put his uniform on, and giving Dusty a confused look.

"Well, I've never seen a baseball player with the number 79 before. I figure you must be in the wrong locker room."

Charlie laughed, knowing that this time it really was a joke – actually a pretty good one for Dusty. "I got the only leftover uniform that actually fit. How does it look?"

"It looks like you're an accountant trying to dress up like the real players, but that's how a uniform always looks on you. It's ok, Chuckster, not everyone has the ripped baseball physique that I do." Dusty said, flexing his muscles.

"Yeah, look at these abs right here." Charlie responded, rubbing Dusty's bulbous stomach.

"Hey, hands off the merchandise," Dusty said, and then turned more serious. "Did you hear the good news? We're going to be battery mates tomorrow. Gordon stopped me on the way in and told me. They must know that only one catcher could handle your ego."

"No, I hadn't heard that yet, but that's great. I was hoping that might happen. That just makes everything easier. Won't need to worry about changing up signs or any of that junk," Charlie said, patting Dusty on the back. He got up and started walking towards the exit to the field.

"Where are you going so quickly?" Dusty asked.

"I want to get out to the field and walk around a little bit, throw the ball around, and shag some batting practice." Charlie had decided that with his three days as a major league baseball player he'd take advantage of every second by being out on the field and taking everything in. Charlie was in a situation that very few players had ever been in. He was a rookie and at the same time he was retiring. There wasn't going to be a next year. There was just now. He didn't have to worry about the future. Charlie felt almost giddy heading out to the field; he was a kid on Christmas day.

Javier Suarez, the starting pitcher today, saw Charlie heading for the door and yelled out, "Hey Rook, you're forgetting something." Charlie turned around to see Javier pointing at a pink Hello Kitty backpack. "Make sure the sunflower seeds get out to the bullpen, eh amigo."

The Hello Kitty backpack was a hazing tradition that the Twins used for all of their rookie pitchers. Clayton and Bryce Hodge already had theirs, and now it looked like Charlie would be joining them. Charlie gave a smile, walked over, and strapped on the backpack to take with him out to the field. He was a little surprised and amazed that within about ten hours of being called up they already had a backpack there waiting for him. Pitchers clearly have too much time on their hands.

Charlie was glad that he at least had one day to adjust to life in the big leagues before having to pitch. As soon as he entered the dugout and stepped out onto the field it was like entering a whole new baseball world, and he had to remind himself that he really belonged here. The dugout was clean and well taken care of. The grass was lush and green. The sound from the speakers came through loud and clear. Even though the game was still a couple hours away there were already people in the stands, and the place smelled like hot dogs. Not the old hot dog and stale beer smell of the minor league parks, but a grilled hot dog smell that made Charlie hungry again.

The next two hours flew by as Charlie played some catch with Clayton, chased a few fly balls in the outfield, and even talked to some fans and signed some autographs.

Charlie had always enjoyed signing for the kids; he just never had that high of a demand. Now that he was a major leaguer all of the kids were after him even though they didn't have any idea who he was. Maybe after tomorrow's game that signature might mean something to some naïve kid.

Javier was the only other lefty on the Twins staff, and he actually had fairly similar stuff to Charlie. Of course, his fastball moved about 6-7 MPH quicker, but other than that their other pitches and control were nearly identical. Charlie decided that he'd chart Javier's pitches tonight. He thought that might help him see what was effective against Cleveland's predominantly right handed hitting lineup. Plus, he just felt comfortable when he was sitting in a dugout with a pencil in hand.

Once the game started, Dusty was sitting there with Charlie talking strategy, and Don Scott thought it would be good for Clayton to sit with them as well and so he convinced Gordon White to let Clayton stay in the dugout for the game instead of being out in the bullpen where he'd typically been stationed. The conversation teetered between serious baseball discussion and humorous jabs at each other.

"Watching Javier pitch is kinda like watching you on steroids," Dusty said. "It would be tough catching him because I would be expecting the ball to hang in the air for two or three more seconds and then bam there it is. He also has that flowing, black hair and that suave Latino attitude that you're lacking."

"Have you asked him out yet?" Charlie responded. "I'm not sure Megan would be happy about this love infatuation you obviously have for him."

"Megan would be so impressed if I could get a guy like that to go out with me that she'd probably be my biggest cheerleader in the whole thing. We'd have to go out Salsa dancing. I bet he's a smooth dancer, don't you think?"

"Probably. He's not using his fastball much, however, is he?" Charlie said trying to keep the conversation focused. He didn't mind the levity, but he also understood the significance of the event that was about to unfold in his life, and wanted to make sure he was prepared. "And he's still being pretty effective. I don't think I'll be using mine very much tomorrow."

"You're right on that," Dusty said. "He's looking strong, except against Darnell Williams of course."

Darnell Williams, called up from Akron after the minor league season ended, hadn't seen a lot of playing time for Cleveland initially. But, thanks to an injury to their starting leftfielder, Darnell had found himself consistently in the lineup against left-handed pitchers. In fact, he'd been playing so well that now he was starting to play against righties as well. He hit his fifth homer in his short time in the majors in the second inning to tie the score at one, and now he led off the fourth inning with a double that hit the wall so hard it looked like it'd leave a dent. He hit such a rope that even though it went 400 feet in the air he still had to dive headfirst into second base and barely made it there underneath the tag. Of course, Darnell is no speedster or seasoned base runner. And the dive was kind of like a belly flop which brought some laughter from the Twins bench.

"What are you going to do with Darnell tomorrow?" Clayton asked.

"Well, hopefully not hit him," Charlie responded, which elicited some more laughs from everyone. "I think I'll probably try and pitch around him as much as possible. He's just hitting too well right now, and the rest of the lineup plays pretty well into my hands I think. I think they're over-aggressiveness will hurt them against me. I'll keep working my way further and further out of the zone. Maybe won't have to throw too many actual strikes."

"You should keep an eye on what their approach is against Jonas Kline in the first game tomorrow, as well," Scott said. "Your pitching styles couldn't be any different, and I think it works out great that you follow him tomorrow. It's just like how you followed Clayton all year long this season, Charlie. And Clayton, you should watch Jonas, too. He pitches the way I'd like to see you pitch."

"Will do, Coach," Clayton replied. One encouraging thing about the troubles that Clayton had been having with the Twins is that he was more receptive now to instruction and realized that he needed to work to become better and not just rely on his God-given natural abilities. "And Charlie, don't worry. If you do hit Darnell tomorrow I'll be sure to find another little guy off to the side somewhere and stay out of your way so you can perform some more Becker-style kung fu on him."

The Twins came through in the clutch scoring four runs in the bottom of the sixth inning and Javier did just enough to preserve the victory. The Twins only used the bullpen for two innings which was a big relief to Gordon White. He was hoping for a complete game from Javier, but knew that was probably expecting too much, and when the lead diminished to 5-4 the Twins went to their set-up man and closer to finish it out. The win meant that the Twins were now two games up and only needed to win one of the last three to make the playoffs. The situation didn't seem nearly as dire as it did just 24 hours earlier. All the Twins needed now was for Jonas Kline to come through in the first game tomorrow, and they wouldn't have to sweat out the uncertainty that was going to come after that.

After the game finished, Charlie was in the locker room changing and was a little surprised to see a couple of reporters come over to him to ask a few questions. So far it was just the local reporters, but he knew that the game tomorrow night would be on ESPN so he'd probably have to talk to the national media sometime before the game. Charlie decided to keep things pretty brief with them as he was in a hurry to get to the hotel and see his family, but he tried to at least take the time to give them a couple of quotes without really saying much. He decided his approach was pretty much just going to be to talk in clichés, and try not to talk too much about himself. He was to the point that he really didn't want to see his name in the paper, and really didn't care that the game tomorrow would be broadcast across the nation. Being in the big leagues was never about popularity for Charlie, it was always about reaching the goal that was set years ago.

When he got finished with the reporters he checked his cell phone and saw that he had 54 text messages and 29 missed calls. He smiled to himself and thought they probably all wanted some free tickets to tomorrow's game. They weren't going to have any luck there. He scanned through the text messages quickly looking for one in particular. He knew that Mr. Marchant would let him know how the football game went, and he also knew that the text would take him at least five minutes to type with his big, clumsy fingers. He found it and read:

Won 21 to 6. playd ok. good luck tmoro. see you tjhere

Charlie jumped in his car for the half mile drive across I-394 to the hotel, and within five minutes was lying beside his wife in bed. As soon as Charlie's head hit the pillow he was out. There were no nightmares, no tossing or turning, no anxiety. On the night before pitching in front of thousands of people in a game that would be broadcast to millions of others it was the most relaxing night of sleep for Charlie in 17 years.

Chapter 27

Minneapolis, MN

Twins Front Office Drops the Ball

By Jason Feldman

Minneapolis – Errors. Sometimes they can cost a run. Sometimes they can cost a win. And, sometimes they can cost a season. As the Twins celebrated an important 5-4 win last night, there was still an ominous hint of anxiety wafting through the air in the home locker room. It wasn't the seventh inning fielding error by Aaron Cummings at third which caused the nervousness. That error only cost the Twins a run, and not a win or a season. No, there was a different sort of error that unleashed the unmistakable stench of fear. It was a mental error. It was an error of omission of thought by the Twins front office which lingered over the locker room. It was an avoidable error. It was an error that might just cause General Manager Dave Duerson or Twins Manager Gordon White or both to lose their jobs if the Twins don't find a way to finish off the division this weekend. Errors can be costly.

Sometimes, however, errors can be forgotten and forgiven. If Jonas Kline shows up for the afternoon game tomorrow and throws the way he's capable, this will all be moot. Kline, at times, has been absolutely unhittable this season. But Kline's nickname, The Elevator, is not because he doesn't enjoy taking the stairs. His season, similar to his career, has been a compilation of ups and downs. If The Elevator is sitting down in the basement, the Twins season might be down there with him. Right along with the professional careers of Duerson and White.

Which brings us back to Duerson and White. Somehow the Twins front office has left us after 159 games with the season on the line in the hands of The Elevator, Mr. Unknown Minor Leaguer, and a big fat question mark. Mr. Unknown is game two starter Charlie Becker. Becker was last seen in Double-A New Britain and has a grand total of ZERO major league innings pitched. So, you'd assume that must mean he is a top prospect, right? An up-and-comer with a live arm, right? Wrong. Becker is a career minor leaguer, with below average minor league numbers. A nobody who has done nothing. At least he's been traveling and working out with the team, right? Surely the front office would have Mr. Unknown participating with the team just in case of disaster. Wrong again. Two days ago he was sitting at home helping coach his local high school football team. Errors. Big ones.

We can't even say wait for tomorrow, because nobody knows what tomorrow will bring. Will it be Clayton Kearns again? Yikes, I sure hope not. Will we try to squeeze out more innings from an already exhausted bullpen? Trouble. Will we try and find a local softball protégé? It's as likely as anything else. I can throw 70 mph heat if they need me. And, we're not getting any help from anyone within the Twins organization about who it will be tomorrow. So we have the fear, the anxiety, the nervousness of Season on the Line Saturday. And we hope for an error-free miracle.

"Well, it could have been worse," Charlie said smiling. He was looking over Karen's shoulder as she was reading the Saturday *Star Tribune*.

"A nobody?" Karen said red in the face. "What an obnoxious jerk. Did he even interview you to try and find anything out about who you were?" Karen did not like anything other than positives being said about her husband, and was all fired up. For Karen, the negativity from the fans was always the most difficult part of attending his games. She was constantly glaring at fans that would yell. Charlie, on the other hand, just took it all in stride.

"I don't remember if I talked to him or not. Karen, it's not a big deal. He's just trying to sell some newspapers."

"The little weasel could at least be a little nicer about it," Karen fired back.

Charlie wrapped his arms around her and kissed her forehead. "Thanks for defending me, honey," he said, which finally seemed to release the tension in Karen's stiff body.

Charlie had been up since 5:00 AM and had already read through the entire Saturday paper, and was halfway through the crossword puzzle before Karen and Timmy got up. He left the Sports section for last and considered just not reading it at all, but he thought it would be kind of fun to see what the media were saying about him. Just like with the fans, Charlie had seen and heard too much over the many years to be bothered by sports writers. He found them humorous as well.

"Charlie, the entire town of Spring Valley is going to be either at the game or watching it on TV today," Karen said, finally putting the newspaper away.

"Oh, come on now, you're exaggerating."

"No, I'm not. They're shutting down the grocery store and both gas stations at 3:00 this afternoon so everyone can either get to the game or to the VFW with the big screen TV. You know how big the Twins are down there, and to have one of their own pitching is just amazing. I didn't know if Timmy and I were going to be able to get out of town with all the people stopping me to congratulate you. I felt like a celebrity."

"Well, I guess I better not get rocked too badly then today. Are you trying to make me nervous?" Charlie asked without really meaning it.

"You know that I'm the one that's going to be nervous. You'll be just fine."

"Just don't go into labor on me in the middle of the game, ok?"

"Deal. Heather, Kenny and your mom will be sitting with us so I'm sure they'll try to keep me calm."

"Yeah, as long as they make the drive up here safely. Kenny's probably going to have the lights and siren going all the way up to the Target Field gates. Heather and Kenny drive too fast."

"Ah, you sound like an old man."

"Thanks, sweetie. Nice to hear that you're going to start with the old man stuff now, too."

"OK, I'm ready," Timmy yelled from the bathroom, interrupting his parents. He ran out with just his swimsuit on. At home if Timmy had been asked to get his teeth brushed and dressed for the day the whole process would take at least 20 minutes, but here in the hotel with swimming as a motivator he was ready to go in about two minutes.

"Alright, buddy, let's do it," Charlie responded, and they headed for the door.

They spent a little bit of time in the pool splashing around before Charlie decided that he better get back to the room and get ready to go. Double headers are long days. The coaching staff wanted everyone at the ballpark by at least 10:00 AM for the 1:05 PM start of the first game. Game two was scheduled for 6:05 PM tonight in a day-night double header type of schedule, except game two was earlier than normal to accommodate the TV people. A strange schedule, but everything about this situation was strange for Charlie so maybe it would affect his Cleveland counterpart more than him. He could always hope.

Charlie pulled into the player's parking lot just ahead of Dusty. He waited for Dusty to park his old, beat up Mazda 626 and walked in with him. It was the first of October and a beautiful day for a baseball game in

Minneapolis. Clear skies, no wind, and a forecast high of 73 degrees were predicted. There wouldn't be any rainouts today.

"Hey, Dusty, ready to go?" Charlie asked.

"I've been ready to go since I found out I was starting yesterday. It feels like it's been weeks, and we still have over eight hours to go. I don't think I've been this nervous for a game in my life. What about you?"

"I'm feeling good. It's going to be a nice day, I think."

"A nice day? Shouldn't you be more nervous or wound up? I'm going crazy here and you're talking about a nice day?"

"Just relax there, big guy. We've been playing this game our whole lives. Since we were little kids we've played hours and hours of baseball. You know what you're doing. It'll go great," Charlie said casually. Charlie seemed to be the only one around him not jittery or anxious about the day.

"Easy for you to say, Chuckster. I was just a kid a few years ago, but you haven't been a kid for a couple decades."

"You worry too much. This is fun. You need to enjoy it."

"What's gotten into you? Since when are you so chipper?"

"Just had a good night sleep is all," Charlie responded with an extra hop in his step. "Let's get it done."

"Ah, crap," Gordon said to Don Scott roughly four hours later. They were sitting next to each other in the dugout, watching Cleveland celebrate yet another home run. "What am I supposed to do now?"

After just over two innings of baseball The Elevator was sitting in the worst possible location - on the basement floor. He just allowed his third homer of the game, and the Indians were now leading 8-1.

"It seems like you've got two options here. Neither one of them is very good," Scott responded, shaking his head. "You could run through your bullpen and hope they stop the bleeding enough to come back or you could consider this game done, rest some of the position players and bullpen, and use Clayton. The bullpen would then have to be used on Sunday. That might be a better option than Clayton on Sunday, anyway, if you need a win."

"I think it's going to have to be Clayton today. We'll just have to deal with Sunday on Sunday. If Becker gets rocked today, too, we're really screwed. He might have to pitch 7 innings regardless of what happens. I don't think I'll take anyone else out yet, just in case, but maybe in a couple innings a few can get some rest."

"Let me call down to the bullpen and talk to Clayton first," Scott said, and then shuffled over to the bullpen phone.

Scott came to the phone, talked for about 30 seconds, and then made his way back to Gordon.

"What'd you say?" Gordon asked him.

"I told him that if he got into this game he wasn't coming out. It didn't matter if he walked the whole fucking lineup straight through. So, ignore all the shit, man up, and get the job done. Then I hung up on him."

"Huh. Does that work with him?"

"I don't know. Never tried it before. That's the most I've sworn in years."

Three batters later the Twins were still trying to finish off the top of the third inning as Gordon White made his way to the mound. The boos that were cascading down from the crowd as Jonas walked off the mound only grew stronger when they saw Clayton Kearns was coming in next. Clayton had been torn apart by the local sports talk shows after his recent rough outings, and the fans were viciously letting him have it. Things just got worse as Clayton proceeded to walk the next batter, and then his first pitch to Darnell Williams came within an inch of hitting him. Darnell got up and just glared at Clayton. He yelled something out towards the mound that Clayton couldn't comprehend, but he knew pretty much what it probably was. Add Darnell to the list of people in the ballpark that currently hated him. Was there anyone left on his side?

Clayton was dejectedly rubbing the ball near the back of the mound when he heard someone yelling at him from the dugout. He looked over there to find Charlie with Dusty's catcher's mask on wielding two baseball bats as weapons while Dusty was in a karate pose with a batting helmet on backwards.

Dusty yelled out, "We've got your back Clayton-san."

Clayton thought it looked hilarious and laughed on the inside. He knew if he broke out a smile with the Twins now down 10-1 in a huge game that a riot might break out and he'd be a dead man. He took a deep breath on the mound and went back to work. The next pitch was still a little bit low, but Darnell thankfully took a cut at it and smoked a one-hopper right at the second baseman who turned a quick 4-6-3 double play to end the inning.

Whether it was the levity of the moment or just pure luck and coincidence is difficult to say, but from that point on Clayton finally put things back together. He got back to back perfect innings, and by the time the seventh inning rolled around the Twins were still losing 10-3, but Clayton had kept the Indians off the board and more importantly had chewed up several innings.

At this point, Charlie and Dusty decided they better start getting prepared for the late game. It was looking more and more like the upcoming game could be the deciding factor on whether the Twins were going to make the playoffs or not. The season was going to be placed squarely on their shoulders. In the locker room the club had a table set up with a variety of lunch meats, cheeses, and breads for the players to eat. Dusty and Charlie thought it best to get a head start on whatever meal this currently was so that the food would be digested and settled before game time. They watched the rest of the game on one of the clubhouse televisions while they ate.

"This is good stuff," Charlie said, stuffing his face with a ham and cheese sandwich on Italian bread.

"Funny you say that," Dusty said, "I think this is probably one of the cheapest meals we've had since I've been up here."

"Well, it tastes good to me," Charlie responded. "Eat up, big guy; you don't want to be thinking about food when you should be helping me win a ballgame."

Dusty was just sitting there watching Charlie eat and keeping an eye on the game. "I don't know how you can be eating right now."

"Dusty, eat. Relax. You see what Clayton's doing out there, right. We're going to do the same thing. Now get some food, and bring me a bag of those potato chips while you're at it."

Dusty finally nibbled on a sandwich and they watched Clayton finish off the ninth inning by only allowing one run. The Twins still ended up losing 11-6, but Clayton threw six and two-thirds innings and completed the game which allowed the others in the Twins bullpen to get some rest. They would be needed tomorrow to try and piece together a win if necessary.

The loss meant the Twins were now just one game up on the Indians with two to play. The Twins would only need to win one of the games to make the playoffs, but as the players came in to the locker room a sense of despair was on many of their faces. They almost all looked at Charlie as they walked past. Seeing him, knowing the season was in his hands, watching him devouring a sandwich, didn't seem to improve anyone's sour mood.

Chapter 28

Minneapolis, MN

In the old Metrodome the Twins bullpen was really just an old, hard bench down the third base line with a couple of mounds next to it. The home relievers were forced to crank their heads to the right if they wanted to catch a glimpse of home plate. If they looked straight ahead all they'd see was the centerfielder and a big baggy for a wall. The bullpens in Target Field, however, are located just to the leftfield side of centerfield. The home and visiting pens are lined up parallel to each other, with the Twins taking the one further back away from the field. It just so happens to be the only one with an overhang as well to provide a little shelter from the elements. When you're playing a game in Minnesota in April it's a little bit of home field advantage. It is not uncommon for there to be snow at that time of the year, and without a dome overhead it isn't always a comfortable 70 degrees to play baseball in. That advantage really wouldn't come into play on a beautiful day like today, however, where it would just about be 70 degrees naturally.

Charlie had already finished a few aspects of his pregame routine. That routine was not as rigid as it was when he first started pitching in the minors. Charlie realized soon after he started pitching in the rookie leagues that a rigid routine was not always a possibility. There were too many unexpected things that could come up, and it was best just to remain flexible and go with the flow. And lately, there were days when Charlie was having too much fun with Timmy to stop and so he just omitted pieces altogether. He didn't take his baseball life so seriously anymore. After all, it didn't mean everything to him like it used to.

Today, with more time available and Timmy sitting with his mom and not on the field with him, Charlie decided to do things more by the book. No matter how much he tried to tell himself differently, this wasn't just a normal day and a normal game. He started with some light jogging in the outfield grass, and then put together a couple of more intense sprints to get his blood flowing and his heart beating. After the running, he performed a detailed stretching routine, extensively covering both his upper and lower body. The stretching routine was the one piece that he did take seriously at all times and didn't stray far from. A lot of younger pitchers neglected their lower half and just concentrated on making sure that the arm was loose. And, there were even some pitchers that didn't do any stretching at all. They'd just take the ball and start chucking it. Because of that, they didn't make it through entire seasons healthy like Charlie almost always had. Pitchers were just as likely to be out with a pulled groin as they were with any sort of shoulder or arm injury.

After the stretching Charlie would first do some lighter short toss in the outfield before moving to long toss of around 100 feet, making sure that the throws were always on a line and not lobbed over. He was not pitching out of a delivery at this point, only throwing. He didn't spend a great deal of time with either the short or long toss, but just enough to start to feel loose. Then, it was time to get out to the bullpen mound to start getting things cranked up. Charlie, Don Scott, and the bullpen catcher, a kid named Ryan Edwards, were the only three out there right now. The rest of the bullpen crew were all either sitting in the dugout, chatting with each other in the outfield grass, or hidden away somewhere in the clubhouse – most likely playing video games and listening to music.

Don was really just out there to watch. He hadn't said a word to Charlie since the entire process started. Charlie knew what to do and so Don wasn't going to mess with him. Edwards was just out there to catch the ball and throw it back. He probably didn't even know Charlie's name, and wasn't talking to Charlie either. The only conversation taking place was Charlie talking to himself. He didn't spend this time concentrating on mechanics, but just tried to free his mind and let his muscle memory take over.

[289]

The only time he'd work on his mechanics in bullpen sessions was between starts, never on game day. Of course, he hadn't had a bullpen session to do that in about a month and a half now.

"Fastball, in," he'd mumble, visualizing a right-handed hitter and trying to hit the spot. It was always right-handed hitters that he would imagine, as he just didn't face lefties very much and probably wouldn't see very many, if any, today.

"Curveball, low and inside." His bread and butter pitch that he'd probably throw 40 times in a game. He'd need this one to be effective today.

"Fastball, out of the zone."

"Curveball, thrown for a strike."

"Try again, curveball, thrown for a strike."

"Curveball, looking for a strikeout."

He'd motion with his hand towards Edwards the type of pitch and location he'd be throwing so not to cross him up too badly. All the communication was done silently. Charlie preferred to work in silence since that's what it is like out on the mound. Pitching can be a lonely task, standing out on the mound with no one else around. All eyes focused on you – the center of everyone's focus. So, Charlie liked to warm-up as if he were alone.

Unlike many other pitchers, Charlie did not throw his warm-up pitches in the same order before every game, and didn't actually throw the same number of pitches every time. He waited to see how his arm felt, and when he felt like he had put each one of his pitches in the exact location he wanted it he moved on to something different. He always made sure that he spent some time out of the full wind-up and some time throwing out of the stretch. Charlie felt just as comfortable in each, but he hoped he wouldn't be out of the stretch very often today.

The stadium was starting to fill up for the start of the second game. After the earlier game Target Field was emptied and then separate admission was charged for the evening game. This was pretty standard procedure for day-night doubleheaders, and the clubs enjoyed those for the double admission money that came in. It looked like there wouldn't be an empty seat in the house for the Saturday evening game, and beer sales were expected to go through the roof on this pleasant evening. They might even sell a couple more hot dogs than normal with the earlier start being closer to supper time.

After Charlie finished his throwing routine he scanned the crowd while holding the ball on the bullpen mound, looking for Karen, Timmy, Kenny, Heather and his mom in the area of the stadium that they said they'd be sitting in. They had decided not to sit in the section with the players' families so that they could all sit together as a group. It wasn't easy finding five good seats in one place, but when the Twins ticket office found out they were looking for seats for the family of the pitcher who held the season in his hands, they worked something out. Don't want to upset the man that was hopefully going to get them their playoff bonus!

He found them sitting three rows back, down the first base line, not far from the Twins dugout. Pretty nice seats actually. Much better than the seats that they sat in a week ago. Was it really just a week ago? So much had happened in such a short period of time. For that matter, Charlie couldn't believe that just two days ago he was at football practice preparing for a high school game.

The only one Charlie didn't see in the crowd was Kenny. Charlie figured he was probably running around getting Timmy something to eat, and smiled to himself. Timmy would keep Kenny busy doing that all game long and Kenny would do it happily until Karen eventually decides to put an end to it. Normally, Heather would be jumping up and down to get Timmy everything he wanted as well, but since the shooting Kenny was trying to do everything he could to keep Heather resting and still. Not that it really worked. Heather wasn't one to passively listen and obey.

"OK, I'm ready," Charlie finally said confidently to Don Scott who was just watching Charlie look around the stadium.

"How do you feel?" Scott asked, speaking for the first time.

"Like I've done this a million times before. I don't feel like a rookie, that's for sure."

"Well, you don't look like one either. Let's get a jacket on your arm and head on back to the dugout."

Charlie finished up pretty much at the time that he hoped to finish in an ideal situation. He had about five minutes until the National Anthem would be played. Enough time for him to get back into the dugout, grab a drink of water, take a deep breath to compose himself, and get lined up for the Anthem.

He stood there next to Dusty who had his shin guards and chest protector on, mask and glove in hand, ready to go. Charlie was staring at his cleats, thinking about the Indian hitters, oblivious to everything going on around him, when the Anthem started. The first line of the Anthem jolted him out of his stupor. Standing before him, out in front of home plate, was a pretty little girl in pigtails, no more than six years old, belting out the Anthem. Here was this girl, out in front of the same nearly 40,000 people that were about to be looking at him, singing with a huge smile on her face. Chills ran all the way down Charlie's body as he listened to her finish the song to the most deafening roar he'd ever heard for a National Anthem.

"Wow!" Dusty said. "Good luck following that one."

"That girl's got a voice and a demeanor like none other. Let's do it," Charlie said, and the team took the field to a continuing roar from the crowd.

Charlie could almost feel the place shaking around him as he took the walk out to the mound to begin warming up. The game hadn't even started yet, and this was already the loudest experience he'd ever had at a game. All of a sudden, the enormity of the moment hit him. Here he was, pitching for the Major League team he grew up living and dying for, in front of all of his friends and family as well as thousands of others watching live. Not to mention the millions of people from all over the world who were watching him on TV.

Charlie made it through his warm-up pitches in the blink of an eye. He didn't even remember throwing them. His head was spinning. All of a sudden the umpire barked out, "Play Ball!", and the Indians leadoff hitter, Michael Gibson, dug in to the batter's box. Charlie's heart was beating fast, his breathing grew heavy, and he was starting to feel light headed. The shaking in his hand that he first experienced as he was on the verge of completing that perfect game against Altoona a month ago returned as well. He stood there, 60 feet, 6 inches away from home plate and looked into Dusty for the signal. The distance felt like miles.

Dusty called for a fastball to start things out. It was kind of funny that Charlie was planning on throwing very few fastballs all game long, yet was going to start out with a fastball. Gibson never swung at the first pitch, especially when he was leading off the game. The plan had been to throw a fastball for strike one every time he came up. Charlie wound up and delivered his first Major League pitch. Unfortunately, the fastball only went about 58 feet, bounced out in front of home plate, caromed off of Dusty face mask and rolled towards the Twins dugout. Not an illustrious start to his Major League career.

Dusty was handed a new ball from the home plate umpire which he tossed back out to Charlie. Charlie caught the ball and took it with him behind the mound to rub it down. His hand was still shaking, and he took his time trying to calm himself down. Charlie normally worked very quickly. He didn't spend a lot of time walking around the mound, and usually delivered the pitch as soon as he received the ball back. He always felt like his fielders behind him performed better if he worked quickly and threw lots of strikes. He thought it helped keep them on their toes. But, he needed to find a way to get control of himself first or there wouldn't be any strikes or any reason for the fielders to be ready. He looked around at the anxious faces in the Twins dugout, and that didn't help. He saw his family sitting nervously in the crowd, and heard the murmuring growing throughout the stadium. It all sounded so clear and loud.

Finally, he got back on the hill and looked in for another sign from Dusty. They were going right back with a fastball to not fall any further behind in the count. Both

Charlie and Dusty knew that Gibson wasn't going to swing. At this point in the season half of the stadium knew he wasn't going to swing. This one went the other direction however, sailing up high around Gibson's eyes for ball two, and the frustration level from the crowd grew.

Charlie was now in a 2-0 count and realized he needed to get it together. He couldn't let himself fall apart the same way he did in the Altoona game, the same way that Clayton did to start his major league career. This time, when he got the ball back from Dusty, he stayed there on the rubber and just closed his eyes for close to ten seconds, asking his dad for some help. He tried to visualize himself when he was at a younger age playing baseball in the backyard with his family. The television announcers were now openly questioning what was going through the mind of this rookie pitcher that appeared rattled. Dusty, not sure exactly what was happening, was about to call time and head out there when Charlie finally opened his eyes again. Almost immediately upon opening them, something amazing happened. Everything around him went silent and almost magically the tunnel to Dusty's mitt appeared. The focus, the being in the moment, being in the game and one with the game all of a sudden came back. It was like his dad, or God, or something was giving him one more chance to be a kid playing a game again, without the world around him.

Charlie took the sign and delivered another fastball, this one going through the inside portion of the plate for a called strike. He threw the next pitch - same pitch, same location. Gibson was taking again, and the count was even. He decided to go with his curveball down and in with the count 2-2 now and that induced a ground ball to the shortstop who made an easy throw to first to get the first out of the inning.

The Indians second hitter stepped into the box and calmly laced a single to left on a sweeping curveball down and in. Charlie put the pitch exactly where he wanted it to go, and yet he still got a line shot hit off of him. The caliber of hitter tonight was obviously going to be much higher than what Charlie was used to seeing in the minors. That pitch, in that spot, hadn't been hit that hard against Charlie all season long.

The third batter of the inning took an outside pitch and went with it, hitting a rocket off the right field wall for a double. Luckily, the ball was hit so hard that it quickly bounced back to the right fielder and the runner wasn't able to score from first. But still, Charlie was in a dangerous first inning jam with the clean-up hitter, Vince Pacelli, coming up and still only one out. Sitting on deck was his old nemesis, the recently scorching hot Darnell Williams who got moved into the five spot for the second game of the double header.

Rather than walk Pacelli to load the bases against Darnell, Gordon White decided that they'd pitch to him and hope for the best. Charlie threw a change-up on the first pitch and Pacelli was so far out in front of it and off balance that he skyrocketed a pop-up in foul ground that the third baseman easily camped under for the second out of the inning. As Charlie took the return throw from the third baseman he breathed out a sigh of relief as that was a huge out in that situation.

Darnell Williams glared out at Charlie as he slowly and confidently strolled to the plate. When Darnell had heard about Charlie being called up yesterday to pitch he was almost as ecstatic as Charlie was for two reasons. One, Darnell had abused Charlie during the regular season with Akron. He had faced him ten times over four games during the season and had hit four homeruns off of him. Two, Darnell did not let go of things easily. He was still upset by the pitch that hit him, as well as embarrassed that he got flipped over onto his back by Charlie. He wanted nothing more than to drop his bat and charge the mound at that very moment, and if this were just a normal regular season game he might have done just that.

"Hey Darnell, how's it going?" Dusty said to him cheerfully behind home plate. "I hear Charlie beat you up last time you saw him."

"Fuck you," Darnell snarled back at him.

Dusty looked into the dugout, and saw Gordon put up four fingers. They were going to intentionally walk Darnell to load the bases. It was a fairly rare move to load the bases in a scoreless game in the top of the first inning, but with the way Darnell had been hitting and with an open base available it seemed like the right call to make. Darnell, of course, wasn't happy about it.

"What the fuck is this?" Darnell said, looking back at Dusty who was standing up with his arm extended.

"Well, Charlie wanted to just hit you again to put you on base, but I guess Gordon only wants to walk you. We'll have to hit you again later," Dusty said, collecting the first pitch.

"Fucking pansies," Darnell growled. "You can't walk me all day. I'll be back."

On the way to first Darnell yelled a few choice words out to Charlie on the mound who just ignored them. He had more pressing things to worry about right now than Darnell. The bases were loaded and he needed to find a way to get out of this inning.

He decided to work the outside part of the plate to the Indian's sixth hitter. He threw a change-up on the corner for a key strike one call. Charlie definitely didn't want to fall behind in the count in this situation, yet he also couldn't just throw it down the middle or he could be down by four. The second pitch, a curveball that was a little further outside, was taken for a ball. Charlie decided to come back inside and try to jam him now, and it worked out perfectly. The curveball came in on the batter's hands and he hit a soft ground ball to the third baseman who stepped on the bag for the final out.

Twenty pitches, two hits, and an intentional walk in the inning, yet Charlie had survived his first inning of Major League baseball without allowing any runs, a huge success in his mind. As Charlie walked to the dugout he realized that this was going to be a battle. Nothing was going to come easy, and he was just going to have to last. He immediately started focusing on what he needed to do to survive the next inning.

Chapter 29

Minneapolis, MN

The next two innings went remarkably well for Charlie. He even got a 1-2-3 second inning with a strikeout, and worked around a one out single in the third. Through three innings he had allowed three hits, struck out one, and hadn't allowed any runs. Now the Twins offense just needed to get something going. The Twins had been put down in order the first two innings, and Dusty was batting with two outs in the bottom of the third. The Twins still hadn't even had a base runner yet. Charlie had some pretty good stuff today, but even with that he knew the odds of him keeping a good hitting Major League team scoreless all game were not too great.

"Give me the rundown, Becker," Scott said, as they watched Dusty at the plate.

"Feel good, Skip."

"It looks like everything is working out there for you. Keep it up."

"Thanks, Skip."

Don Scott could tell by Charlie's short, choppy responses that he wasn't interested in talking right now; that he was locked in. Don considered this a good thing and sat back down to watch Dusty hit. Dusty, never a great hitter anyway, was no match for the Cleveland righty and he went down swinging on three pitches. It was time for Charlie to get back to the mound to keep the game scoreless.

Charlie had finished the third inning by getting the Indians clean-up hitter, Vince Pacelli, on a fly ball to the warning track in left. He left another change-up a little bit too far over the plate, and almost paid for it. It was a 3-0 pitch, and he didn't want to walk him with Darnell Williams standing on deck and fortunately Pacelli just barely got underneath it.

Now, with Darnell standing in there, Charlie decided that he couldn't make that same mistake with his change-up again. The Indian hitters were starting to realize that he wasn't using his fastball very often, and that was allowing them to have better timing on the change-up. He'd have to remember to squeeze a fastball out a little more frequently to keep them honest. For Darnell, he decided to work the outside part of the plate with his curveball and not give him anything that he could pull. His first pitch to Darnell was just outside for ball one. His second, same curveball, caught the corner and Darnell took it for a strike and turned around to glare at the umpire.

Charlie had a decision to make, now. Keep working the outside portion of the plate or try to catch Darnell leaning out there and bust him in. He decided he still didn't want to give Darnell anything to turn on, so he put another slow curveball on the outside portion of the plate. This one caught just a little too much of the plate, however, and Darnell went with the pitch to right.

"Shoot," Charlie said to himself almost immediately after Darnell hit it, turning his head. "Go foul."

The ball was not crushed, but with a short porch of 328 feet down the line in right field it wouldn't need to be crushed to go out. Charlie watched helplessly as the ball stayed to his left of the foul pole for a homerun. Darnell let out a deep, guttural yell as he slowly ran around the bases, looking at Charlie the entire way.

Charlie just called for another ball from Dusty and got ready to get back to work. He couldn't let this one slip up snowball into something greater. The next hitter, however, used an inside-out swing on a curveball in and blooped a little pop-up. It landed just out of reach of the second baseman down the right field line for a double to keep the pressure on. Down 1-0, and with the Twins bats silent so far, Charlie knew that he couldn't let the game get any further out of hand. Gordon White also realized he couldn't allow it to get any further away so he called time to make a visit to the mound.

"Charlie, bottom of the order coming up here. Make sure you go right after these guys. We don't want the top of the order coming up with any runners on base. Throw strikes," Gordon said.

"Got it, Skip," Charlie responded.

"Listen, I've got no one warming up in the bullpen because I've got no one left. This is up to you. Go get them!" Gordon said, and headed back to the dugout.

"Fastball?" Dusty asked, before he left.

"Yeah, let's go right after them. I'll keep it away."

Charlie succeeded in keeping it away, hitting the outside corner for strike one. He went back out there on the second pitch and the batter tapped one to the second baseman who easily got him at first, advancing the runner to third.

Now it was decision time in the dugout. They really had three options. 1) Walk the eight hitter to try and get a double play ball from the speedy nine hole hitter. 2) Bring the infield in to try and cut down the runner at the plate on a ground ball. This could allow for a big inning, however, if a ground ball leaked through the infield somewhere. Or 3) Keep the infield back and allow a run to score on a ground ball, but ensure the second out of the inning and keep the top of the order from coming up.

Gordon almost immediately decided that option number 1 wasn't really an option. Even if they did get a ground ball from the ninth hitter it would have to be hit right at an infielder to get a double play out of it. They don't want to walk the eighth hitter and then see the top of the order coming up with runners on base.

"What do you think, Don?" Gordon said to his old friend sitting next to him.

"Charlie will be able to get a ground ball here; it's just going to be a gamble on if he hits it at someone or in a hole. I think you should bring them in. We're not exactly scoring loads of runs lately. Two runs might be too many," Don replied.

"I agree. Let's bring them in," Gordon said, telling one of his bench coaches to line up the defense accordingly.

It turned out to be a good decision as Charlie induced a check-swing ground ball that bounced a couple of times before being scooped up by the shortstop who fired to first. The runner on third had to hold up. If the infield had been back everyone might have been safe.

Charlie knew that he still had work to do. He couldn't ease up. He struck out this hitter the first time up with three curveballs down and in, but was concerned about going right back at it again. Would the batter make adjustments and sit on that pitch after seeing it three times already? Charlie decided that he better waste a pitch first, just in case. He threw an inside fastball and, sure enough, the batter was sitting on a curveball. He swung late and was underneath it, popping it up in the infield. The Twins first baseman camped underneath it and the Twins were out of the inning with no further damage.

Charlie took some congratulations from his teammates and quickly hurried back to his self-designated spot in the dugout without talking to anyone to focus on the next inning. He hoped the Twins would find a way to put some runs on the board soon.

Chapter 30

Minneapolis, MN

"Yeah, baby, that's what I'm talking about!" Clayton yelled at Dusty who was sitting right next to him.

Despite being shoulder to shoulder Dusty couldn't hear a word that Clayton said, but he got the general message. Target Field had become whipped up into a frenzy as the Twins went from down one to up two in one swift swing of the bat. The place was rocking and rolling. Dusty held his hand up in the air to give Clayton a high five, and let out a whooping noise.

Dusty had been the one to get it all started, leading off the bottom of the sixth inning with a line drive single to left, only the second hit the Twins had managed up to that point. Any offense that Dusty provided was just a nice bonus. When the next hitter, the leadoff batter, knocked a ground ball to the shortstop Dusty knew he had a job to do. He came barreling in to the second baseman and took him out with an aggressive slide. He was out at second, but Dusty made sure that there would be no throw to first and no double play.

After a strikeout and a walk the Twins finally came up with the big hit they'd been looking for. The ball was tattooed into the seats in left field, and all of a sudden the Twins were simply nine outs away from the playoffs.

Charlie, meanwhile, had for the past two innings been doing what Charlie does. He'd throw strikes, get ground balls, allow a couple of hits, yet somehow managed to work his way out of trouble. He allowed a pair of singles in the fifth, but was saved by a double play ball off the bat of his new favorite Indian Vince Pacelli.

Darnell Williams once again victimized him leading off the sixth inning, but at least this time Charlie kept it in the ball park by a couple of feet. The leadoff double didn't come around to score thanks to a key strikeout and a couple fine defensive plays by the infielders. Through six innings he'd already allowed eight hits, but only one run had crossed the plate.

His Indian counterpart, however, had only allowed three hits and had struck out seven batters yet had given up three runs. Baseball can be a crazy game. The homerun that he allowed didn't come at a very opportune time for the Tribe.

"Is my man ok over there?" Clayton asked Dusty, nodding his head in Charlie's general direction. Charlie was just sitting there staring out into the field while the rest of the dugout was starting to settle back down after the homerun celebration.

"Kind of funny, isn't it?" Dusty replied. "I've never seen him like this. It's completely opposite of the normal Chuckster. So calm and focused. I'm not sure how to handle it, so I'm just leaving him alone."

"I think that's probably a good idea. I bet he doesn't want to talk to you anyway."

"Whatever, funny man. You're just happy now because everyone in Twins Nation doesn't hate you anymore. You were going to be like the Bill Buckner of the Twins."

"I think they still hate me actually. Just maybe not quite as much now. Hopefully they'll forget about me completely if we finish this thing off today. How's Charlie's stuff?"

"Not bad. He's putting the ball where he wants it most of the time. He just needs to hang in there for a couple more outs," Dusty said, jumping to his feet to get to his spot back behind home plate.

After Charlie had completed his warm-up pitches he saw a pinch-hitter coming out to lead off the top of the seventh. It made some sense as the nine hitter hadn't been able to get the ball out of the infield against Charlie in his first two at bats today. Charlie, figuring the Indians were looking for a base runner and so would be taking some pitches, went right after him and retired him on a lazy fly ball to center for the first out of the seventh.

Then things once again got a little dicey for Charlie. Michael Gibson, the Indians leadoff hitter, legged out an infield single. After another fly out to center, Charlie gave up another base hit. Now there were runners on the corners with two outs, and things were starting to get tense in the crowd as well as in the Twins dugout.

"Is Bernard ready?" Gordon White asked the pitching coach who was just getting off the phone.

"Bad news. His arm's tight, Gordon," He responded. "I don't think he's going to be able to go. He just went too many innings on Thursday."

"Dammit. He should have let us know earlier that his arm was tight. Well, I guess it's better to know now than after he blows the game for us. Who else could we use?"

"Montgomery is ready to close the game out, but we can't go to him yet. I can get the kid, Hodge, warmed up."

"Alright, get him ready in case of emergency. I'm going to stick with Becker for now. He's had success against this guy today. I'd rather not use Hodge unless we have to."

Gordon called time to once again visit Charlie out on the mound. This conversation wasn't much different from the last one. Essentially, Charlie needed to get out of this jam because there was nowhere else to turn.

Vince Pacelli was back up at the plate with runners on base yet again. He had already stranded five runners on base, and Charlie needed to find a way to add a couple more to that number. Pacelli had thrown his helmet angrily down after grounding into a double play in the fifth, and Charlie could almost see the steam coming out of his ears at the plate.

Charlie decided to use that anger, and hopefully the aggressiveness that came along with it, against him. He threw a first pitch fastball, something he'd never normally do to a fastball hitter like Pacelli. Charlie didn't throw it for a strike, however. He put it up around Pacelli's shoulders, and sure enough Pacelli almost swung out of his cleats. Even a slow fastball like Charlie's is difficult to catch up with that high in the zone and Pacelli was behind it and immediately in an 0-1 hole.

Charlie learned early on from his dad that when a hitter swings at a high fastball for strike one it was time to "climb the ladder". He put the next fastball up a couple of inches higher – right around chin level. Once again Pacelli took a huge cut at it and missed it completely.

At this point, Charlie had little choice with what he was going to throw next. Even a fastball hitter like Pacelli wouldn't be able to touch the ball up around his eyeballs, and if he wasn't smart enough to hold off and take a pitch than Charlie would just have to make him pay. At this point in the season Dusty and Charlie were on the same page. Dusty was almost standing as he called for the pitch with his mitt up at head level. Charlie put it where he wanted it and sure enough, Pacelli couldn't hold back. He took a wild hack at the pitch that was by the brim of his helmet and once again swung and missed.

Charlie recorded his third strikeout of the game and was out of the inning unscathed. Pacelli, who almost fell to the ground after the swing, took his bat, slammed it onto the plate and then snapped it over his knee into two pieces. That was something Charlie hadn't seen in the minors. Charlie walked calmly back to the dugout oblivious to the fact that the crowd was on its feet going crazy. The noise level was like nothing heard at Target Field in its short existence. The fans could smell victory and the playoffs, and were on their feet for the seventh inning stretch. Charlie had thrown 97 pitches thus far and felt as if he could finish the game if called upon to do so. He thought he could easily get his pitch count up around 130 without it affecting his pitches. He'd actually only end up throwing three more (the last three pitches of his professional career) for an even 100 pitches, but those three would end up being three of the most crucial of his life.

Chapter 31

Minneapolis, MN

The Twins offense didn't give Charlie much time to rest. After a stirring rendition of "Take Me Out to the Ballgame", eight pitches, and three ground balls, the Twins were back out on the field to start the eighth inning. It felt like the blink of an eye. Charlie actually preferred to get right back out there as quickly as possible. Long innings just meant that his arm would start to get cold. In fact, if an inning lasted more than about twenty minutes Charlie would grab a ball and start throwing. This kept him loose, but it also limited the number of pitches he could throw in a game. Today he hadn't been forced into doing that once, hence the fresh arm despite the 97 pitches thrown. The Twins one big inning where they scored all of their runs was still over pretty quickly. It was the half innings in which Charlie was pitching that were the longer ones. Actually, the amount of time the Twins were in the field compared to the time they were at the plate was in approximately a two to one ratio.

Charlie's least favorite Indian, Darnell Williams, was back up at the plate to lead off the eighth inning. This was the fourth time that Williams had been up today and the third time he'd led off an inning. The only time Darnell had been up with anyone on base was the first inning when he was intentionally walked. This was ideal for Charlie. The Indians weren't planning on Vince Pacelli having arguably his worst game of the season. If Pacelli had been on base even one time ahead of Williams this might be a whole different ballgame.

Charlie decided, since nothing else seemed to be working, that he'd go with a fastball this time around. Looking back on this game later, Charlie was amazed with how many fastballs he actually threw. He hadn't been expecting to throw more than a couple, and it ended up that he used that pitch almost as frequently as his curveball. Each game he pitched throughout his career was a little bit different than the others. He didn't really have a ton of speed on his fastball today. It hovered right around 89-90 miles per hour, but he'd slowed his changeup down so much that it could be effective at times.

Darnell Williams was so locked in that somehow, he wasn't fooled. He turned on the inside fastball and smoked a double down the third base line. Just like that, with one pitch thrown, the Indians were threatening again. The tying run was coming to the plate, and Charlie was going to have to fight his way out of trouble once more. The whole game had been a constant battle of working out of tough situations.

Charlie was still feeling alright about things, however. He felt like he knew the pitch he wanted to throw here to this batter, and he'd had success with the curveball down and in on him up to this point. He delivered the curveball in the perfect location and got the expected result. The ball was dribbled softly towards the normally sure-handed second baseman who inexplicably booted the ball. Instead of one out and a runner on third, the Indians now had runners on the corners with nobody down and the go ahead run coming to the plate.

Time was called as the Indians sent a pinch runner to first – a speedster named Reggie Hughes who stole 43 bases in the minors this season. He'd likely be heading to second at some point in the inning. It was just a matter of when.

"Is Montgomery ready?" Gordon asked the pitching coach.

"Yeah, he can go if you need him."

"What do you think, Don?" Gordon would normally just go to the pitching coach with any questions like this, but since Don knew Charlie better than anyone he was finding himself looking to Don for advice. Most likely all of this working with Don was pissing the pitching coach off, but he didn't have time to worry about feelings right now. The season, and possibly his managerial career, was hanging in the balance.

"Has Montgomery given you two innings of relief before?" Don asked.

"No, this would be the first time since he's been in the league, but I think he can handle it."

"Does he hold on runners well?"

"No, he's awful. Hughes will be at second after one pitch," Gordon replied.

"I'd give Charlie a chance here then," Don said, and then paused for a moment. "Hey, I know this isn't normal, but can I go out there and talk to him?"

"Sure. We're not doing anything else by the book. Why start now?" Gordon said, in almost a defeated tone.

It was an extremely unorthodox move for anyone other than the pitching coach or the manager to take a visit to the mound. In fact, except for games where the manager had been tossed, Gordon White couldn't remember ever being at a game where it had happened. This would further alienate the pitching coach, but for the last month or so he'd just been making Gordon irate anyway with his decisions. If they weren't in a pennant race with the season nearly over he'd have been fired. Gordon would also take some heat from the media for allowing someone different to visit the mound. He could imagine the ESPN announcers right now bashing Gordon for losing his mind and wondering who was running the show. None of that would matter if they won, however. Winning cures all ills.

As Don Scott limped slowly out to the mound none of those thoughts were in his head. He didn't care about the politics or what the talking heads upstairs were saying, he just knew he had something important to talk about with his pitcher.

"Hey fellas, we're a long ways from Altoona," Don said casually to Dusty and Charlie on the mound. Dusty broke into a big smile while Charlie just listened intently, ready to get back to business. "Here's the thing. Hughes over there on first is going to steal. He's stretching over there like he's preparing for the 100 yard dash. I keep expecting him to pull out the starter's blocks. My guess is that he's going right away. First pitch – you know how those base stealers get antsy over there. They're going to try and put the tying runner in scoring position and they aren't going to bunt here with this guy. Charlie, has Hughes seen you somewhere in the minors before?"

"No, I don't think so. I think I'd remember him."

"Good. I want you to give him your slow-ass pickoff move where you make it obvious that you're throwing over there twice. Play it up like it's the best move that you've got. Then, take the sign from Dusty and ignore him over there.

Don't even give him a look – like you're just concentrating on the pitch. Then give him the good one. The ump at first, Martinez, won't call a balk. I've known him for years, he's oblivious. He'll ring the guy up if you get him, though. He likes the spotlight. Go get 'em boys!" Scott said, and was gone – walking even slower than normal to try to get Hughes excited to run.

Charlie really had no expectation of this actually working, but he figured he'd at least give it a shot. What would it hurt? His main focus, however, was trying to keep the runner close and induce another ground ball at someone for a double play. He'd already got two ground balls from this batter earlier today and struck him out the other time he faced him. A double play ball would allow the runner to score, but the Twins would still have a lead and two outs in the inning. That was a trade that he'd be more than willing to make. In his mind, that was his best case scenario.

Charlie came to the set and looked directly over at Hughes on first. He picked his leg straight up in the air and with his body momentum moving straight ahead threw it to first. He threw the ball hard over there, not the lob that he sometimes gave. He wanted Hughes to think he was trying to pick him off with this move to give him some confidence in his lead. Hughes got back safely and easily without even going to a slide. This is where they'd see if the plan had any chance for success. Would Hughes expand his lead or would he stay close to the bag? Even Charlie's best pickoff move wouldn't get Hughes with a lead that small.

Charlie again came to the set and what he saw looked promising. Hughes had taken another step away from the bag. His fingers were moving and his look was focused. Once more Charlie made an obvious move towards first base and Hughes got back in safely. This time he dove back towards the base however. It wasn't that close, but it was a lot closer than last time and for the first time Charlie thought that the old man in the dugout might be on to something.

Charlie looked in to Dusty for the fake sign and, for the third time, came to the set. It didn't look like Hughes expanded his lead any, but he also hadn't cut it back either. Charlie tried not to look over at first too carefully, but he could sense that this had a chance. He lifted his right leg with his knee slightly rotated behind the left one. It was technically a balk, but Charlie knew from experience he could get away with it. The whole time he kept his line of sight on Dusty until the last moment when he sprang into action. Just as his leg barely started coming towards home plate his eyes snapped back towards first and his arm moved that way as well. Hughes, thinking the ball was about to be pitched had committed. He was two steps on his way towards second when he heard the first base coach yell out "back" and realized that he was a goner. Charlie gave the throw to the first baseman at chest level who took a big step in towards the mound to get a better angle for the throw to second. Hughes was still going, trying to beat the throw to the bag, but even with his speed he didn't have a chance. He was out diving headfirst into second in a play that would be cursed by Indian fans for years. Darnell considered making a break for home, but with his lack of speed he wisely decided to stay put.

The first base coach argued passively for a balk with the umpire, but it never got much steam. It was more like a conversation. The Cleveland manager was too pissed at Hughes to pay any attention to arguing with the ump, and didn't even consider that it could possibly be a balk. Not that arguing would have done a whole lot of good anyway, they weren't about to change a call.

The Twins dugout, meanwhile, exploded with excitement and energy. Clayton couldn't find enough teammates to high five so he tracked down the bat boys – frightening them with his exuberance. Gordon, after a quick pump of the fist, was quickly focused again. There were still decisions that needed to be made.

"I'm going to stay with him here, now. I'd really rather have Montgomery just pitch one inning like he has most of the year. Even if a run comes in here we'll still have the lead," Gordon said in Don's general direction.

Don just nodded back. He was more amazed that it actually worked than excited about it. Rarely does a coach make a strategic in-game decision that so obviously has the desired result and benefits the team like that. Don realized a few years back that he'd never end up being a Major League manager, and he was content with that. But, for one moment, he proved to himself that he could cut it up in the big leagues. Don wouldn't show any emotion about that right now, but he felt good about himself.

Charlie also showed little emotion on the mound. Dusty was on his way back out there to talk things over. He needed a second to calm down after that big play, himself.

"What do you want to do here, Chuckster?"

"I know I can get a groundball out of him. I'm just hoping it's at someone. I'd like to get it to third so Darnell can't score. So let's really go down and inside with the curve. Everything inside."

"Are you going to work out of the stretch or the wind-up?"

"The stretch. It doesn't matter to me. Might as well keep him close."

"Sounds good. Just remember, Darnell's run doesn't mean much. Don't lose the hitter; he's the run that matters," Dusty said, and was back to the plate.

Dusty had a good point. If the runner scored, the Twins would still be up one, but a homer here would tie things up. Charlie could try once or twice to get that groundball, but eventually he'd need to make sure that he got an out in whatever way he could. He truly did feel just as comfortable out of the stretch, but he could change to the wind-up if he didn't locate out of the stretch.

Charlie peered in to Dusty to get the sign and came to the set. He wanted to get a lot of drop on the curveball so that it would be pounded into the ground. He held the ball with a tight grip across the seams and delivered. He put a little too much drop on the pitch and it bounced at the batter's feet as he danced out of the way. This type of pitch would typically be blocked by Dusty right at the plate, but it took a strange hop out of the dirt where the batter had dug in and caromed off of Dusty's chest protector, rolling slowly towards the Indians dugout. The ball didn't move very far away but Dusty couldn't find it.

"Over there!" Charlie yelled, pointing towards the baseball and running in to cover the plate.

Darnell Williams froze initially. But, after noticing that Dusty didn't know where the ball was he broke towards home. If Darnell had left immediately he would have been safe easily, and if Dusty had seen the ball initially Darnell wouldn't have gone towards home at all. It was not a smart move to make the second out of the inning at home plate, especially when being down by two runs. In fact, it was plain stupid. If Darnell got thrown out at home he'd be committing the second huge base running gaffe of the inning.

Now, with Dusty closing in on the ball quickly and Darnell stuck halfway between third and home, Darnell realized that he was in trouble. Charlie was there on the third base side of home plate waiting for the throw from

Dusty. Darnell knew he only had one shot at scoring, and that was to take Charlie out. He had to make sure he dislodged the baseball from Charlie's glove or he'd be out at home easily.

Charlie, focusing on Dusty tracking down the baseball, didn't notice that he was standing on the third base side of home, directly in the base path until it was too late. He caught the ball in plenty of time to apply the tag, but when he looked up to do it he saw the intensity in Darnell's eyes and realized that he was going to take a hit. He held his ground and braced himself for the contact. Darnell hit him full force right in the chest and came down hard right on top of him – the full weight of his body landing squarely on Charlie's shoulder. Charlie let out a scream of agony. A shot of pain ran from his left shoulder all the way down to his fingers.

For what felt like an eternity to everyone involved the umpire stood looking down at the carnage to see if Charlie held on to the baseball. Finally, as Darnell was rolling off of him, Charlie held up his glove hand to show the umpire that he had held on to the ball and the umpire bellowed "He's out!"

Charlie lowered his glove and stayed there on the ground for a second as Gordon and the trainer came running out to check on him. Right as they arrived at home Charlie got back up on his feet. The initial shot of pain was gone as the adrenaline of the moment again filled his body.

"Charlie, are you alright?" Gordon asked, concerned.

"Yeah, I think so. It just hurt initially. I think I'm going to be ok. I'm good." Charlie was trying to convince himself, as well as Gordon, that he could continue on.

"We're good here, Charlie. You can be done if you're hurt. You don't have to be a hero. The bullpen can handle it now. Don't feel like you have to keep going," Gordon said.

"Let's try it out. I'd like to give it a shot," Charlie said, taking the ball to the mound.

Charlie would get a warm-up toss after being injured and he planned on trying it out quickly before Gordon gave him the hook. Now that there were two outs with nobody on base, Charlie wanted to at least finish the inning, knowing that he'd almost certainly not be back for the ninth regardless of what happened next.

Charlie got to the mound and, with Gordon and the trainer standing by watching his every move, he took the ball in his hand to give it a go. He was back doing the same wind-up that his dad taught him from the time he was a little boy. He rocked back with his right foot, bringing his hands together. His left hand felt a little bit numb as he gripped the baseball. He raised his right knee up steadily, always completely on balance. His dad used to have him stand like that in the "stork position" to help him become comfortable there. He turned his shoulders and kept his hands on the left side of his body to help him rotate his hips.

He brought his glove hand forward, pointing the way to the catcher's mitt.

But, just as he was starting to bring his left arm forward, a shot of pain ran back through his arm again and he winced. He brought his arm forward at half speed and hung on to the baseball, taking a step forward and bending over to finish the follow-through. He clutched on to his shoulder with his glove hand and knew he was finished.

Charlie looked up at Gordon and shook his head. He couldn't do it. He handed the ball to Gordon who patted him on the back and said, "You got us here, Charlie. We'll bring it home. Great work today."

The crowd, having been silent while Charlie was being looked at, exploded in applause as he took a step off the mound. For the first time all game he heard the noise and the cheering, and it was like a bolt of energy that caused him to stop dead in his tracks. He was frozen for a second as a chill ran down his body at the sight of nearly 40,000 people on their feet cheering for him. The sound and wave of energy engulfed him as Gordon was calling in Montgomery from the bullpen. He started walking again back towards the dugout and looked over to where his family was sitting. He saw Karen, with tears rolling down her cheeks, cheering while holding on to Timmy who was also yelling happily while holding his hands over his ears to block out some of the deafening noise.

Charlie gave a quick smile up towards his family before he entered the dugout and then was mobbed by his new teammates congratulating him. He got through all of the right-handed high fives when Clayton came up to him and picked him up, giving him a big bear hug.

Charlie, after finally being set back down on the ground, gave him a shove backwards and said with a smile, "You left me to battle Darnell all by myself again."

"I knew you had it all under control," Clayton responded. "You're a beast!"

The crowd, meanwhile, was still going crazy as Montgomery was going through his warm-up throws. Don came up and shook Charlie's hand, and told him that he still had some work to do.

"You need to go out there for a curtain call, Becker."

"No, that's ok, Skip. They cheered for me. I don't need the attention. I'm good."

"Charlie, I'm serious. You either need to go out there and wave to the crowd on your own or I'm going to throw you out of the dugout myself, and I know you don't want to mess with me."

Charlie finally relented, climbing up to the top step of the dugout to give the crowd a quick wave of his right hand while flashing his smile at everyone. Target Field once again exploded in noise, and Charlie got back to his seat just in time to see Montgomery's first pitch – a strike, traveling roughly ten miles an hour faster than anything he had thrown all game. The eighth inning was over quickly.

Chapter 32

Minneapolis, MN

"We should get you back into the training room now and get you some treatment," the trainer said to Charlie as the Twins were coming to bat in the bottom of the 8th inning.

"No way. I'm staying here."

"You need to get some ice on your shoulder immediately. We need to control the swelling."

"That's fine. You bring some ice out here to me and I'll be glad to put it on my shoulder. But I'm not going back there. I have a front row seat to watch my hometown team win a game that I started to send us to the playoffs. I'm not going back there to watch it on TV. I'll be watching games on TV the rest of my life."

The trainer eventually relented and left Charlie alone. Charlie knew his baseball career was finished so it was pointless to get any treatment on his arm. He wasn't ever going to pitch again even with a healthy arm. This felt to Charlie like the same injury he had years ago and so it wouldn't have even mattered if he wanted to continue playing baseball. He wasn't going to go through the rehab again. Now he was finished and could leave without any regrets or thoughts of coming back. The injury was actually another blessing in a day chalk full of blessings.

"I'm sorry, Chuckster," Dusty said, sliding next to him on the bench.

"About what?"

"I should have blocked that ball. It's a play I should make. A play I normally make. I feel terrible about getting you injured."

"Dusty, you didn't get me injured," Charlie said, putting his hand on Dusty's shoulder. "If anything I got myself injured by squeezing that ball so tight and throwing that pitch into the ground. It all turned out well, though."

"Still, I should have moved my body over quicker. Now you're going to have to go through all the rehab and stuff. What a pain in the neck."

"Listen Dusty. The injury doesn't matter. I was never going to pitch again anyway. I'm retired. Here's a secret for you. I actually retired a month ago. This is the end," Charlie said, as the bottom of the eighth finished. "Now forget about this injury that doesn't matter and get out there and get me my win."

Dusty finally relaxed and gave Charlie a smile. "Alright, Chuckster. Just don't forget about me when your big social security checks start rolling in."

Charlie was watching Montgomery finish up his warm-up tosses before the start of the ninth inning when the trainer came back with a huge pack of ice and an ace bandage. The trainer strapped it on Charlie's shoulder and every time he had to move his arm it hurt now. The adrenaline had completely worn off and he was starting to feel it.

After the trainer finished, Charlie sat there by himself again at the end of the bench. This time, however, even with the throbbing pain from his shoulder he looked out of the dugout with a goofy smile on his face. He didn't so much watch the action on the field as he did the people in the crowd. Charlie had never been a people watcher in the past, but today was a new day.

His eyes were drawn to a couple of guys in the first row of the second deck. They each had a beer in both hands. Charlie recognized that familiar gaze of intoxication in the eyes of one of the young men wearing a Twins jersey. Somehow, even with the fan's team on the brink of a championship, he looked sad. Winning and drinking can't mask everything. *Montgomery induces a ground ball to short for the first out of the ninth.*

Charlie turned his attention to a vendor back behind home plate, still working, walking up and down the aisles. It looked like he was selling peanuts. The man was a little bit older and slower. Probably not moving as well as he did a couple years back. His attention wasn't on the game either. He had a job to do and his eyes were constantly moving, looking for the next sale. Ploddingly trying to finish his job. Working up to the very last out. He was too busy to appreciate what was going on around him. *A pop-up to second, and now there are two outs in the ninth.*

Charlie's eyes next caught a family sitting in the last row of the lower deck. Not the best seats in the house, definitely worse views than the others he'd been watching, yet they also seemed the happiest. There was a boy about ten years old keeping score on a program. Next to him was another younger boy eating some popcorn, and a little girl sleeping on her mom's lap. The dad looked like he had his hands full with helping one son keep score, and helping the other not spill his drink. *Strike one on the batter.*

The dad was laughing at something his younger son said through a mouth full of popcorn, picked him up, and set him on his lap. He was stealing handfuls of popcorn from his son when he wasn't looking. *Strike two.*

Everyone was on their feet now with the older son being one of the first to stand. He was obviously intently involved in the game, whereas the younger boy was intently involved in his food. Both were having a great time. The older boy, standing up on his seat in the back row, nudged his dad and brother and must have told them to stand up as well. The stadium was now quite loud, yet the little girl continued to sleep peacefully. *Strike three. Game over.*

The Twins poured out of the dugout to mob Montgomery out on the pitcher's mound. Dusty was the first one out there, and Montgomery jumped up into his arms before the rest of the team arrived. When the team did arrive it was one big jumbled, mass of humanity. Charlie was one of the last Twins out of the dugout. He wasn't going to go into that mix with his shoulder all wrapped up in ice. These weren't really his teammates anyway. He hadn't played 160 games with them. Just the one. A big one, but one nonetheless. He walked a couple steps out on to the field, a safe distance away from the celebrating teammates, and was congratulated by a few of the coaches that were also staying on the outskirts of the celebration. Charlie shook a few hands, answered some quick questions on how his shoulder was feeling, did a short, quick interview with ESPN, and then inched away from everyone.

He made his way over to the area where his family was sitting and called them down to the railing. His mom made it there first, and he gave her a big hug. Karen, holding Timmy to keep him close by, came next and also grabbed him in a hug.

"You did it, Charlie," she said into his ear.

"We did it, Karen." he responded. "I'm going to take Timmy down on the field for a bit. I love you."

He grabbed Timmy from Karen and set him down on the soft grass. "Can I run the bases, Dad?" Timmy asked. By now the players were starting to head back into the clubhouse to continue the celebration with some champagne. It would be a fun time, but one that Charlie was going to avoid for several reasons.

"Go ahead, Timmy."

After a few seconds of standing behind home plate alone, alternating between watching Timmy circle the bases and the crowd filing out, Gordon White came up to him to congratulate him one more time.

"I just ran into Dave Duerson. He wanted me to let you know that you can travel with us for the playoffs. We fly out to Anaheim on Monday. We can do some rehab while we're out there."

"Tell Dave I said thanks. I appreciate the gesture," Charlie said, as Timmy ran across home plate and jumped up in his dad's arms. "But I'm going to have to decline. My baseball days are done. Timmy and I, we're going home."

Epilogue

Spring Valley, MN

"How are you feeling, Charlie?" Karen asked him as he came sleepily down the stairs to get some coffee.

"I feel more nervous than I did before throwing that first pitch with the Twins 11 months ago. Terrified might be a better word," Charlie responded.

"You'll be fine once you get started."

"I don't think I slept at all last night. I just kept thinking about today and what's going to happen."

"You're good on no sleep. It will be great. I'm going to wake up the kids so we can get them over to your mom's house."

"Alright, I'll just be in here shaking like a leaf."

A few minutes later Karen came into the living room carrying a kid in each arm. Timmy, not used to being woken up in the morning, was half asleep in his mom's right arm while little Sophia was wide awake and smiling at her daddy.

Charlie and Karen each took a kid and started the process of getting them dressed for the day - Charlie with Timmy and Karen with Sophia. Ten minutes later, they were out the door and over to Ellen's house. Charlie missed them almost immediately, but could console himself with the fact that he'd be seeing them again soon. There were no week long road trips anywhere in his future.

A long, slow hour passed as Charlie waited for things to begin. Finally, there he was standing in front of 28 blank faces that were all staring right back at him, not very excited about the start of a new year. His new life had begun.

"Good morning. This is my first year teaching, but some of you might recognize me as the new varsity football coach. My name is Mr. Becker, but you can call me Mr. B..."

Made in the USA
Charleston, SC
13 December 2012